About the author

Susan Parry began writing when her twin daughters were small, and she was working full time as a university professor at Imperial College. She now devotes her time to consultancy work, including forensic studies and archaeological investigations that form the basis for her writing. Her husband, Mark, is retired so they are now able to spend more time together in the family home in Swaledale, where the views from her farmhouse provide inspiration. Together they have walked many of the areas described in the books, accompanied by their Airedale terrier. Her grown up daughters, Elspeth and Alice both have careers in crime – on the right side of the law. Visit her website at www.SusanParry.co.uk.

By Susan Parry

PURPLE SHROUD

SUSAN PARRY

Viridian Publishing

First published in the United Kingdom in 2011 by
Viridian Publishing

Viridian Publishing
PO Box 746
Woking
Surrey
GU24 0AZ

www.viridian-publishing.co.uk
e-mail: viridian.tc@virgin.net

ISBN 978-0-9567891-0-5

For Alice

Chapter 1

At first Mills thought it was a grouse sitting partially hidden but it didn't move as she made her way carefully through the thick heather. The bird had clearly been dead for some time, its large wings spread gracefully, exposing the almost white chest feathers. Her walk above Gunnerside had been a bird-watching expedition but this was not how she'd expected to see this impressive raptor. She assumed it was a buzzard but reached for her identification manual. The size was right, it must be at least sixty centimetres in length, but the photograph certainly didn't do justice to the beautiful red-brown plumage that was just visible at the shoulders. She took a close-up shot then stood admiring the bird, thinking that she would much rather have seen it circling overhead, silhouetted against the early morning sun.

Instinctively she bent down to touch the soft feathers at its neck, and felt a plastic tag attached to its wing. Very gently she turned the bird over, releasing it carefully from the tiny twigs of heather that clung to the feathers. She knew that the numbered tag could mean only one thing. Looking at the long forked tail feathers and the damage to its back confirmed her fears: this was a red kite that had been shot. She, of all people, had just disturbed a crime scene. She took more photographs then hurried back down to Mossy Bank; uncertain who would be available at seven o'clock on a Sunday morning but anxious to inform the authorities as soon as possible.

Earl, impatient for his breakfast, stared up at her, whining gently, as she tried a series of phone numbers. Eventually, after a few false starts, she got through to a trained wildlife crime officer in the North Yorkshire police who was available to come over to Swaledale that afternoon.

'And you're sure it's a red kite?' he'd asked.

'Oh yes, positive.'

She told him about the number on the tag and he asked for the colour.

'Sounds like it were released last year,' he said. 'It's not the first time. Let's hope it's the last.'

Earl was pawing at her leg; he would start his low bark if she didn't feed him soon.

'I'll be over about two,' the officer said and put down the phone.

'Just be patient, Earl,' she called as she went to the larder to find his food.

The dog bounced round her as she filled his bowl, which clattered as she placed it on the stone floor. He took less than a minute to empty it, pushing it round the tiny kitchen noisily in an effort to remove every scrap. Mills made toast, eating as she brought her laptop to the kitchen table. Soon she was scanning websites on red kites, finding out as much as she could about their release in the region and any similar crimes. It seemed more common to find birds that had died from eating poisoned bait but there had been previous examples of a bird being shot in the mistaken belief that they took live birds such as pigeons. Was it possible that someone had thought this one was taking grouse?

With breakfast over, Earl was becoming eager for his walk. Mills slammed the laptop shut, grabbed his lead and opened the front door.

'Come on then, let's go.'

He didn't need any encouragement. Before she reached the gate he was over the low wall and racing up the lane. Generally he was well behaved so she wasn't concerned until he disappeared off in the direction of the Manor House. There was no sign of him when she reached the end of the drive so she stood yelling and whistling but with no response. Frustrated, Mills eventually wandered slowly back to the cottage calling half-heartedly. It was not the first time he'd disappeared and on the last occasion he'd been hanging around at the farm making a nuisance of himself. She settled down in front of her laptop, promising to go out again in an hour or so if he wasn't back by then.

She had found some information about the tagging system used for the release of red kites which showed how the colours related to years and locations. The hour was nearly up as she went to fetch a notepad from the sitting room but was distracted by the sight of Earl's head peering through the front gate. She flung the front door open and called him, expecting him to leap over the wall but he stared at her forlornly until she let him in. Limping through to the kitchen, panting loudly, he took a long drink from his water bowl before slumping down heavily onto the cool flagstones. Mills sighed. She hadn't budgeted for another trip to the vet this month. He pulled away when she felt his leg but didn't make a sound. He was a tough animal and rarely complained but she could tell he was in pain. She hoped it was just a strain from jumping too many walls.

By the time the wildlife crime officer arrived, Mills felt she was reasonably well-informed about the habits of red kites. The middle-aged man dressed in walking trousers and open-neck checked shirt introduced himself as George Herbert and asked her how she had found the bird.

'Did you move it at all?' he asked.

She blushed, hesitating before admitting that she'd turned it over.

He laughed. 'That's ok. I just wondered if it's in the same spot.'

'Oh yes. I wouldn't touch it once I realised it was a crime scene.'

He looked as if he was going to ask her something but then carried on towards his vehicle. She told him they would have to leave the Land Rover behind and walk the one and half kilometres across the moorland by foot.

'No problem. It's a grand day for it,' he replied with a grin.

He collected a rucksack before they set off. Mills slowed to peer down the drive to the Manor, trying to detect how Earl had hurt himself. There were no cars about so she assumed the place was empty. She ran to catch up with George who was striding ahead at a fast pace and fell in beside him, asking about how he'd come to be doing the wildlife crime officer role.

'I thought it'd be interesting to do the training. That's not to say that I don't do the usual stuff but it means I get the chance to be involved in protection. I were always interested in wildlife but that's because of being brought up on a farm like.'

'I thought farmers didn't really like having red kites up here.'

'No, that's not true. Just a few misguided ones.'

She indicated where the path forked and they turned to climb up the narrow track towards the top of the fell.

'It's not far now,' she said.

'Well it's a grand view up here,' George said eventually.

He was not a great conversationalist and Mills was pleased when they reached the outcrop of rocks close to where she had found the bird.

'It's over there.' She led the way into the heather, standing aside to let him view the scene.

He was obviously affected by it. He stood silently as if contemplating how anyone could carry out such a despicable act. He appeared unaware he was alternately rubbing his chin and then running his hands over his hair. Eventually he reached into his rucksack for a camera and took a series of photographs before finally turning the bird over and taking another set. He replaced the camera and pulled out some sheets of paper which he studied for a while.

'It *were* released last year,' he said, his finger following a list of numbers. 'Aye, a male released in July.'

Mills could hardly watch as he packed up the bird ready to transport it down to his vehicle. He swung the rucksack onto his back and set off without speaking, with the parcel in his arms held awkwardly out in front of him away from his body.

'I suppose this is the downside of your job,' Mills commented, following him back onto the path.

'Aye.'

They moved in silence for a few minutes before he continued. 'This is serious. Whoever did this is breaking the law.'

'The Wildlife and Countryside Act?' Mills had done her homework.

'Aye.'

She'd read that disturbing a red kite nest by taking eggs or even just photographing them could result in a big fine or possibly imprisonment.

'Could someone get a prison sentence for it?' she asked.

'Aye but only up to six months. Six years wouldn't be enough for 'em.'

Mills murmured her agreement. George marched on, stiffly holding out his precious bundle until they reached his vehicle, where he laid it delicately on the back seat.

'Would you like a drink... tea or something?' she asked, wondering what would happen next and thinking he might want to make some notes on how she found the bird.

'No thanks. I've got to get over to the North York Moors as soon as I've taken this 'un back. There's been an incident out there.'

'Not another bird... ?'

'No... summat altogether more serious than this.'

'So what will happen to the kite?' She'd thought she would be able to ask him all about it before he left.

'A post-mortem followed by a thorough investigation. We'll need a full statement from you but I've got to go now.'

He leapt into the driver's seat and slammed the door. Mills watched him turn the vehicle round and disappear back down the lane.

She went into the cottage expecting Earl to be greeting her noisily but he simply lifted his head when she came into the kitchen then settled back down again. She massaged his leg and he grunted quietly.

'You'd better give it a good rest, young man,' she told him and went through to the garden.

Although she'd only been in Laurel Cottage for a few months she'd been able to plant a few flowers and make a start on a small vegetable plot. There was little space but it was surprising how much could be crammed into pots around the place. She picked a few lettuce leaves and chewed them thoughtfully, examining the small green tomatoes; it would be several more weeks before they were ripe enough, she concluded. She sat for a few minutes on the bench in the warm shelter of the wall that separated her garden from next door. She could hear their television – probably sport, the old man liked his sport. Still, this won't get anything done, she thought, collecting the trowel and fork from the tiny shed and going inside.

'D'you want to come out?' she asked the lurcher as she passed through the kitchen. She wedged the front door open in case he changed his mind and started on the flower bed by the front wall. She'd been putting off the weeding for a while now because of the flies – possibly some manure had been applied last year, whatever the cause it made gardening at the front quite unpleasant, she decided.

There was no sound except the buzzing of the insects until a car engine broke the silence. She peered over the wall as a Range Rover, with a man and woman in the front, moved slowly past. Mills ducked down until they had passed then lifted her head so she could see where it was going. The car moved beyond the row of cottages and made a right turn. Mills concluded they must be visiting Mossy Bank Manor – they looked far too posh for Ivy Cottage, the tiny place next door.

It only took an hour to clear the weeds from the tiny patch in front of the cottage. Mills straightened up and carried the garden implements indoors, glancing over to check that Earl was still in his bed before going through to lock everything away in the shed.

'Walkies!' she shouted as she washed her hands at the kitchen sink.

At first there was no response but gradually he lifted his head and stretched. It was unusual for him not to be excited by the chance of a run - Mills had learnt early on that the dog was only really happy when he had his freedom. It was as if he could not feel properly relaxed unless he was out on the moors. Phil hadn't warned her; there was no mention of his constant desire to be outside. He'd told her that Earl was the easiest dog in the world to look after: 'Just food, a walk and a comfy bed is all he needs,' he had said, before going to Colombia for an unspecified time, leaving her with his dog, a lead and enough food for one week.

'Ok, I'll go on my own,' she called, as she made for the front door.

There was a scuffling and pattering of feet as he caught her up. The slight breeze out in the open made the air cooler away from the cottages. No-one else was around despite the fact that, like her, at least half the owners lived in their cottages all the year round, and the holiday lets were beginning to fill up now the school holidays had begun. Earl's head hung down as he limped slowly beside her and she decided that she would only take him to where the lane became a rough track before going back. But as they reached the turning to the Manor he froze, refusing to go any further. She attached his lead and tugged but he was a strong animal and stood his ground, peering nervously at the entrance to the house.

Mills looked down the drive, shaded by high stone walls on either side covered in ivy and honeysuckle. The cottage on the left was barely visible for foliage, which was presumably why it was called Ivy Cottage. She could see the black Range Rover parked on the wide area in front of Mossy Bank Manor.

'Look there's nothing to be scared of.' She began to walk towards the house. 'Come along!' she called as she looked back at him.

Earl watched her, motionless. Mills kept going, determined to show him that it was safe. Then she turned her gaze towards the house and stopped. A figure was moving from behind the car towards the house – a man dressed entirely in black, with big black leather boots, a studded belt. She could only glimpse his back for a few seconds before he had slammed the front door. Had he rushed inside to avoid her? Or was it Earl he was afraid of? The dog had started barking, loudly, urgently. She walked quickly back to the lane then turned to watch, soothing the dog with a gentle pat on his side.

'It's all right. He won't hurt you,' she said, without knowing why.

Chapter 2

Customers at the "Lion Inn" heard the woman before they saw her. She was shouting, almost screaming, as she ran towards the pub. Her two small girls were in tears as she dragged them along, their feet lifting off the ground as they tried to keep up with her. She stopped by the road, bent over double with the effort to catch her breath, then collapsed to the ground with her children clutching her in distress. A tall man in walking clothes strolled calmly over and crouched down beside her.

'What is it?' he asked calmly.

'The man... on the moor... he's dead!'

The walker motioned to his companion who obediently joined him.

'Look after the children, love. I need to call the station.'

It was not the Sunday lunch Mitch had planned when he'd invited Jemma out on their second date. He didn't want to abandon her, or spoil her day by asking her to act as nanny but, once he suspected it was murder and officers were on their way, he had to secure the scene.

The woman's hand was shaking as she sipped water from a pint glass. She kept glancing over to where Jemma was comforting her daughters.

'They'll be fine with her. She's a teacher,' he reassured her. 'Do you feel able to show me where you saw the body?'

She nodded and stiffly walked across to her daughters, who were looking round nervously as the crowd stared at them.

'Mummy will be back soon. You stay with this nice lady.'

They nodded solemnly.

The track ran down onto a lower path that levelled out across the valley.

'Is it near the path?' Mitch asked.

'No. We... we were playing. The girls were running around in the heather when they...'

'Ok. You show me.' He talked quietly, walking slowly, keeping her calm at all costs. She was still shaking even though the afternoon was warm.

'There!'

He could see a rucksack lying in the heather.

'Is that yours?'

'Yes. I must've left it when I...'

'So the body is there too?'

She nodded.

'Stay here,' he ordered.

The man was lying face down in the heather. There was no pulse and the body was stiff – he'd been dead for some time. He looked like a walker but that was just supposition because he was on the Coast to Coast route. It was difficult to tell what injuries he'd sustained and Mitch knew not to disturb anything. He moved away edging backwards slowly until he reached the woman.

'May I go back now please?' she asked. 'My children...'

'Yes, of course. Please stay at the pub until we've had a chance to make some notes, will you?'

She turned without speaking, walking quickly along the track until she disappeared from view; leaving Inspector Mitch Turner to ponder on the man in the heather.

When the scene was finally secured, he felt able to return to the "Lion Inn", offering to take a statement from the distraught mother while she waited for her husband to arrive. Apparently she was spending the day with her children while he had a day's fishing. Unfortunately his special treat would end abruptly and Mitch, who was a keen angler, could sympathise. He spoke briefly to Jemma, who agreed to keep the girls entertained while he spoke to their mother again.

'Just tell me exactly what happened.' He spoke gently, leaning across the small table in the bar, which was almost empty now.

She repeated what she had told him before about their walk and how her daughters had found the body as they played in the heather.

'Did they... or you... disturb anything?'

'You mean like move him, or touch him?' She paused. 'I touched his neck, to feel for a pulse.' She pulled a face and shivered.

The sunshine was almost blinding as Mitch stood outside, waiting for her husband to arrive. Jemma joined them with the two girls. They seemed quite relaxed, hanging onto Jemma's hands and smiling shyly at Mitch. He thought what a great mother she would make, dismissing the idea quickly, as if somehow she might guess what he was thinking.

As soon as the family were reunited, he followed Jemma to her car, apologising once more for the ruined afternoon.

'Don't be silly, Mitch. It's not your fault. I'll call you in the week if you want me to.'

'Of course I do,' he said, wondering whether he should give her a kiss on the cheek. By the time he had made up his mind, the car was reversing away and Jemma was waving goodbye.

'Damn,' he said quietly.

He spent the rest of the afternoon with officers from Pickering. Some of them were not entirely unhappy at being dragged away from a Sunday afternoon with the family; this was their job and nothing was more serious than a murder investigation. As the most senior officer present, Mitch was able to take charge of the scene and initiate the investigation. He waited on the track as the local force secured the area with tape, and chatted to the officers going about their duties. Within an hour a flimsy tent had been erected over the body and they were waiting for the pathologist to arrive. It was another half an hour before Mitch saw a familiar figure striding down the track towards him. Doc Strickland, Diana, was already dressed to protect the crime scene and Mitch guessed she'd got ready in the car park. It was a hot day and he could see her face was wet with sweat when she reached him. It was not a time for pleasantries and he directed her into the tent as she pulled the hood over her hair.

While he waited for her to re-emerge, the crime scene investigators arrived. They came from a civilian outfit so he didn't recognise them and when they introduced themselves he asked them to wait until Diana had finished. Meanwhile he briefed them on how the body had been found. The photographer began wandering about inside the tape, taking shots of the area outside the tent while his forensic colleagues delved into their cases, preparing for when they could begin their examination.

The pathologist pulled off her protective suit as soon as she reappeared. Her short blonde hair was sticking up; sweat was running down the side of her nose.

'Good grief, Mitch, it's warm in there.'

'So? What do we have?' he asked, motioning to the forensic team that they could move into the tent.

'Male aged thirty to forty, stabbed in the chest and stomach with a small blade knife, just a few centimetres. He died in the last thirty-six hours judging by the rigor mortis.' She wiped her forehead with a tissue she had retrieved from the pocket of her jeans.

'Can you be more precise than that?' Mitch knew that if the body was stiff it had been dead over twelve hours but he didn't want to irritate her by being too demanding.

'I can't be definite until the post mortem but it's certainly more than a few hours. Say between twelve and thirty-six.'

'That's what I thought.'

'Did you, Mitch? Quite the CSI, aren't we?'

'Can we move the body once the investigations team are done?' he asked to cover his embarrassment.

'I don't see why not.' She studied the ground for a second. 'There is something that worries me though. I'd expect a lot more blood at the scene. The wounds were small but there are a lot of them; it was quite a frenzied attack. He was on his stomach and the lividity suggests he was killed where he lay, but there's very little blood.'

'What do you mean – he was killed? It definitely wasn't suicide?'

She ignored his question. 'I may be sticking my neck out but it could mean he was killed somewhere else and moved. But it would have had to have been very soon afterwards or at least within a few hours.'

'Sorry, what's lividity?'

'It's the way the blood settles with gravity. In this case it confirms he was lying face down, just as he was found.'

'Could he have been lying in the same way somewhere else before he was moved?'

She looked puzzled. 'Perhaps. I need to see what the post mortem shows up. The blood loss is important and I'll have a better idea when I know how much he lost. Meanwhile you might want to look for signs of blood around here.'

Mitch watched her walk quickly back up the track towards the road, digesting what she had told him. If the body had been moved he would have to organise a thorough search of the area before dark. He'd assumed that the man had lain in the heather since the previous day but if the body had been moved, there could be witnesses in the area now. He told the two nearest constables to accompany him back to the pub and then ran, leaving the local sergeant in charge – he had to stop any more of the customers leaving the "Lion Inn" and question any visitors that remained in the car park by the road. This could be his first mistake in the investigation.

He relaxed as he walked the last few metres to the pub. He'd left one of the constables in the car park, where there were several families enjoying a picnic. The pub was still busy with customers lingering over their Sunday lunch. They were happy to stay and answer questions once he had explained why they were there.

'What's your name, constable?' Mitch asked.

'Robbins, sir.'

'Right. I want you to take statements from anyone who has seen anything... anything suspicious... today or yesterday if they were around here then. Say as little as you can about what has happened. All they need to know is what we've told them – someone was found dead on the Coast to Coast. They don't need to know the details. And tell me if anyone has any intelligence that might be important. Can you manage?'

'Yes, there's help coming up from Pickering and Malton, sir.'

'Good. I'll get back down to the site; we might have identification if we're lucky.'

He wasn't feeling very lucky as he made his way from the car park, where the other constable had drawn a blank.

'No-one's seen anything, sir. Nothing to report so far.'

'Well, keep at it and don't come back down when you've finished – go and help your colleague in the pub.'

'Yes, sir!' he said enthusiastically, clearly looking forward to getting into some shade.

The forensics team spent several hours before they began packing up. They had found no wallet, cards or money on the body, no clues to who he was or what he had been doing on the moor. There was no sign of the knife that killed him in the immediate area and it was noted that there was very little blood considering the man had been stabbed many times.

'Did he have a rucksack?' asked a middle-aged woman, who was the senior member of the team.

'We haven't found one,' said the sergeant.

'He's got sturdy boots so I assume he was on the Coast to Coast walk,' she continued. 'Even if he was out for the day you'd think he'd be carrying a map or something to drink.'

'We'll see if he stopped at the pub once we have a photograph to show them,' Mitch said. 'Meanwhile we'll get a more extensive search carried out before dark.' In case he was stabbed somewhere else, he thought. The problem was, if he had died elsewhere the investigation might have to be extended a very long way.

More officers arrived to help with the search, which began at Mitch's request at six o'clock. They would have a few hours before it was too dark to continue. The body lay on the moor until dusk fell, when it was finally carried slowly up the track to the car park. There were no parents and children to witness the chilling sight of the body bag being carefully transferred into the back of the black van. Mitch watched the vehicle move off towards Scarborough, where the post mortem would take place, hopefully within a few hours but certainly early the following day. They had promised him.

'... and so I'll be around while the investigation is completed,' Mitch explained on the phone.

He was hoping Jemma would offer to put him up since he would be working so near her village but she simply expressed mild interest and told him to drop in when he was passing. Hardly surprising, he convinced himself – she's only known me five minutes. However, nothing could diminish his delight at being asked to head up the investigation and he whistled as he packed his bag.

He was up early next morning, first to arrive at the mobile incident room which had been set up in the car park of the "Lion Inn". He busied himself putting together the relevant information, ready for the nine o'clock briefing. So far there was little to go on but the post mortem had shown that the man had been stabbed at a different location, and then moved to where he was found after he was dead. This would suggest more than one person was involved since he was a well-built man of six foot. Times were a bit vague but it seemed that the attacker or attackers had killed the walker on the Saturday afternoon or evening, moving him after a few hours to where he was found on Sunday afternoon. As far as Mitch was concerned the most urgent duties were to find any potential witnesses out walking the Coast to Coast path over the weekend. This would mean sending officers to the accommodation used by walkers on Friday and Saturday nights.

There were just fifteen officers waiting outside for him when he began the briefing. He'd hoped for more.

'Here's a list of local B&Bs and campsites used by people walking the Coast to Coast,' he said, handing round copies. I want to know who was on the walk this weekend, I need names and addresses and I want you to follow them up; find out where this man was staying. There's no camping equipment so...'

'But there's no rucksack neither, sir.'

'I know. Either he wasn't walking far, or the rucksack – and maybe camping gear – is missing. Those of you on the search need to keep a look out for them.'

The search team was divided into two groups, each under the command of a sergeant, before leaving to carry out a search of the moorland or local accommodation. Mitch rang Newby Wiske to ask for more support and later that morning he was joined by Nina and Hazel.

'Good morning, ladies!'

They looked at each other and shrugged.

'Am I glad to see you! I need you to sort out paperwork while I supervise the search.'

He escaped almost immediately, leaving the women to get up to speed as best they could.

On the moor, the line of officers was spreading out and moving slowly forward, accompanied by a couple of spaniels. If the searchers hadn't been in uniform they could have been mistaken for beaters working the moor for grouse. It was slow, tedious work and disappointing; by the end of the morning they had found nothing. Mitch called the dog handlers aside, asking them to move out along the route of the Coast to Coast path after lunch, one in each direction.

'It's a long shot but we know the body was moved... so let's start by tracking back both ways to see if it's come from along the path. We'll let the lads finish on the moor for the rest of the day before we decide what's next.'

He remained to watch the line of figures moving ponderously through the purple heather, waiting, hoping for a shout. After half an hour he left them to it, returning to the incident room, where he hoped he might find a cup of tea and a sandwich.

The furniture had been arranged neatly so that three chairs had access to desk space.

'It makes room for a filing cabinet. We'll need somewhere to store documents, Mitch,' Hazel said in the tone she used when she would not be contradicted. Mitch didn't waste effort trying. He knew he would be dependent on Hazel's long experience to keep information logged as it was received. He needed to concentrate his efforts on raising more help from headquarters.

'There are sandwiches on the desk,' Nina offered. 'And tea in the flask.'

The portacabin was uncomfortably hot and before long Mitch decided to head back out to see how things were progressing, leaving the two friends having a well earned break.

'Is there no intelligence on the victim at all?' Nina asked as she selected an egg and cress sandwich. 'No identification on the body?'

'Nothing,' her friend replied. 'No belongings at all, which is pretty weird for a walker even this time of year. He was wearing heavy boots, which suggests he was a serious hiker. Nothing from fingerprints or dental records yet but they'll be doing all the forensics. We'd better get on with the accommodation checks, they've almost exhausted the list Mitch gave them this morning and I've only found another ten B&Bs so far.' She handed Nina a mug of tea and returned to her desk.

By the time Mitch addressed the team outside the incident room at the end of the day, he'd been back to headquarters to brief the Chief Superintendent. His boss would have to face the press in the morning so he'd expected some progress to report. Although nothing had been said, his disappointment was palpable. It was in sombre mood that Mitch asked his team for any intelligence that had been gained during the day.

'Nina, have we covered all the locations where the man could have stayed on Friday night?'

'Yes, guv. Everywhere within a twenty mile radius.'

'Only twenty?'

'He wouldn't have wanted to walk too far off the path, sir.'

'Anything?'

'No single men meeting his description, sir.'

'And what makes you think he was alone?' He asked sharply. 'Surely someone was with him before he died?'

Hazel rested her hand gently on Nina's arm, indicating that she would answer. 'They were all checked for men matching the victim's description, sir. Single, or in a group.'

Mitch nodded. 'Ok. That would suggest he was camping as we thought. It makes sense, although it means that he must've been stripped of all his belongings including camping equipment.'

'D'you think they dumped them around here?'

'It's possible, sergeant. We'll resume the search in the morning and extend it east and west. Now, what about the search team, sergeant – anything?'

'Nothing. The moor where the body was found is as clean as a whistle.'

'And the dogs?'

'Nothing so far... but it was too late to work them for long this evening. We've only done a kilometre so there's another to do tomorrow.'

'Right then. We'll continue tomorrow with the dog teams looking for somewhere local where the stabbing took place and the rest of you can follow on with a wider search for camping gear, in case it was dumped. It's more likely to be close to where they killed him. Until we find something we'll be no closer to finding a motive.'

Once the men had dispersed, Mitch turned to Hazel.

'I can't wait for forensics before we start to identify the victim. Set up a team at HQ tomorrow – I'll give you two or three men, I can't spare more.'

Hazel smiled at Nina, packed up her bag and left.

'You can hold the fort here tomorrow, can't you?'

'Yes, of course. Is there anything you want me to do in particular?'

'No. Just answer the phone and keep the tea topped up,' he replied with a laugh.

It was meant light-heartedly but it irritated Nina. All too often she was left in the office "holding the fort".

Left alone in the portacabin after Mitch had slammed the door behind him, she stared across the desk. There was very little intelligence so far and the board was dominated by a map of the Coast to Coast path. It was a walk she'd been keen to complete in the days before her accident... followed by her pregnancy... then her husband's illness. But now it was a possibility again, perhaps when Rosie was a bit older. She was sitting almost exactly at the half-way stage and it occurred to her that it could be quite a few days before anyone would miss the dead man if they planned to meet him at the finish in Robin Hood Bay – assuming he had been walking in that direction. Everyone had someone who would notice you were missing, even if it was only the milkman or the delivery man from Amazon. Their victim probably had family, work colleagues, friends and associates who would only be asking about him next week... *unless they were expecting a call.* She rang Hazel's number at HQ, leaving a message reminding her to make a general check for "missing persons" – it was possible that someone had already noticed.

She was locking up when the phone rang. Cursing, she hurriedly turned the key again and lunged across the desk.

'Hi, it's Diane Strickland. Is Mitch around?'

'Sorry, he's gone. It's Nina.'

They exchanged pleasantries but Nina was keen to know what the pathologist wanted.

'Did you have anything on the stabbing?'

'It may be nothing but I thought I should let you know. He appears to have been on some quite unusual medication for his age. I'll send the report over but let Mitch know he was taking propanolol.'

'What's that?'

'It's a beta blocker.

Chapter 3

Mills had spotted the young man several times during the week as she passed the Manor on her early morning walk with Earl. She was unable to prove that the lad dressed entirely in black had ill-treated Earl in some way but she had her suspicions. The dog was still jumpy when they approached the Manor, speeding up until he was well clear of the entrance to the driveway. This morning the coast was clear and they were up onto the moor without a sign of him. It was a beautiful morning, warm and fragrant after the overnight rain. A curlew's call pierced the air but it wasn't the bird Mills had seen when she lowered the binoculars, looking anxiously for Earl. He was away in the heather, unaware that the young man in black was coming down the track towards them. She called him but it was too late. The second the dog saw him he was off back towards the village leaving Mills no option but to follow.

As soon as Earl was settled indoors, Mills headed back up the lane.

'Excuse me!' she shouted. 'I'd like a word!' She knew it sounded weird. 'I want to ask you something,' she added more quietly.

He was only a teenager, standing a few metres away now, at the entrance to the Manor. He stopped, waiting obediently in silence.

Mills stood awkwardly as her face reddened. 'My dog... I...'

'Is it all right?' His accent indicated he was a southerner, like her. His voice was what she called "posh". Private school, she guessed.

'Why?' She knew he'd done something to the dog.

'I just wondered.'

'Do you know something?'

'Like what?'

'Like he's been frightened by something or someone.' She looked him in the eyes, noticing that he had used black makeup to outline top and bottom eyelids, giving him a bizarre appearance.

He looked at the ground, muttering that he had to get back, and then ran down the drive towards the house. His jacket glinted in the sunlight, highlighting the words "Devil's Advocate" picked out in studs across the back. His gait was strangely affected by the rigid black boots that were laced up half way up his calves.

Later that morning, when her neighbour called round to present her with homemade biscuits, Mills asked if she knew who was staying at the Manor.

'Just the owners: the Banfords. They spend the summer every year. Have done since Olive passed on, bless her.'

'You mean her son?' Mills was trying to remember the name of the man she had met when she visited her grandmother years ago.

'Yes. Daniel...'

'...and his wife, Penny - I remember her! She was really...' She pulled herself up short, appreciating that she may be talking to a friend of the family.

'Stuck up?'

Mills laughed. Then she understood who the lad was. 'So the Goth is their son?'

'Yes. Gareth's going through a funny phase. His sister is the same but she's not with them this year. Gone abroad with friends apparently.'

'Well poor Gareth doesn't seem very in tune with his surroundings. He must be really hot in all that gear for a start!'

They exchanged stories of teenage fashion fads they had experienced themselves for a few minutes until the phone rang and her neighbour excused herself.

'I'm sorry, Dad, but it really isn't a good time. I'm just leaving to get to Harrogate.'

'You know I wouldn't ask if it wasn't important, Mills. Fiona is really getting depressed being stuck in with the baby all the time. A break for just a few days would make all the difference. Please?'

Mills sighed as she finally gave in, regretting it even as she replaced the receiver. The cottage had only two bedrooms, and if the baby really did cry non-stop... it would be unbearable. Having them there for even a short break would be very disruptive, just as she was trying to get into a routine of working at home part of the time. She looked at Earl, wondering how he would take to her guests. He was lounging in his bed enjoying a rest after his morning run.

'Just you be a good boy while I'm out,' she told him. 'I'm only going to see Brenda; I'll be back this afternoon.'

It was like an oven when she climbed into the Mini. She opened the windows on both sides before setting off, hoping that the air flow would cool it down in due course. As she drove through the lanes she thought about Daniel and Penny Banford. They had inherited the Manor when her grandmother's friend Olive died – well been murdered as it turned out. She had no desire to renew her acquaintance with either of them.

An hour later she was sitting in the office of the forensic laboratory, sipping a glass of chilled water with the new owner, Brenda Yardley. The room had been transformed since Mills had last sat there. Now it was dominated by an antique desk covered in untidy piles of paper. The chairs were shabby but comfortable and a tray with teapot and cups sat precariously on a small stool beside her.

'I expect you're wondering why I asked you to come over today,' Brenda began, as she poured the tea.

'Well, I...'

'I want you to meet Timothy. He's my newest acquisition in the lab,' she said with a laugh. 'He's very bright but knows nothing about soil. I thought you might be able to help him.'

'How?'

'By acting as a consultant of course.' She wagged a finger at her. 'I said I would be able to find you some work – you've not got a job yet, have you?'

'No, not really.' Mills reddened. 'I've some teaching at the university and I'm still waiting to hear about a job with the National Park.'

'Good! Because I think you can help us get going with some soil analysis.'

Brenda looked very pleased with herself; Mills hoped she was up to the task.

'We've got the clothes and boots from a stabbing, where we think the body has been moved after it was dead. We can do most of the work ourselves but I can't cover the mud on the boots and clothes. I thought of you immediately.'

'Why?'

'Because you know about digging up things. I'm sure you have someone at the university who can help.'

It was typical of Brenda, she was so positive and confident, Mills thought. But she was right. It would only be a matter of getting the analysis done in the department.

'Do you want to match the mud on the boots with a particular area?' Mills asked.

'Not that simple, girl. We have mud on the boots and soil from where he was found. Can you tell us where the mud on the boots came from?'

'Well, it would be easier to say where it didn't come from but we can try.'

'Excellent! I'll introduce you to Timothy and he can sort out the samples for you.'

Timothy was a young graduate, fresh from a forensic science degree course. When Brenda introduced Mills as Dr Sanderson, he looked suitably impressed, shaking hands with a nervous smile. Left alone with him, Mills asked to look at the samples of mud taken from the boots. There were two bags marked left and right boot. A third bag was full of soil from where the body was discovered. Timothy carefully transferred a small amount of the contents from each into new plastic bags, labelled them up and handed them over.

Mills thanked him as she signed the chain of custody forms and put her head round Brenda's door as she left.

She was on the phone but broke off her conversation. 'Are you off already? Got everything you need? Thanks for helping. This could be the start of a whole new area for the lab – and for you.'

As it happened, Mills had investigated soils in her undergraduate days and she'd worked on peat for her doctorate thesis. So she was fairly sure she could provide useful information for Brenda, once she'd had the soils analysed at the university. In the car park she called the department to speak to the laboratory, telling them that she would be over right away. Before handing over the samples she would need to look at them under a microscope to see what minerals were in them.

Hazel was at headquarters, keeping Nina updated by phone. '...but nothing from the fingerprints; no criminal record.'

'What about the dental records?'

'Give us a chance. I'm still waiting for the chart.' Hazel tried to keep the irritation from her voice.

'Anyone reported missing yet?'

'Not based on a description. Although it's early days – I haven't done the form for the Missing Persons Bureau yet. Mitch reckons he should've been reported missing by now, if he was going to be.'

'That's rubbish!' Nina sounded indignant. 'He wouldn't necessarily have been in regular contact with his family if he was doing the Coast to Coast walk.'

Hazel didn't want to extend the call longer than necessary. 'Look, I've got to complete the "mispers" form. It's supposed to be in within forty-eight hours. Bye.'

She returned to her keyboard and opened the Police OnLine Knowledge Area. The Missing Persons Bureau needed as much information as possible about the unidentified body to do a proper search, and she still needed the DNA and dental charts to add to the photographs and fingerprints.

Hazel greeted Mitch with the completed form when he arrived back in the afternoon to update his superiors. The dogs were still working the paths but the meticulous search had made little progress. His boss had wanted to release a statement to the press before the end of the day and apparently he could barely disguise his disappointment.

'Never mind, sir. Perhaps something will turn up from the MPB.' Hazel knew she didn't sound convincing.

Mitch sighed and settled behind his computer. The two colleagues worked in silence for two hours without speaking. Finally, his phone rang.

'Yes?'

Hazel was trying to understand what was being said but Mitch was only interjecting occasionally to confirm whatever was being asked. Finally he replaced the receiver with a smile.

'Good news?' Hazel asked.

'News, anyway,' he replied. 'The dogs have found something on the moor to the west of where the body was found. About a mile back along the path.'

'Is it a match?'

He gave a hollow laugh. 'It's definitely blood but we won't know if it's a match until we get the DNA report.'

'Wow. So he staggered a mile before he died?'

'I don't think so, Hazel. They think he was carried from where he was killed to where he was found.'

'What would someone do that for?'

'If we knew that, Hazel, we'd be nearer finding the killer... or killers.'

She shrugged and rang Nina, who already knew the outcome of the dog search and sounded excited.

'At least it means someone might have seen something odd... out of the ordinary.'

'I thought they'd already spoken to all the local people and walkers yesterday, Nina.'

'They did, but we didn't know he was being carted about then. We need to go over it again.'

'Well you can suggest that to Mitch but he's had the search team reduced by half already today.' Hazel knew that Nina wouldn't give up once she had an idea.

'Don't worry. I'll make the calls now. I can talk to the B&Bs again for a start.'

Hazel smiled as she put down the phone.

Nina called Nige to warn him that she would be late... again.

'No problem. I'll pick Rosie up early; I've got no lectures this afternoon. It'll be easier to write the paper I'm working on at home anyway.'

Nina returned to her work, knowing that everything would be under control – sort of. Rosie would get to bed later than she should, there would be no proper dinner prepared and Nige would be asleep in front of the telly when she returned, however late it was.

It was a good time to ring the accommodation list again before their guests arrived back for the evening. She opened her folder of neatly typed names and phone numbers, working meticulously through from A. The questions she was asking them had changed, in some respects more specific and yet still rather vague. The responses were sometimes entertaining, for example the farmer's wife who thought anyone who wouldn't eat meat was an extremely dubious character. But no-one had received a guest that was unexpected, who arrived late or left very early. No-one had a late cancellation or a guest not turning up at all. No men arriving alone or in a pair fitted the deceased's description. In fact everything was very normal over the weekend. All of which suggested to Nina that he must have been camping, which created a huge problem because he wouldn't necessarily have been using a recognised campsite.

Come on Nina, she told herself, you still have to check them out. So she started a new list for local campsites and typed in the contact details. It didn't take long. It was clear that the best place to camp in the area was just outside – by the "Lion Inn". She quickly tidied her desk, locking up before stepping into the pub next door.

There was a police vehicle parked outside the cottage when Mills arrived back from the university on Tuesday evening. As soon as she drew up behind it, the driver emerged carrying a folder. She didn't recognise the wildlife officer at first and it must have shown in her face because he gave his name as he came to meet her.

'I'm sorry, George, I didn't recognise you in uniform,' she muttered self-consciously, leading the way into the kitchen.

Earl stretched as he climbed lethargically out of his basket and came towards them yawning. The dog sank to the floor and lay at the man's feet as he stroked him gently. Mills offered tea and while the kettle was boiling, George asked her to describe exactly how she had found the dead bird. He wrote slowly and she waited for him to complete each sentence before continuing. Finally he pushed the paper over to her for a signature. Then he explained what had happened at the post mortem on the red kite she'd found on the moor.

'... and so we've made poor progress. Unless we find the person or people concerned there's nowt we can do.'

'You say it was a high-powered air rifle?'

'Yes. A point two-two; the most powerful weapon you can keep without a licence. We've got pellets and they're being analysed but they're common enough. It'll be hard to prove even if we find the killer.'

'Who would want to kill such a beautiful bird?' Mills wondered aloud.

'You'd be surprised.' George's voice was quiet but it didn't hide his anger. 'Farmers, gamekeepers, kids who think it's clever.'

Mills thought of the young man in black staying at the Manor.

'Anyway, I'd best be going.' George drained his mug and handed it to her. 'Thanks for the tea.'

'Finished for the day?'

'I've got to be going back to Pickering. They're recalling the team over there.'

'Team?'

'There's a murder investigation going on. I expect you've seen on the telly. I'm part of the search team.'

'How interesting.'

'Not really, miss. Just a routine search.'

Mills knew better than to ask for more details. She'd seen the brief press release being read out by the senior investigating officer. The message that came across was that they had no idea who the man was or why he was there.

'I sometimes get involved in forensic work,' Mills offered, hoping that he might be willing to discuss the case on a professional footing. 'I'm doing some work for Brenda Yardley's lab at the moment, as it happens.'

'Aye?' He looked uninterested. 'I don't know 'owt about forensics. I just do as I'm told like. If I'm asked to look for a weapon, I look for a weapon.'

'Don't you have dogs for that?'

'Aye, we have.'

It was like getting blood out of a stone, thought Mills – which would have been funny if she had been able to share the pun.

'If it's the stabbing, I've been asked to get soil samples analysed.' She waited for his response.

'Oh aye.'

'Yes. They think the body may have been moved.'

'Do they? 'Appen that's why we've to search further afield like.' He stood up and walked towards the front door. 'I must be going.'

'Well thanks for coming round to let me know,' Mills offered.

'I came to ask you to keep an eye open – if you see anyone with an air rifle who looks suspicious let me know.' He offered her a scrap of paper with a phone number. 'It's my number. You can leave a message if you like.'

When she showed George out, Earl tagged along beside him as far as the gate. Mills wondered if the dog was missing male company. 'Time for a walk,' she said quietly, shutting the front door behind her. He kept close to her when, as they approached the Manor, a black Range Rover sped out of the drive, screeching to a halt in the middle of the road only metres from them. Earl bolted back to the cottage, leaving Mills waving apologetically despite an irritation that increased when the driver lowered his window and leaned out.

'Sorry. By the way, I'm Daniel Banford and this is my wife, Penny. I think we're neighbours.'

Mills wanted to catch Earl but remained awkwardly beside the car. 'Yes, I know. I mean, we've met before. I live in my grandmother's cottage...'

'Can't stop I'm afraid – got to pick up my son – but you must come for drinks. We've got a few people round tomorrow, say six o'clock?'

She nodded but before she could speak he revved the engine and was off down the road.

'So we've drawn a blank on the accommodation front, have we?' Mitch was looking more stressed than Nina had ever remembered seeing him.

'I'm sorry. I thought he would have used the pub campsite but they had no single men booked in that night.'

'What about groups – or couples?'

'I did ask.' She referred to her notes. 'There was a group of lasses and two couples.'

'Could he have booked in with someone – before he was killed?'

'None of the men fitted his description. I asked.'

'None of them?'

'No.'

'Bit of a mystery man then,' her boss muttered, pushing his hair back with his hand and rubbing his forehead. His superiors were demanding information for the press but with the exception of the blood they had found nothing new. He'd asked for the DNA matching to be fast-tracked and had been waiting for the call all morning.

'Well, you wait here and keep me informed of any progress. I'd better go and see the Chief Superintendent.'

His meeting did not go well. He was soon at his desk again, begging Nina to give him something he could work with.

'Sorry, we've drawn a blank with "missing persons". It suggests he's a loner.'

'Didn't look that way though, did it? Smart walking gear. Expensive boots. Stylish haircut.'

'Stylish?'

'Well...I mean... you know...nicely cut.'

Nina smiled. You couldn't accuse Mitch of being stylish. 'I know.' She chewed a fingernail.

'Talk to Hazel, Nina. You've checked out the campsites. See if she can find any other places this man might have stayed: barns, outhouses...'

'Hedges? Haystacks? What about ditches?'

Mitch's lips tightened. 'Just ask her, please. I've got to get on with the press release.'

Nina sent her friend an e-mail, knowing it would be unlikely that she could rouse enough support to arrange another search. The response was short and to the point. Nina shrugged; she was more interested in the medication they had found on the body. She looked up the forensic medical examiner's mobile number and left a message.

'Hi Naomi, it's Nina from Newby Wiske. I really need your help with some intelligence. A drug found in our stabbing victim; it's called propranolol – why would you take that?'

She didn't expect to hear from her that day so was surprised when Naomi poked her head round the door in the afternoon.

'I've only just turned my phone on – I was at the young offenders' prison up the road so I had to leave it in the car. Thought I'd drop in on the way home.'

Nina made tea for them both and explained the background to the case. Naomi immediately recognised the name of the drug, and asked whether there had been any sign of angina or heart problems at all.'

'No. Why d'you ask?'

'It's a beta-blocker, commonly used for hypertension. Did the PM pick up any angina or heart failure.'

Nina picked up the paperwork. 'I didn't see anything in the report,' she said, checking as she spoke.

Naomi held her mug, without drinking. 'I suppose an irregular heartbeat or high blood pressure wouldn't necessarily have shown up.'

'Wasn't he a bit young for that?' asked Nina. 'It says here he was in his thirties.'

'Not necessarily, especially if he was a smoker or overweight.'

'No, no. He was fit apparently. Worked out and not a smoker or heavy drinker.'

'Just unlucky then,' Naomi suggested as she drank her tea.

'Thanks,' Nina called out as the door closed. She picked up the post mortem report to re-read it in the light of what Naomi had told her. There was definitely nothing to suggest he'd had a heart problem.

An e-mail popped up on her screen. Hazel's messages were always brief and to the point. *Rucksack found on the C to C path near where the blood found.*

Chapter 4

Mills hadn't felt so positive for months. Since before Phil went to Colombia, if she was honest. But this morning, looking down at the village from above, she was feeling great. Earl was way ahead on some mission so she called his name, wanting to get back down to the cottage so she could leave for the university. The departmental technician had responded really quickly to her request to test the soil and mud from the stabbing, including an additional sample sent by Brenda from a new potential crime scene, and Mills had arranged a meeting at ten to discuss the results.

'All right to pop in to Earl at lunch time?' Mills shouted to her neighbour as she leant over the back wall. Muriel waved back through her kitchen window.

'Right you are, love!'

It was a mutual arrangement which involved feeding Muriel's cat if she was away overnight.

On days like this Mills enjoyed driving the bright red mini. It suited her mood as well as the weather. She turned on the radio, singing along to the music, shouting answers to the quiz questions and remarking out loud when a contestant got the answer wrong. There was even a space left in the car park.

The senior technician met her in the corridor outside the laboratory.

'Come to my office, Mills. I've printed the results out for you so you can see the patterns.'

Mills was intrigued. She'd not given her any information about the soils.

'Look.' The woman turned on her computer monitor, 'The samples fall into two sets. You didn't say where they came from but it's obvious they form two separate coherent groups.' She pointed at a graph where there were red triangles in a bunch at the top right corner and blue circles at the bottom towards the left. Mills tried to follow what she was saying.

'Don't worry,' she continued, 'I've plotted the iron content against a ratio with another element.'

'Right,' said Mills. 'So this means that the red triangles have a lot more iron in them than these?' She pointed at the group of blue circles.

'Absolutely! Do you know where the samples are from?'

The woman knew they were forensic samples because Mills had told her. It was obvious since they had chain of custody forms with them.

'Not really.' It wasn't really a lie, Mills thought. She knew they came from two different locations but not exactly where without her notes.

The senior technician was clearly disappointed. 'I'll send you the files by e-mail,' she said, rather frostily, as she turned off the screen. 'It would be nice to know if the work has been useful.'

'Of course, I'll let you know... as soon as I've found out.' Mills smiled and expressed her gratitude several times before leaving to install herself in the library.

It was another hour before the files appeared in her 'Inbox' and she was able to put numbers against the squares and circles on the diagram. She made a list of samples from where the body was found, entering the iron content beside them. The values were higher than normal, which puzzled Mills until she inspected a map of the area and realised it was the site of iron extraction years ago. Excitedly she did the same for the site to the west of the road, where the blood was found. All the iron values were well below the first set. She looked at the samples of mud from the victim and nodded. The iron was low and matched them; he'd not walked on the iron-rich soil but must have been carried there.

She quickly sent an e-mail to the technician, thanking her for her help and letting her know it had proved a valuable point. Then she rang Brenda to give her the news.

'Mills, that's really good news. Can you send me the information so I can pass it on straightway? I'll need a formal report of course but that can wait until tomorrow.'

'No rush then?'

'You know me. I like to keep on top of things. This has been really useful, Mills. I'm sure we can do more of this if you would like to.'

Mitch had called off the search for the weapon at three, asking Nina and Hazel to return to HQ for a briefing.

'The rucksack was nearly empty – no tent and nothing to identify him. It looks as though it was turned out – everything stuffed in, higgledy-piggledy. The DNA report on the blood indicates a match with the victim so we have to assume he was stabbed on the path to the west of Blakey Ridge. Which means he must've been moved to where he was found to the east of the road. The question is, why?'

'And which direction was he walking in?' added Nina.

'Why's that so important?' Hazel asked sharply.

Nina frowned. 'Was he taken back to where he'd come from or further on?'

'The Coast to Coast walk is from west to east,' said Mitch.

'It can be done either way,' Nina said confidently. 'It's something to do with the pub. He would have been planning to stay somewhere round there, at the pub or its campsite – it's the obvious overnight stop.'

No-one said anything so she continued. 'Most people travel eastwards, so let's assume he was approaching the pub on the Saturday evening when he was stabbed. Someone else coming along the same way might have found him... but... wait... Moving the body to the east of Blakey Ridge would mean he wouldn't be found until the next day when people set off!'

'Doesn't seem much point in moving a body unless you're playing for time,' Hazel agreed.

'And if he was travelling to the west,' continued Nina, 'he would be setting off from the Ridge in broad daylight. They would have to move him in the light, wouldn't they?'

'It's a bloody peculiar business, if you ask me. We need a psychologist to explain it. What is the usual reason for someone to move a body, girls?'

'To hide it,' answered Hazel immediately.

'They didn't do a good job then.'

Mitch was looking tired, Nina thought.

'To play for time. To confuse the investigation,' she said.

'Well they've certainly done that.' He pushed back his hair and sighed.

'If the assailant flees he would leave everything as it is. If he was local he'd be more likely to try to cover his tracks,' Hazel suggested.

'Do you think he or they are local?' Mitch was looking at Nina.

'Perhaps.'

'There's no DNA or dental match. No-one resembling him reported missing – it's as if he doesn't exist.'

Hazel was staring at the photograph. 'His hair. It's so neat. It reminds me of my ex. He was in the Yorkshire Regiment.'

'If he was services we'd have an ID by now,' Mitch said.

'Only if he was one of ours.'

They stared at each other.

'At last!' Mitch sounded triumphant. 'Hazel, get on to the MOD straightaway. They should be able to help with the right contacts abroad.' Mitch was heading for the door.

'Guv?' Nina called. 'Whichever way he was walking, he must have stayed somewhere the night before. I could try the last stops in both directions again.'

'Well, this time make sure you include foreigners. I reckon Hazel's onto something there.'

Stupidly, Mills hadn't asked Daniel what sort of "drinks do" she was invited to at the Manor. So she'd been peering out of the front window whenever a vehicle went up the lane. Three cars had passed in the last twenty minutes: two four by fours and a VW Beetle. Encouraged by the Beetle she settled Earl in the kitchen and stepped into the evening sunshine. She could put it off no longer.

The front door was ajar but she rang the bell and waited. After a moment, the teenage lad appeared, dressed in black and, yes, it was eyeliner.

'Come in.' His voice was quiet. 'Mum and Dad are in there.' He pointed at the door into what she knew was the sitting room. It hadn't changed very much. Daniel and Penny were deep in conversation with the other guests: two middle-aged men in tweeds. Mills hovered, uncertain how to introduce herself since they hadn't noticed her entrance and the lad had disappeared.

'Hello Millie!' The cheery woman's voice came from behind her.

'Naomi?' She recognised the face immediately. It was Daniel's sister, who Mills had made good friends with during her stay with her grandmother, years ago.

'Come into the kitchen and get a drink.' Her friend took her by the arm, almost pulling her out into the hall. 'I was gobsmacked when I heard you were living in Mossy Bank,' she said, grabbing a bottle from the refrigerator. 'White ok?' She poured a glass without waiting for an answer.

Mills explained the arrangement she had with her grandmother to stay in Laurel Cottage while she needed somewhere to live. Then she described how she had progressed from the schoolgirl that Naomi had known to a fully qualified archaeologist working for the university – sometimes.

'... and I do some forensic work for a lab in Harrogate.' She mentioned it because she knew Naomi would be interested, since she was a police surgeon.

'A forensic medical examiner, please!' Naomi corrected her. 'Same job just a new name.'

Penny came into the kitchen with empty glasses, to refresh the drinks and collect more nibbles. She said a cursory hello to Mills and disappeared again.

'Should we go in and be sociable?' Mills asked.

'Don't worry; they're far too busy trying to impress the Scotsman. He's brought his son down to train with the local keeper. They're all over him because he's invited them to shoot on his estate.'

'Oh, talk of the devil.' Loud voices from the hall preceded the entrance of Daniel's son. He was accompanied by a lad of similar age or perhaps a bit older. In contrast, he was dressed very traditionally, emulating his father's choice of tweeds. They made an incongruous pair.

'So how's my favourite nephew? Bored out of your mind yet, Gareth?'

'This is Fergus,' he replied gruffly.

'Hello Fergus.'

'Hi. You should call me Gus. You must be Naomi.' Although his accent was strong, it was a pleasant sound which, for some reason, made Mills think of the word "brogue".

'I am.' Naomi sounded amused. 'And this is Millie.'

'Mills.' She felt awkward correcting her friend.

'Right, Mills.'

Naomi filled the silences by asking the boys questions in turn. Gareth was bored by college, bored by the Yorkshire Dales and generally wished he wasn't there. Gus, on the other hand, was excited by the opportunity to train as a gamekeeper. His father apparently ran a large estate in Scotland and he wanted his son to come south to train with an experienced gamekeeper.

'... but of course I've been working with my dad's keeper for years on the moors at home, so I know what to do,' he said airily.

Gareth was expressionless as he took two cans of coke from the refrigerator and indicated to Gus that they should retreat – from further embarrassment, Mills suspected.

She and Naomi giggled when the pair had gone.

'How old d'you think Fergus is?' Mills asked.

'He's left school... just. And he's been helping his father on the shoots. I doubt he's more than nineteen.'

'And Gareth?'

'Seventeen.'

'What is Gareth's sister doing now?'

'Oh Lucy's in the States with friends. She's the apple of her Dad's eye. Poor Gareth doesn't get a look in regarding parental pride, I'm afraid.'

'He doesn't exactly fit in here, does he?' Mills suggested.

'But he's a good lad, whatever his parents say.' Naomi laughed, topping up her glass and handing Mills the bottle. 'Anyway, how's *your* family?'

'Gran's fine. I think she likes her apartment in Harrogate. Dad's married to Fiona and they have a baby girl. In fact they're coming to stay next week.'

'That's nice.'

'No it's not. It'll be awful. It's bound to end in tears, I know it. The cottage is too small for us all and the dog will be out of sorts with a baby crying. And I'm supposed to be helping with an archaeology course the National Park is running so I won't be round much anyway. I told them it wasn't a good idea but...'

'There's always Ivy Cottage,' Naomi said brightly. 'You know it's mine. The house next door?'

Indeed, Mills did know that Naomi had inherited the cottage next to the Manor from her mother.

'So what about it?' Naomi insisted.

'Do you rent it out now?' In the past it had been a holiday cottage, perhaps this was the answer, thought Mills.

'Not officially. I have friends stay there. I don't use it much myself – although now I know you're in the village I might come up more often.'

'So Dad and Fiona could use it? Are you sure?'

'Of course. We have to preserve your sanity, don't we?' She stood up. 'Hey, why don't you come and see what I've done to it since you last saw it? It's time I was going anyway and I think we've done our duty.'

Mills insisted they went in to speak to Daniel and Penny although her hosts didn't seem concerned that they'd neglected them. Naomi called up the stairs to Gareth but there was no response above the music coming from overhead. Mills noticed a gun bag leaning in the corner against the wall as she stood in the hall.

'Is that a shot gun?' she asked.

'Dan's got several. He's quite the country squire these days.'

'Does Gareth use it?'

'Heavens no. Dan wouldn't let him. He's not allowed more than the air rifle.'

'Air rifle? Is that legal?'

'Oh yes. It's quite powerful but it doesn't need a licence. Dan takes pot shots at the rabbits with it.'

Mills said nothing but thought of the red kite lying motionless in the heather as she followed Naomi into Ivy Cottage. It had been redecorated throughout in a simple country style that gave it charm and comfort. Mills declared it perfect for her family, insisting that her father contribute a sensible rent for its use. They agreed a sum and Naomi handed over the key.

Back in Laurel Cottage, Mills checked her e-mails while the microwave heated her supper. Brenda appeared delighted with the results of the soil analyses, which definitely showed that the victim had not walked to the spot where he was found and probably had not even been in that area on the day prior to his death. You might be required as an expert witness, warned Brenda.

She ate quickly, and gave Earl a quick run, noticing that the four wheel drive vehicles were still at the Manor. While the dog wolfed his dinner, she rang her father with the good news. Fiona answered, sounding weary, almost tearful.

'Oh Mills, it's super to speak to a human being. I've been stuck in the apartment all day without seeing a soul and your father's still not home.'

'How's baby?'

'She's been grumpy all day.' She was clearly close to tears.

'She's probably just teething.'

'That's what they say but sometimes I just think she hates me!' Now she was definitely crying.

Mills was at a loss. She cajoled, empathised and comforted her stepmother but it was beyond her sphere of experience. Fiona's problem was exacerbated by living in an apartment in Canary Wharf where Mills doubted there would a mother and baby group in the immediate area. When she told Fiona about Ivy Cottage it went quiet at the other end. Mills put all the advantages to her, but her response was not enthusiastic.

'You mean we'll be doing our own cooking? Are there any shops? Where is the nearest Waitrose?'

'It'll be fine,' Mills reassured her. 'There are supermarkets in all the local towns and they'll deliver everything, even nappies. And the cottage has a washing machine, a microwave – all mod cons.'

'Is there a television?' She sounded calmer now.

'Of course. Anyway, I expect you'll want to have the odd evening out, won't you?'

'Oh yes Mills, thank you!'

'I'll find a local baby-sitter and make sure she's free,' Mills offered sweetly.

'We've had a minor breakthrough.' Mitch was smiling, Hazel noted. She'd not seen that for a few days.

'What's that, guv?'

'Forensics has shown that the soil on the victim's boots comes from the area where we found his blood – the supposed murder scene – and not from where he was found. That means he didn't walk east of Blakey Ridge that day.'

'So they carried him?'

'Yes.' Mitch was still smiling. 'Let Nina know she needs only check accommodation to the west. It should speed things up.'

Hazel contacted her colleague immediately.

'I hope it hasn't wasted your time?' she added when she finished explaining the progress that had been made.

'No, not at all. I assumed a bigger chance of a westward journey so I started at Ingleby Cross which would have been the last stop before Blakey Ridge. I'm there now.'

'Don't forget about the overseas visitors,' warned Hazel.

'I won't.'

Nina had contacted the police at Richmond and was accompanied by two young constables. She divided the accommodation list into guest houses, B&Bs and campsites and they took one category each. She ensured she had campsites because she had a hunch it was the most likely place to find something. She was armed with a photograph of the victim which was a good enough likeness if anyone thought they may have seen him from the written description. It wasn't her wish to flaunt a dead man's face to all and sundry.

Campsite owners were busy people during the day with farms to run or other jobs to go to. It was difficult to get an answer to a phone call. In desperation Nina drove down to the last site on her list, on the off-chance someone was around the site even if they weren't answering calls. The road to the farm was a long rough track through three fields, each with a gate to open and close. Nina hoped it wouldn't be a wild goose chase. The farmhouse was hidden by a stand of deciduous trees, until she turned a corner and entered the yard.

She braked hard when she saw a child's tricycle and toys lying around, pulling up near the side door. It was open and she could hear music inside but no-one answered her knock. She peered around outside, picking her way carefully to the back of the house where a woman was playing with two children. According to her list, this was Mrs Holt.

'I'm sorry to disturb you...' Nina began.

The woman shielded her eyes from the sun as she surveyed Nina, who stood self-consciously in her black pencil skirt and white blouse.

'Well, you don't look like a camper!' The woman's comment was sharp but not unfriendly.

Nina identified herself and asked if she could question her about her guests who were walking the Coast to Coast path.

'Is it about the lad that were found over at Blakey?' she asked.

'It is I'm afraid Mrs Holt.'

'Call me Doreen.' She gave her boys the football she'd been holding, directing Nina to a bench in the shade of the farmhouse wall.

'Fire away, then.'

'You've heard about the incident?'

'Oh aye. The walkers, they talk about nowt else,' she said as she settled her large bulk beside Nina. 'Shaken them up, especially the women like. Some were considering giving up before going that far along.'

'I see. Well I'm making enquiries about the men.' She described the victim carefully, asking her to recollect anyone fitting that description that had stayed on what would have been the friday night.

'Let me fetch me bookings.'

While she waited Nina watched the boys playing football, enjoying the cool breeze, listening to the curlew overhead. The view from the garden was spectacular. Nina dreamt of the day when she, Nige and Rosie, and maybe a boy later, could afford somewhere in the country.

Mrs Holt returned with an exercise book, flicking through the pages.

'Right. There's none that spring to mind. But I don't scrutinise them like.'

'He might have been from overseas,' Nina offered.

'Overseas, you say?' She stared at the page. 'We had a couple here that night. American – well he was.

I can't say I recollect her speaking. So do you think he was American?'

'Perhaps.' Nina took the photograph of the dead man's face from the folder. 'I have a photograph of the man...' She waited to see Doreen's reaction.

The woman must have sensed her reticence. 'Don't you fret yourself girl. I've seen plenty of dead bodies in my time. I was a nurse before I married farming folk.'

'It's just his face.' She handed it over.

The woman held the photo at arm's length, considering it. 'Good looking even in death, God rest his soul. But is it Mr Eisenhower?'

'Was that the name he gave?'

'That's what I've got down here: Mr and Mrs Eisenhower. Not that I'm fussed. I don't ask for marriage certificates here.'

'Do you think it was his real name? Did you see a credit card, for example?'

'Credit card, love? What d'you think we are, the Holiday Inn?' Her laughter was deep and hollow.

'Do you have an address, anything that might help identify him?' Nina tried to keep the frustration from her voice.

'No, sorry. Just a name and cash on the nail, that's all we ask.'

Nina who was not going to admit she had no idea what the rules were regarding maintaining records of campers, smiled and asked her to confirm whether the photo was of "Mr Eisenhower".

'It might be.' She was still holding the photograph.

'Doreen, I'd like you to try to remember him while I read out the details we have, to see if it fits his description.'

Nina read out his height, hair colour, eye colour and many other details, including his slim hands and the fact that he would have had a very upright posture. When she had finished, Doreen sat in silence for a while. Then she nodded slowly.

'I think it could fit his description. I remember his hair – how did you say? Neat and well managed? It was very different to the scallywags that usually come through.'

'If you think it could be him, we can check. We can use fingerprinting to confirm it or even DNA if we can find anything suitable.' As she said it Nina wondered what on earth would carry either from a campsite. It would take a full statement to ascertain any possible sources.

She took a detailed set of notes, telling Doreen that she would require a statement later. Meanwhile she asked her to think about exactly what Mr Eisenhower and his wife had done while they were on the site.

As soon as she had a signal, she rang her constables, who had found nothing. She told them to call it a day and she returned to HQ, where she sat with Hazel, trying to establish how she could link that campsite to the man lying in the morgue. Unable to come up with anything plausible, she spent the rest of the afternoon typing in her notes. When Mitch appeared, she read them aloud for his benefit.

'The couple arrived on foot at about five o'clock. They seemed tired but put the tent up immediately – a small, three-man tent. The man did all the talking. The woman was preparing a meal. He had an American accent and was very polite, calling Doreen ma'am. He was amicable but not particularly talkative. She describes him as average height to tall and fit looking.' Hazel giggled. 'I mean athletic, although she did say he was good-looking, as it happens.'

Mitch had been sitting at his desk without speaking but now he asked, 'What about the woman?'

'She was thin, tall with medium length blonde hair. There was a wedding ring, she noticed that. They paid on arrival in cash and left early the next day.'

Mitch looked at his watch. 'Organise a CSI team for tomorrow. Get down there with them and cover every inch of that site. We have got to find a link. It's all we've got.'

When he'd gone Hazel said, 'It's been days since they were there. You'll be lucky to find anything now.'

The CSI team consisted of three very young women, Nina observed as they set about planning the evaluation of the entire area where the American had pitched his tent. It was taped off in sections before the line moved meticulously forward, using tweezers to collect anything there. It took several hours, resulting in a number of bags containing bits of fluff and debris.

'Has the site been tidied up since last week?' Nina enquired as she sat in the farm kitchen with Doreen.

'How d'you mean?'

'Rubbish collected, paper and cans binned?'

'No. We expect the campers to do that.'

Nina could see the team were getting close to the tape, so she wandered out to speak to them.

'Another ten minutes and we'll be done,' the leader confirmed.

'And is there anything?'

She shook her head at Nina. 'Nothing much.'

Nina watched, her gaze following the ground they had covered and then beyond the tape. Something white in the grass caught her eye and for a moment she looked at it, puzzling over what it might be. Then she sprinted back into the kitchen.

'Doreen... the American... did you notice if he was chewing gum?'

Chapter 5

Mills had taken Earl down to Ivelet Bridge to cool off in the Swale. A dipper hopped unnoticed by the dog as he paddled on the smooth stones. The afternoon had been hot and humid but a slight breeze was developing as she sat in the shade. She needed to think. The call from the National Park Office had been a shock: the person in charge of the summer school was in hospital and would not be well enough to attend. They wanted her to take his place and lead the week's course on archaeology on the moors instead of simply assisting. Naturally she was flattered and glad of the money but she was concerned about the amount of work involved. They assumed she would know of people she could call on to help her.

Earl climbed up the bank and shook himself vigorously, settling at her feet. She patted his damp back, wondering how she could find a helper. Her colleagues and their students had left for the summer to carry out work on sites which were mainly abroad. Wherever they had gone they wouldn't return for a week in the Dales. She would make enquiries of course but was sure it was a hopeless task.

She was conscious of movement behind her just before Earl leapt up barking and growling. She turned to see Gareth marching down the hill from the village towards them. Grabbing at Earl's collar she ordered him to sit, then called the teenager to stop. He obeyed, turning bright red in the face as he did.

'Sorry, he's usually so good with people.' The dog was pulling away as she dug in her pockets for treats, handing a few to Gareth.

'Would you mind giving him one? He won't be able to resist.'

Earl moved cautiously and snatched it away.

'We don't have a dog,' Gareth admitted. 'He's cool. What is he?'

'A lurcher. He's not really mine. He belongs to a friend who's working abroad.'

'Mum and Dad won't have pets. She says it's a health hazard but Dad's scared of dogs.' He continued to hand out the treats until they were finished.

Earl settled back at her feet and Gareth perched on the end of the bench, gently moving his hand in front of the dog's nose until he condescended to lick the boy's hand.

Mills finally broke the silence. 'Are you off somewhere?'

'No. It's boring at home so I came for a walk. I wasn't following you.'

It hadn't occurred to her that he was, she thought. He is a strange lad.

'Naomi says you're an archaeologist.'

'Yes,' she said. 'Are you interested in it?'

'A bit. I've seen some stuff on TV that's quite cool.'

'So are you at college?' She chose her words carefully.

'Sixth-form college, yes. I'm doing my A levels next year.'

'What subjects?'

'Maths, history, chemistry and art.'

'Not a bad combination. What do you want to do after?'

'Dunno. Dad wants me to go to Cambridge. He went there. I'd rather be in London.'

'To study what?'

'Dunno.'

He stood up and starting walking down towards the bridge. Earl started barking again.

'Wait!' shouted Mills.

He turned quickly, almost expectantly.

'Would you like to help me with a job here in a couple of weeks?'

Nina was updating the report forms with the latest intelligence, including the chewing gum find. She was so agitated about the result of the test that she couldn't concentrate. If the gum gave a match to the victim's DNA it would prove he had been accompanied by a woman and they would know he was American. The name he had given – Eisenhower – would be checked anyway; it was the only information they had so far since there was no address and he'd paid by cash. On the other hand, if it wasn't his DNA then it could belong to anyone – the killer, the wife or girlfriend, or even an innocent camper.

Hazel had teased her constantly since the find, leaving a pack of gum on her desk with a note saying "chew on this buster!" Mitch had been pleased that he had something he could tell his Chief Super. As far as he was concerned the longer they took to get the results the better but Nina had asked for the test to be fast-tracked and later that afternoon Brenda rang to give her the news personally.

'Nina, you're a star! It's a perfect match to the victim.'

She rushed out of the office to find anyone willing to listen. Hazel, who was outside smoking, threw down her cigarette, grinding it into the lawn, telling her to find Mitch, even if he was in with the Chief Super. That was exactly where he was but she paced up and down at the end of the corridor until he emerged looking pensive.

'I've got some news for you!' She explained the result as they walked back to the office together, where Hazel was waiting. She watched with satisfaction as his demeanour changed and he became organised and in command again.

'Right. This is what we needed. It means we have a profile – get it posted. We have a woman in the picture now too.'

Nina had been thinking about her next step. 'Do you want me to work back along the Coast to Coast path, checking campsites on previous nights?'

'Yes.'

'I'll check for American mispers and the usual things: the embassy and US servicemen...'

'Services? Who mentioned services before?' Mitch interrupted. 'Could he be doing military training up here?'

Something else was worrying Nina. 'Guv, do you think the woman killed him? If she did she must've had help to move him so far.'

'And where is she?' asked Hazel. 'Why hasn't she turned up?'

'Perhaps she's dead too,' said Mitch.

They were all quiet for a while. Then, just as Nina was going to ask the question, Mitch said, 'We're not searching for another body unless we know there is one.' His tone suggested the discussion was over.

Nina and Hazel took up positions at their desks for the rest of the afternoon, making one call after another. By the end of the day, Nina had a list of just three addresses to visit where the couple had camped overnight on route. Hazel had drawn a blank with the embassy and was not getting far with the US police, so was relying on making a contact with the military. So far she had been unable to reach the relevant authorities.

'I'll keep trying tonight,' she said. 'There's no point in the morning with the time difference.'

Daniel Banford was striding down the lane as Mills parked outside Laurel Cottage. He waved, so she waved back as she turned through the gate and up her path.

'Hold on!' he called. 'I want to see you!'

Oh dear, thought Mills as she turned with a smile, hoping it was nothing serious.

'I understand that my boy's going to do some archaeological thing with you.' He sounded out of breath.

'Yes. He's offered to help me with a course I'm running... if that's ok?'

'My wife and I think it's so good of you to give him a chance to be honest.' He was standing at the gate, sweat pouring down his face and Mills wondered why he was dressed in a waistcoat and tweed jacket on such a sweltering day. 'He's going through a funny stage,' he continued. 'Can't make sense of him myself. No doubt he'll work through it. Quite different to his sister.'

'I'm sure he's fine.' Mills could hear Earl inside, scratching the unopened front door.

'The problem is, Penny... my wife and I... we're supposed to be going to Scotland the week after next.'

'Oh dear...'

'It's not a problem for Gareth to stay here but... I wonder... would you keep an eye on him? He can be a bit... juvenile. I, that is, we'd feel happier if you were to keep an eye on things.'

There was the sound of whining from inside the cottage.

'No problem, really.'

'That's excellent. Penny will be relieved to hear it.'

He turned and strode back up the lane, leaving Mills to wonder if she had been wise to accept responsibility.

Gradually the pieces were beginning to fall into place. Nina had located three overnight stops where Mr Eisenhower and friend had pitched their little tent: Borrowdale on Friday, Shap on Sunday and Keld on the Tuesday. It would only be a matter of time to locate where they stayed in-between once there was an item in the press. She reckoned that bookings must have been made ahead too and found that Mr and Mrs Eisenhower had booked a site beyond Blakey, at Little Beck. The owner confirmed that no-one had shown up.

Then she did what she should have done before now, she rang the "Lion Inn" at Blakey. Sure enough, they also had a booking under Eisenhower.

'But you said there were no "no shows",' Nina objected.

'There weren't.'

'The couple arrived?'

'Yes.'

'But I gave you a description. You said you hadn't seen him.'

'I didn't. The description was not him.'

She drove over with the photograph of the victim. The car park was empty now the incident room had been removed and there was nothing to show it had even been there. She was struck by a cold wind when she climbed out of the car and reached back inside for a jacket.

'So you're absolutely sure it wasn't him. Are you certain he didn't have an accent?'

'Yes. I was working on Saturday. They came in for a meal.'

'How did they pay?'

The young man looked puzzled. 'I'd have to ask. I don't have access to receipts.'

In the end she agreed to wait until the next day for the information, leaving strict instructions for any receipts to be retained if payment was by card.

As she drove back across to Newby Wiske, she went through the intelligence so far. She knew that as soon as she was in the office, Mitch would want a report.

'The American and the woman were booked to finish the walk at Robin Hood's Bay last Monday. These are the sites they definitely stayed on and the owners have confirmed the use of the name Eisenhower. More importantly, no-one appeared at the site booked for Sunday night.

'What happened on Saturday night?' Mitch asked.

'A couple stayed under the name Eisenhower but it wasn't him.'

Mitch swore under his breath. 'We need a description of that woman,' he said.

'I could go to the sites where they've been seen with the artist. A likeness could be shown on "Crimewatch"... we can organise press coverage.' Nina enjoyed working with the police artist.

'No, Nina, we won't,' Mitch sounded irritable. 'We're waiting for a response from the States. It's too sensitive until we hear from them.'

'Seriously?'

Hazel would normally have argued, thought Nina, but even she seemed to sense there was no point.

'Ok, I'll get the artist's impression prepared for when we can go ahead.'

'Good girl.'

Nina gritted her teeth and smiled.

As soon as Mitch had left, Hazel reacted as expected. 'What the hell does that mean? Do they think it's some terrorist plot on the moors? Come off it. It'll be some jealous wife or mistress and the sooner we get her picture published the better.'

Finally, after a long wait, Hazel received the call she had been waiting for; a Major Henderson could meet her at Catterick Garrison that afternoon. Brenda Yardley's expertise on clothing had confirmed that the victim was dressed principally in items of USA origin, except for the rugby shirt from the "Black Sheep Brewery". Nina's visit to the brewery shop had drawn a blank although Nige was pleased to receive some samples when she returned home. However, it did suggest the victim might have been a visitor to the area.

Hazel was directed to the Major's office by a polite young man dressed in fatigues who explained that

Major Henderson was in temporary accommodation during his visit to the base. It was a small room with just a desk and two wooden chairs. The soldier saluted, shutting the door quietly as he withdrew.

'Would you prefer to sit outside? There's nothing to keep us inside.' He was a clean shaven man; tall and tanned.

Hazel smiled and followed him down the corridor and out into the fresh air.

'D'you mind if I smoke?' he asked, reaching into his pocket.

'No...' She hesitated. He'd already taken a cigarette from the packet and was lighting it with a silver lighter. She was fumbling in her bag, searching for her own when the Major began to apologise.

'Gee, I guess I didn't expect...' He offered her a Marlboro, leaving Hazel thoroughly embarrassed. She accepted but was left feeling she was the one on the back foot.

'So,' the Major said, 'you've got a body you think may be one of ours?'

'We have reason to think he may be American, yes. Possibly in the services.'

'Why?'

'Why what?'

'Why d'you believe he's in the US military?'

It was just a hunch, initiated by the short haircut – she could hardly tell him that.

'It's normal procedure if we exhaust our mispers... our missing persons... to look further afield.'

He paused to flick the ash from his cigarette and indicated that they should sit on the bench across the road. 'I've been making enquiries and I don't think it's possible that he's one of ours. There's no reason for US personnel to be up here. We do have guys at RAF Leeming. I can check it out if you'd like me to?'

Hazel, anticipating she'd be fobbed off, was ready to apply more pressure but he appeared to be trying to help. They smoked in silence, watching the soldiers moving to and fro across the area between buildings. It was pleasant in the shade but as soon as she stubbed out her cigarette she jumped up.

'How soon can you get back to me, Major Henderson?' She hoped she sounded officious.

'If you accompany me back to the office, I can make the call now.'

She followed obediently, sitting quietly while he rang first one then another administrator until he found the appropriate member of staff to contact. Hazel was impressed by the way he commanded his subordinates to respond immediately, and then listened while he spoke to a senior officer at Leeming.

'...yes, sir, that's correct.... Thank you, sir..... Right, sir, I'll tell her.' He turned with a smile, shaking his head. 'There's no-one missing over there. He wants a full report. I'll write a note and send it over. Everything in triplicate round here.'

Hazel was planning what to do next.

His teeth were really white when he smiled. 'I'm sorry not to be more help, ma'am.'

'Can I ask you something, Major Henderson?..'

'Please call me Robert. What is it?'

'We've contacted the US Embassy and now we've spoken to you. Is there anyone else who can tell us if there is an American citizen missing?'

'I don't think the US Government has any more control over their citizens abroad than yours does. It's quite possible that somebody could disappear without it being noticed for a while.'

He stood up, offering his hand. 'I'll do what I can to ensure he's not one of ours.'

She noted his strong handshake.

'Please let me know if anything does turn up. It's really important we find out who he is.'

He examined the card before placing it inside his jacket. 'I have your number,' he said with a smile.

On returning to HQ she was careful to avoid reference to Major Henderson, preferring to report the negative results of her visit without recollecting the officer's good looks and captivating American drawl. Her resolve lasted just two hours until Nina took a call, quickly handing over the phone, mouthing the word "Catterick", which caused Hazel to blush.

'I hope you don't mind me calling you at work but I wondered if you'd like to have dinner.'

Nina spent the next three days visiting the campsites where Mr Eisenhower had stayed, developing a picture of his female partner. She was accompanying Karen, a very experienced police artist, who had a remarkable talent for developing an impression of her subject from verbal descriptions, to the point where witnesses agreed it was a true likeness. At the same time Nina was assembling more detailed profiles of both the mystery woman and the victim. The woman was quiet but those who had heard her speak were sure she was English, possibly local. It appeared the man was quite communicative, chatting to the site owners about their route and the local area. At Keld the owner remembered he had arrived wearing the Black Sheep Brewery shirt and they had discussed the tour he had taken of the brewery. At Kirkby Stephen he'd remarked that he'd enjoyed fish and chips in the town. Nina followed up all the leads but they led her no further forward.

However, the profile of the woman was going well. They now had a good likeness which was being gradually tweaked. Nina decided they'd done enough when, in Borrowdale, the last of the witnesses recognised the woman from the artist's impression they showed her.

'Oh aye, I remember them. They stayed Friday night, it was pouring down. I said they could sit in by the fire in the kitchen if they wanted. I was going to my sister's, I see her once a week if I can.'

'What was she like to speak to?' Nina asked, reaching for her notebook.

'I don't recall. She were very quiet.' She bit her lip. 'The reason I remember her was more because of what she left behind.' She paused as if wishing to be prompted but Nina simply waited, knowing the woman wanted to tell her.

'It was in the bathroom bin,' the woman offered. 'I saw the packet. It was one of them pregnancy testing kits.'

Nina wondered how to put the next question delicately. 'Would you happen to know whether it had shown positive?'

'Oh, aye. It were.'

Chapter 6

Mills found a handwritten note from Penny Banford on her doormat in the hall, thanking her for agreeing to "keep an eye" on young Gareth and letting her know they would return in ten days – a contact number was enclosed. It was bad enough that Dad and Fiona were descending on her, without having to take responsibility for an adolescent as well. On her way up to Ivy Cottage to air the rooms and turn on the refrigerator, she was weighed down with groceries she'd picked up in town. She was going to be too busy preparing for the course in the following week to devote all her time to her family and hoped that by stocking them up with essentials she might get more time to herself.

The tiny cottage was ideal for her father and his wife. The smaller of the two bedrooms had a cot for the young baby and the kitchen was equipped with everything - all modern conveniences. Mills noticed there was an open fire in the tiny sitting room but if the weather remained warm there would be no necessity for any heating.

The sound of shooting drew her upstairs to the back of the cottage. The grouse season hadn't started – perhaps a farmer after rabbits? From the small bedroom she could see down into the large walled garden next door. The sound was coming from the Manor, as if someone was shooting through an upper window into the vegetable garden below. Another shot sounded as a rabbit bolted under the gate.

Daniel and Penny had gone so Mills knew it could only be Gareth using the air rifle. She hurried down stairs, ready to tackle him but thought better of it. She would, however, contact George Herbert, as he had asked her to. She would tell him of her suspicions about the air rifle and he would deal with them as he thought fit.

By the time she was in Laurel Cottage with the phone in her hand she'd had a change of heart. If Gareth was in trouble with the police while his parents were away, she would be responsible. Not only would she be involved but she might lose the help she so badly needed on the summer school. Guiltily she replaced the receiver and started making supper.

As soon as she'd eaten she continued work on the course. Fortunately the general plan had been established months ago and all the necessary permissions and risk assessments had been completed and approved. She sat with the huge file of paperwork in front of her, staring at the list of participants. There were ten youngsters aged fourteen to eighteen, from a variety of schools in the Yorkshire area. There had been competition to join the course and she feared they were coming with high expectations. Each day was designed to highlight a different aspect of archaeological investigation which began with the simple stuff: how to make notes and use maps but soon moved on to recording information correctly. The more challenging days on analysis and geophysical interpretation would be handled by experts but she would have to take the young students through the practical stages of excavation, which was probably what they looked forward to most of all since many of them would be studying archaeology "A" level.

The site selected for the excavation was unfamiliar to her. It was in the heart of the Dales close to Settle. It was chosen for ease of access since there was no desire to herd ten teenagers far across the moors, possibly in inclement weather. The site was close to the road so they would not have to carry the tools too far. Flint artefacts had been uncovered on a previous excavation and it was sufficiently well characterised that the involvement of students was not considered a problem, provided they were carefully supervised.

Mills was relieved to discover that she would be provided with a minibus and driver to ferry her charges about. The paperwork confirmed that the equipment had been booked with her department at the University of North Yorkshire and, in fact, would arrive in a bus also provided by the university. She e-mailed Jake to find out who would be driving only to discover that Nige had volunteered, since he would be demonstrating the geophysical analysis during the week. Suddenly things were looking up. If Nige was driving he could be persuaded to help and Gareth would be assisting her. Yes, Gareth. She leant back in her chair to consider the best course of action. It was no good – she would have to talk to him about the gun at some stage but maybe it would be best once the course had started.

Mills had left the front door open to cool the house while she prepared a salad to go with the cold meat she'd bought for the evening meal. Dad and Fiona said they'd arrive around six and she'd told them to come down once they were settled in the cottage. She'd bought strawberries, meringues and cream to concoct a rather impressive pavlova.

At half past six her father called from the front door as he appeared with the baby in his arms. Over his shoulder was a large bag, presumably full of Flora's paraphernalia.

'Oh, I thought she'd be ready for bed,' said Mills.

Her father was holding the sleeping baby at arms length, offering her to Mills, but she ignored the gesture and began laying the table.

'Where's Fiona?'

'She'll be along. She's getting ready.'

'Well, sit down. I'll open the wine.'

He lowered the baby onto the sofa and sat down beside her, dumping the bag on the floor. Earl wandered over to investigate.

Mills handed her father a glass of red wine.

'Good journey?' she asked.

'Don't ask. I'm knackered.'

Everything was ready by the time Fiona arrived. She was wearing a spotty dress and had clearly decided to make it a "night out". She was fully made up and was wearing earrings, bracelet and necklace. Her perfume pervaded the air.

Mills grabbed Earl, dragging him back into the kitchen and began serving the meal. While they were eating, Mills asked whether they had any plans for the week. She explained that she would be busy after the weekend running the course but would try to see them in the evenings.

'You should walk over to Gunnerside Gill while you're here – I could take you tomorrow.'

'We'd love to, Millie,' her father said, 'but I can't carry Flora very far. It hurts my back.'

'Buy a carrier, Dad. That's what people do. Put her on your back.'

'I don't think Fi wants to go,' he said looking across at his new wife, who was nearly asleep on the sofa.

'Of course she does,' Mills urged. 'You still go to the gym, don't you Fiona?'

'Yes, more than ever.' She perked up visibly. 'They have a crèche.'

'She's there nearly all weekend. She calls it her "me time".'

'If you can use those cross-trainer things you can do a few hills. You must get a carrier for Flora, Dad.'

'When the shops are open,' he replied. 'I thought we could have a lie-in tomorrow with a very late lunch at the pub we passed on the way down here.'

The meal went well, Mills thought, as she opened another bottle of wine, but the mood changed as soon as Flora woke up. Fiona became anxious to leave and her husband jumped up ready to help.

'She wants her bottle. She always wants a feed at this time. We'd better go, Hugh.'

Mills offered to warm the milk but Fiona was adamant they should go. Reluctantly her father collected the baby things together and followed his wife who was clutching the wailing offspring.

'Mills, you know we do appreciate you organising this little break for Fi,' her father said awkwardly.

'No problem, Dad. I hope you all enjoy it.'

'Better go,' he said sheepishly, looking over his shoulder at his wife and baby disappearing up the lane, 'or I'll be for it!'

When Robert Henderson suggested "The Nag's Head" at Pickhill, Hazel offered to meet him there but he insisted on coming to fetch her "so she could have a drink". She was immediately concerned about his motives and by the time the car drew up outside her block of flats – a BMW Z4, she noticed – she was feeling surprisingly apprehensive, aware she would be dependent on him driving her back later. The short drive to Pickhill was awkward with the conversation around the weather becoming embarrassingly protracted. She didn't know the pub and was not particularly impressed by the exterior as they turned into the car park.

Her opinion changed immediately they were shown to their table and Robert had selected a bottle of chenin blanc. She made herself sip it slowly as they studied the menu, both selecting fish. Conversation was easier after the second glass. Although it wasn't like her to open up about her divorce, Hazel found herself relating the whole sorry story. When she'd finished unburdening herself, she asked him if he'd been married. They were interrupted by the main course arriving and the subject changed to memorable meals.

They were talking like old friends now. In fact, if asked, Hazel would have said there was no spark of romance there at all now. By sharing their stories they'd somehow lost any mystery and promise that was there potentially, as far as Hazel was concerned.

'So, tell me about your work,' Robert asked, refilling her glass. 'It must be fascinating.'

Hazel laughed. 'Fascinating? You've got to be joking! Most of it's so mundane you wouldn't believe it.'

'But the case you're on. A murder? That *must* be interesting.'

'A lot of paperwork mainly. But what about you? I don't really know what you do.'

He shrugged. 'I'm just a major in the US Air Force.'

'So what does that involve?'

'This and that... paperwork mainly.'

They both laughed.

She tried again. 'Do you fly?'

He grinned. 'I'm not superman, you know.'

They laughed again but she sensed he was avoiding the question and waited, indicating she expected an answer.

'I have to travel a lot with the Force but I'm not a pilot, no.'

They looked at the dessert menu but in the end just ordered coffees. Robert picked up the bottle, inspecting the small amount of wine remaining before preparing to top up Hazel's glass. She covered it with her hand to indicate that she had had more than enough.

'So have you managed to solve your murder yet?'

'No.'

'Have you found out the identity of the body?'

His questioning was beginning to irritate her.

'No. I don't suppose you've heard of any missing personnel?'

'Zilch. I'm sorry.'

She wasn't sure that he was sorry.

At the end of the evening he drove her home and she thanked him for a pleasant evening. He said he was glad she'd enjoyed it. There was no "we must do it again sometime" no fumbling embrace, not even a peck on the cheek. She climbed the steps feeling slightly used, convinced all he really wanted was some intelligence about the murder. Oh yes, she was sure that's what it was. He was from that oxymoron joke – military intelligence.

They'd agreed to meet up at the pub in the early evening, allowing everyone to have a restful day, except Mills, who had plenty of preparation to complete for the course. She reluctantly packed everything away at six and made her way down to Muker.

The pub looked busy with a number of people choosing to remain outside in the last of the sun. Fiona was seated at a table with Flora.

'Hugh's inside getting drinks,' she called.

Mills went in to help her father by carrying the white wine out for Fiona.

'Did you have a nice day?' she asked him.

'All right,' he said.

Mills detected he was being polite. 'What's up, Dad?'

'Nothing. It's just that Fi didn't sleep very well. It was rather noisy in the cottage last night.'

'Noisy?'

'From the big house. They were having a party I think.' He lowered his voice as they went out into the sunshine. 'Music very late.'

Almost immediately Fiona began moaning about her lack of sleep. When Mills explained that Gareth's parents were away, she demanded that she contact them to complain.

'I'll speak to him about it. I'm sure you won't have any more problems.' It reminded her that she had a favour to ask of them. 'Will you be around on Tuesday?'

Her father looked at Fiona. 'We can be if you want. Why?'

'It's just that Muriel can't take Earl out and I'll be away all day with the course.'

'We'll make sure we are. It'll be fun.'

Fiona said nothing.

'Thanks, Dad. I'll get some menus.'

They sat making small talk while they waited for their food but it was clear that everyone was relieved when it arrived. Mills watched as Flora, the centre of attention throughout the meal, was passed from Fiona to her father and back as they ate in relays.

'She's always difficult at this time,' Fiona explained. 'It's colic.'

'Colic?'

Her father laughed. 'Don't ask me.'

'All babies are like it at her age.' Fiona was jiggling the little bundle up and down on her knee. 'She probably needs a feed.'

They left as soon as they'd finished eating, much to the delight of a family of four who'd been eyeing their table for some time. They said their goodbyes with Mills promising to drop in the following evening.

'Have a nice day tomorrow then!' she called as they climbed into their respective cars.

'That's if we get some sleep tonight,' was Fiona's response.

Mills was up at six to walk Earl and had everything ready when Nige arrived with the van at eight. Gareth was supposed to be at Laurel Cottage by then. Mills told Nige to wait and marched up the lane to find him. She was passing Ivy Cottage when she heard a sound from an upstairs window. Her father, still in his pyjamas was leaning out, trying to attract her attention. His whispers were hardly audible.

'Hold on Dad, I just need to go next door.'

She hammered on the door of the Manor then returned to the cottage. Her father had come downstairs to inform her that the music had gone on until four in the morning and Fiona was very upset.

'Ok, Dad.'

Gareth was stumbling down the drive pulling on his leather jacket.

'Come on, we've got to leave!' she shouted at him over her shoulder as she almost ran back down the lane.

She muttered under her breath to Nige about Gareth's behaviour but her friend told her to chill out.

'They're all like that at his age,' he said.

She planned to tackle the teenager on the way but he sat slumped forward with his eyes closed, leaving her to fume over the fact they would be late on the first day despite Nige's attempt to speed in the old minivan.

There was a line of cars parked by the field where the course was taking place. A handful of teenagers were sitting in the cars with their parents. She indicated to them to join her in the field and, by the time everyone had arrived, she was surrounded by the participants and their parents. Although the students had come from a number of different schools there were two brothers, Oscar and Piers, and two boys who knew each other: Jay and Stuart, who liked to be known as Stu. The youngest member of the group was Mike, a small lad with ginger hair who had come in his school uniform, causing some comments from the others, particularly a girl who was dressed precociously in shorts and a crop top. Mills, noting her painted fingernails, wondered whether she would last the course. The three other girls seemed more normal.

Mills began by explaining what they would be doing and handed out sheets with the programme for the week. The adults stood watching until she could stand it no longer, pointedly telling them what time to pick their offspring up. Fortunately several took the hint, leading the others away. Just one man was left and Mills gave him a quizzical look.

'I'd like to stay if I may. I have an interest in archaeology.'

Mills explained it was not possible because of insurance and CRB checking.

'But I haven't been CRB checked,' Gareth pointed out when the man finally left.

'That's ok,' said Mills, 'I'm supervising you.' She was distracted by a car screeching to a halt at the gate. A young man with a thatch of blond hair emerged, racing across the field towards them as the car revved and disappeared.

'You must be Zak,' Mills said, referring to her list of names.

'Yes, miss.'

Nige grinned at Mills.

The morning seemed to go all right although it was difficult for Mills to judge because the students said very little, simply following her instructions to the letter. She gave them thirty minutes for lunch and sat with Gareth surveying the group. She wished she had thought about how to get them talking amongst themselves, although Nige was doing a grand job going round each of them in turn, chatting and getting others to join in the conversation. Mills noticed that the only ones not involved were the brothers and the girl with the fingernails, called Emily. She was fiddling with her mobile phone. She nudged Gareth, suggesting he speak to the students but he blushed crimson and muttered something inaudible.

'Good party was it... last night, Gareth?'

'Party?'

'There was loud music...'

'Was there?'

'Did you have friends round?'

'Sort of.'

'Are you planning to have them round again?'

'Maybe.'

'Could you tell them to keep the music down please? My dad and his wife are sleeping at Ivy Cottage and it's very disturbing.'

He made no response.

Mills got up to hide her irritation and went over to Emily. 'I don't think there's a signal here,' she said by way of introduction.

'No.'

'Are you enjoying the course so far?'

'Can't say. We ain't done much have we?'

'How d'you mean?'

'Well, I'm doing it for "A" level, so's Stu and Jay. We thought it'd be more like challenging.'

Mills spent a few minutes explaining that there was a range of experience in the class and they would be doing more complex work later in the week, then announced that it was time to start some real work. She split the class into two groups, allocating one to Gareth and taking the other herself. Nige took the opportunity to fiddle with his geophysics equipment in preparation for the surveying demonstration later in the week. He'd even offered to set up an area on the other side of the field where the students could use ground penetrating radar to search for an artefact, with a prize for the team that found it first. He'd prepare the site on and off during the week when he wasn't required and they could run the competition on the last day of the course.

Everything seemed to be going well until about halfway through the afternoon when Mills noticed a disturbance in the group working with Gareth. Amy stood up, shouted something at him then marched across to Mills. She fixed her with a glare, complaining she wasn't being allowed to take the lead. Mills had asked Gareth to let each of them do some soil removal in turn. Apparently Amy had had her turn but didn't want to relinquish the tools. Mills, having established that the girl had done one year of the A level course, gave her some record sheets and asked her to start making notes for the group. That seemed to satisfy her and she went back brandishing the paperwork.

A little later Mills was interrupted by Emily who requested her record sheets since she was also an A level student.

'Perhaps you could work with Amy,' Mills suggested.

'No way. She's a stuck up cow!'

Mills ignored her. 'You'll have to share the pencil,' she said, handing over the sheets.

'I have my own pens,' she replied, flouncing off.

Mills had had no problems with her own group. Thankfully the two friends, Stu and Jay, were pleasant enough. Both Jennifer and Zoe were quite shy and Oscar had settled down once he was separated from his brother. She realised that she'd split the class in a way that had resulted in an even distribution of personalities and wandered over to the other group. She noted that they'd made excellent progress and Gareth was being very sensible.

'We've found an artefact,' announced little Mike, pushing his spectacles back up onto the bridge of his nose as he stood up.

'Really?'

Mills jumped down into the pit and examined where they were clearing.

It was difficult to say whether there was anything there but their enthusiasm was infectious. Piers handed her the brush and she spent a few minutes working quickly until the soil began to expose a solid surface.

'Yes, you're right. I think we've got our first find.'

The resulting cheers and whistles attracted the attention of the others and soon the entire class was huddled over the trench as Mills supervised Zak, allowing him to brush the edges until the tool was exposed. It was a poor specimen but it could have been treasure trove as far as the teenagers were concerned. They took pictures on their mobile phones and some tried to send them to their friends or family, unsuccessfully. All other work ceased, allowing Mills to give a lecture of sorts on how the tools were made while everyone sat round in the sun drinking the bottled water Nige fetched from the van.

Parents were soon arriving and Mills was able to clear the field by five. She was keen to get away on time so she could see what sort of day Dad and Fiona had had. She'd meant to tackle Gareth again but was too tired to begin now. So she sat back and closed her eyes as they set off, the van jolting her awake as they went over Ivelet Bridge.

When they arrived in Mossy Bank, they watched Gareth trudge up the lane. Nige said he had to dash; Nina was on early shift so he wanted to get back.

'I've hardly seen her in the last week. There's a big investigation on.'

'Is it the stabbing on the North York Moors?'

'How d'you know about that?'

'It has been in the news you know... and I got some analyses done for the forensics lab.'

'Wow, did you? Nina hasn't said much... I don't think there's much to go on.'

He started the engine, turned the minibus in the road and set off with a wave.

'See you tomorrow,' Mills called.

She wanted to prepare for the next day but knew she should see that Fiona and Dad were all right, so she gave Earl a quick walk before rushing back up the lane. Loud music was coming from the Manor as she went through the open door at Ivy Cottage.

The scene was one of tranquillity. Her father was sprawled on the sofa watching TV. There was no sign of Fiona.

'She's having a bath... there isn't a shower.'

'It's the ceiling, Dad, it's too low.'

He nodded as if in agreement while continuing to watch the TV.

'I can sit in if you want to go out this evening,' she offered.

His disappointment was obvious. 'No, no. It's fine. We're just chilling out.' His eyes didn't leave the screen.

'Dad, don't forget, Fiona will want to go out while she's on holiday. I don't mind baby-sitting one day this week.'

'Right, I'll tell her.'

There were footsteps on the stairs. Fiona stood in the doorway, looking tired. Mills decided it was probably because she was wearing no make-up.

'She's nearly asleep,' Fiona said, almost accusingly.

'Come in sweetheart. Fi's making dinner aren't you darling?'

'Trying to,' she replied tersely.

'Can I help?' Mills asked automatically.

'No, I can manage.' She disappeared into the kitchen.

'I'd better go,' Mills said, wondering whether they would mind if she left them for the evening.

'Yes, of course.' Her father looked relieved.

'You should be cooking, Dad.'

'I know,' he sighed. 'I know.'

Nina had been at work for an hour when Hazel arrived. She insisted on hearing about her friend's date with "The Major" and was surprised when Hazel insisted he was only fishing for information.

'Rubbish, Hazel. You know he fancies you. He took you to dinner for goodness sake.'

'Business expenses, I expect. They probably ordered him to.'

'They? Why would they order him to?'

'Because they've got something to hide, Nina. I'm sure they know something about the body and they're hiding it. They've told him to find out what we know.'

Nina laughed. 'I don't believe you'll tell Mitch that.'

'Probably not. Coffee?'

As soon as Mitch appeared, Hazel told him that her contact had told her they had no trace of a Mr Eisenhower in the US military.

Nina grinned at her friend but she was ignored.

'Does that mean I can now release the artist's impression of the woman, guv?'

'Wait until I get the official word – I'll chase it with the Super.'

'Crimewatch?' asked Hazel.

'There ought to be enough media interest for a picture in the national press and TV,' Nina suggested.

'As soon as I give the word,' Mitch promised. 'We'll aim for the evening news.'

Nina spent much of the day updating reports and getting loose ends sorted out. She went through the intelligence again, something she often did when a case seemed to be at a standstill. Occasionally something that seemed irrelevant got overlooked and became important later on when it made more sense. Only this time she could see nothing helpful. One lead that had gone nowhere was the propanolol, the drug for high blood pressure. It could only confirm an identity not establish it. Naomi had explained about its use for heart problems and angina but someone with angina would hardly be walking a long distance footpath, surely?

She searched for propanolol on the internet, browsing the medical information until she reached a rather different site. It was a press release about a snooker player called Bill Werbeniuk who took propanolol. It wasn't clear whether it was for his heart or to steady his hands but it was clear that it was a drug that was banned in snooker. Intrigued she searched further to find that an Olympic pistol shooter from North Korea had had his medals removed for using it and since 2010 the drug was a banned substance in several Olympic sports, including archery, shooting and gymnastics.

Was it possible that their man was using the drug to steady his aim in some sport or other? And, if so, would examination of his hands or fingers give an indication of whether he was an archer or a shooter or even a professional golf player?

Chapter 7

Mills watched the two groups of students sitting sharing their packed lunches. It was good to see that they had finally sorted themselves out. Surprisingly, Zoe, who Mills found quiet and withdrawn, had emerged as a leader due to her experience of archaeology. The group dynamics was less transparent in the other team but, because Amy and Emily disliked each other so much, Piers had begun to act as peacemaker, with the result that the rest of them looked to him for guidance.

Amy had continued to show off her apparent knowledge which was quite superficial, obviously irritating everyone. Emily had again arrived in very short shorts and a cropped top which was distracting Piers and Zak, who spent most of the morning observing her legs rather than the record sheets. Oblivious of the testosterone filled atmosphere, Mike was thoroughly enjoying himself, sometimes explaining with excitement then becoming embarrassed as the older ones were amused by his behaviour. By lunch-time it appeared that the team was working well.

Mills had made enough lunch to share with Nige, who was tucking into one of the giant sausage rolls from the bakery in Reeth.

'Been anywhere interesting recently?' Mills asked.

'Nah,' he said, flakes of pastry flew from his mouth. 'I've been busy though.'

He brushed crumbs from his shirt.

'How's that?'

'I've been researching calluses.'

Mills thought she'd misheard.

'You know, hard skin. Calluses in sportsmen... and women of course,' he added quickly.

'Why?'

'Just ask me about calluses on hands, like for snooker players. When you think about it, there are loads of sports where you get calluses on your fingers.'

'Such as?'

'Well, first of all there's snooker players. They get them here.' He indicated the area between his forefinger and thumb, mimicking the action of the cue. 'Then there's archery where you get them across here.' This time he pointed to the first three fingers of his right hand. 'Of course it depends whether you're left-handed or right-handed.' He took another sausage roll. 'Then there's shooting. If it's rifle, it affects your shoulder but in pistol shooting it's on the knuckle of the middle finger.'

'What about tennis players?'

'Ah. No. You see I wanted sports where you need a steady hand.'

'But why?' Mills knew he was avoiding the question.

'I found golf. You get them in all sorts of places if you're not playing properly but if you're good it should just be on the left-hand, if you're right-handed, at the bottom of the last three fingers.'

'Fascinating. I suppose in darts you get a callus on your forefinger from lifting the beer glass.'

'You may mock but this could be important.'

Before she had the chance to find out why he was doing this research, Amy marched over to them, standing over them, blocking out the sun.

'I thought you should know that alcohol is being passed round my group.'

Mills was taken aback for a few seconds. 'Right,' she said while working out what she should do.

'I thought you'd want to know,' Amy said accusingly.

Nige chipped in, 'Thank you Amy. Could you ask Gareth to come over... when you sit down again.'

'You do realise we're in *loco parentis*.' Mills said when Amy was gone. 'I had to be CRB checked to do this.'

'Well I am, but is Gareth?' Nige asked as the teenager came towards them.

Mills went hot and cold; she hadn't even thought about it.

'Is it about Zak's ginger beer?' he asked when he flung himself down beside them.

'Ginger beer?' Mills felt relief – it was all a misunderstanding.

'Yes, a bottle of "Crabbies". Piers asked to try it then Mike wanted some.'

'But ginger beer isn't alcoholic,' Mills pointed out.

'That one is,' said Nige.

Mills sighed. 'Ok. It's no big deal... but it mustn't happen again. I'll have a word with Zak – he shouldn't be drinking anyway.' She suspected that Zak knew exactly what he was doing when he let the youngest member of the group drink it.

It seemed strangely quiet when Mills walked into the cottage that evening. There was no sign of Earl but she assumed that he was out with her father, since he had agreed to look after him for her. It was a luxury to unpack her rucksack and sort out the paperwork without having to rush out with the dog. But by the time she'd showered and poured herself a beer, she decided she should go up to Ivy Cottage to collect him.

As she started up the lane she saw her father coming down. There was no sign of Earl.

'Have you decided to keep him?' she shouted as soon as they were near enough.

Her father's face was drawn. He waited until they were together before he said, 'I can't find him, Millie.'

'What d'you mean?'

'He ran off when we were up there.'

'He does that, Dad. He'll only be gone half an hour or so.'

'No, that was at lunch-time. He's been gone for hours.' He seemed distraught.

'Please don't worry. I'll go up and find him.'

'I've been searching all afternoon. I've been all over.' He was pulling his hand through his thinning hair.

'Go back to the cottage and have a drink, Dad. He'll be fine. I'll go up and find him.'

They walked together as far as the entrance to the Manor in silence.

'Is Fiona all right?' Mills asked, thinking that her day must have been spoiled.

'She's fine. She and Flora have been sleeping in the sunshine most of the day while I've been worrying about that wretched dog of yours. Are you sure you don't want me to...'

'Get yourself a beer. I put some in the fridge – unless you've drunk them all already.'

'Thanks, Millie. Let me know how you get on.'

Relieved not to have to put a brave face on any longer, Mills almost ran up the track and onto the moor. She would walk their favourite path and take a large circuit round the fell. She should have brought the whistle but he so rarely needed it now he had settled in. Was it the fact that her father was a stranger. On any other evening Mills would have found it a pleasant walk but tonight she was getting hotter and more concerned as she tramped across the heather. By eight o'clock she was tired and tearful. There was no sign of Earl and silence followed when she called. She made her way back to the path that followed the contour round to join the main track.

That was when she heard barking and, looking up, saw a figure taking a parallel course higher up the fell. It was a local farmer who she sometimes met out on the moor. She waved and carried on until their paths met.

'How do,' he said, calling his collie to his side.

She asked him if he'd seen the lurcher on his travels.

'No, but I'll keep an eye open like.'

They parted. He walked down towards the village, whistling his dog when it ventured too far, leaving Mills looking down at the Manor, wondering what to do next. There would be another couple of hours before dark and they shouldn't be wasted. She resolved to get a warm jacket and a torch before setting off again.

Her father must have been looking out for her because he intercepted her as she reached the lane.

'Any luck?'

'Not yet. I'm getting some things and going back up in a minute.'

She rushed on to the cottage, not wanting to waste precious time. He was there when she went back but this time he too was wearing a fleece and carrying a torch.

'You don't need to come, Dad.'

'I do.'

It was a sombre patrol across the moors. Neither spoke as they trudged through the heather whistling and calling the lurcher. After two hours Mills suggested they called it a day despite her father's protestations.

'There's no point, Dad. He'll be miles away now. If anyone finds him they'll let me know.'

'Yes.' She could tell he wasn't convinced. 'Yes.' His voice took on an optimistic tone. 'D'you remember when your hamster went missing? I told you then we'd find it and we did, didn't we? What was it called again?'

'Cheeky. It was called Cheeky.' She didn't remind him that it was the rabbit they'd found behind the shed. The hamster was dead at the bottom of the airing cupboard.

Mills refused to go back to Ivy Cottage for a hot drink but said goodnight and carried on home. It was only then, when she was alone that she allowed herself a few tears, the result of exhaustion and anxiety that had been building up for hours. She wanted a strong drink but knew she might need to be alert later, in case she had the call she was dreading – that Earl had been found dead or injured as the result of some horrible road accident. She reported Earl missing before going to bed but only partly undressed, ready to jump up if the phone rang. But when it began to get light she'd heard nothing and sat in the garden drinking tea for hours before she got ready for another day of teaching.

Normally Mills would have confided in Nige but Gareth was waiting when she came out of the cottage and she didn't want to talk about Earl in front of him. Nige and he discussed the rugby – apparently England was playing Wales on Saturday – while she looked out of the window, wondering what to do. However, there was little time for brooding that morning. Amy's father was waiting to speak to her, concerned about the report of underage drinking that had been going on at the site.

When she explained it was a mistake and she'd dealt with it, he seemed satisfied but after he'd gone Amy muttered that her mother was ringing the University to complain anyway and she was nearly not allowed to attend the course again. The rest of the group was subdued as they all gathered for Nige's demonstration of the geophysics and Mills was left to consider what to do next.

She was pleased to see Gareth listening intently to Nige as he explained how they would be spending the day. Of all the kids, he made the most bizarre spectacle; standing in the middle of the field dressed entirely in black with knee high boots and leather jacket. Everyone else wore clothes for the heat and were in T-shirts, shorts or jeans. Nige, of course, was in his signature plaid shirt but even he had his sleeves rolled up and was in baggy khaki shorts below his knees.

In the afternoon Nige allowed small groups of three to walk the equipment across the site. It was while Stu and Jay were taking their turn that a university vehicle parked at the gate and she recognised the man who stepped out as the lecturer she'd spoken to when the course was set up. It was obvious why he'd come.

'I had a call...thought I'd pop over since there's no signal...'

'I suppose it was Amy's mother?'

'Yes.' He looked down at her over his glasses.

She explained what had occurred and that she'd already spoken to Amy's father. He seemed satisfied with her account.

'But there was something else. Apparently there's a young man helping out – I don't know his name.'

Mills felt herself redden. 'I know. I'm sorry. I didn't think it would... he's a boy who... I just needed...'

'I require a note of his details, for insurance, you know.'

'Yes... and I suppose he should have been checked... you know.... for...'

'Ah, a CRB check.' He considered for a moment. 'How old is he?'

'Seventeen.'

'Are we paying him?'

'I suppose so. I haven't really...'

He rubbed his chin. 'I think it would be best if we registered him on the course. Then he's covered by insurance. He can help but not formally.'

Mills was concerned that she'd called it a job when speaking to Gareth, indicating a payment, and told the lecturer so.

'We can give him an *ex gratia* sum at the end, if you want.'

He seemed happy that the problem had been solved. Warning Mills to keep an eye open for any further drinking incidents, he waved across at Nige and turned to walk back to the gate. To her surprise, Gareth was delighted with the arrangement.

'You mean I can be one of the students?' he asked.

'Yes but you're still going to help me and Nige with the groups.'

'That's so cool,' he replied, striding off to tell his new friends the good news.

Mills frowned. There was something about him that worried her, particularly the reaction Earl had had towards him and that air rifle in the hall at the Manor. Yet he seemed a perfectly nice young man in the dealings she'd had with him. She sighed as she wandered over to look after Jennifer, Oscar and Zoe. They were making excellent progress in their investigation reports and were keen to move on to the photography session.

'So, how are we getting on?' she asked, trying to sound enthusiastic.

'He's asked me for another date,' Hazel announced apropos of nothing at all.

'I'm sorry?' Nina was sending a message to the pathologist to ask her to look for hardened skin on the dead man's hands, following Nige's detailed descriptions of where it would occur for each sport requiring a steady hand.

'Major Bob... he rang this morning.'

'What here?'

'Of course here, he doesn't know my home number.'

'You said he wouldn't call again.'

'I know. He must need more information about the case.'

'He may just fancy you.'

Hazel laughed. 'I don't think so.'

'Will you go?'

Hazel looked pensive. 'I don't know. What d'you think?'

'It's your duty, Hazel. It may be important for the case.' She was teasing her friend but Hazel was taking it very seriously.

'I suppose you're right. If the US military know something about it, then I'd better try to find out. I'll ring him back and suggest Saturday.'

Nina excused herself on the pretext of making coffee, allowing her friend to make the call in private. When she returned, Hazel gave her the thumbs up.

'Apparently he's taking me to "The Star" at Harome, which is really posh.'

'Can you do me a favour when you see him? See if he has any calluses on his hands.'

It was a request that required an explanation. As Hazel listened she became increasingly incredulous.

'I'll look but I really don't think that's likely. He told me – he's a paper pusher.'

The pathologist returned her call just before Nina left to pick Rosie up from the nursery.

'Thank you so much for getting back to me. I hope the message about calluses didn't sound too weird.'

'Well, I have to admit, it's a new one on me but I can see why you're asking. It would explain the use of the propanolol which didn't make any sense in the absence of heart problems.'

'It's just an idea. I hope the descriptions made sense.'

'Yes. You've been busy.'

'So...?'

'Well. It's more a matter of what isn't there.'

'Really?' Nina tried to hide her disappointment.

'Nothing on the fingers that indicate archery and nothing on the rest of the hand that match snooker or golf. There is a small amount of hardening on the left hand in the skin on the knuckle of the middle finger but it's not recent. If he's a shooter he must be left handed.'

'Does anything else point to left-handedness?'

'Oh, let me see...' The phone went quiet for about a minute. 'Yes, I've got something in my notes here. The musculature indicates he could be left-handed.'

'So do you think he could be a shooter? A pistol shooter, presumably?'

'He could be. Why? Do you have something indicating that?'

'No, not really. It's a sort of hunch at the moment.'

'Fair enough.'

'Can you send me a note about the knuckle?'

'Yes, of course. Let me know if you need any more information... and good luck!'

Nina could think of nothing else as she collected Rosie and drove home. Was it possible that their mystery American was a pistol shooter? Did he do it professionally or was it part of something more clandestine? More importantly, would Mitch take her seriously when she told him?

Mills could hardly bear to enter the cottage that evening. It felt empty and cold despite the sunshine outside. The answer machine was flashing; she felt sick when she saw there were five messages. One by one she listened. No message. No message. No message. Finally – a familiar voice.

'It's Dad. There's been some news. Call me.'

She prepared to run up the lane but stopped to pick up the last message, her heart pounding. It was the farmer from down the dale.

'Hi, it's David. I think I've found your dog. I took 'im down to the surgery but he's in a bad way, I'm afraid.'

She grabbed her keys, slamming the door behind her. She was in the car and down the lane before she realised that she didn't know which vet Earl had been taken to. Turning round, she sped up to Ivy Cottage. She left the engine running and before she could knock, Fiona opened the door carrying Flora.

'Hugh! Hugh! It's Millie!'

There was a cry from inside and he ran out, engulfing her in his arms.

'They've found him but he's in a bad way, Millie. We'll take my car. He's in Leyburn.'

Mills was grateful to her father for offering to drive. It meant there would be room to bring Earl back in comfort if he was well enough. On the way her father explained how David had found Earl in one of his fields. The dog seemed to be paralysed. After trying to contact Mills, David decided to take the dog straight to the vet then drove to Mossy Bank to find her. Muriel had pointed him to Ivy Cottage where he had spoken to Fiona, her father being out searching the fells again.

Mills found herself shaking as they waited to speak to the vet. When he finally appeared they were shown into a back room where Earl lay inert in a cage like a large rag toy.

'What's wrong with him?' she asked, the lump in her throat preventing her from speaking in more than a whisper.

'We're not certain but we think it's poison.'

'Poison? You mean someone...'

'No, no. He's ingested poison somehow, possibly a toxic chemical. The dog's stomach contained some blue pellets, which suggests a pesticide such as metaldehyde.'

'You mean slug pellets?'

'Possibly.'

She'd put some on the vegetables but didn't think they were a danger to him where the pots were. Was it possible she was at fault?

'I'm unsure at present; I would have expected to see muscle spasms but his muscles are very weak – it's more like a paralysis. We're getting the blue granules analysed. Meanwhile we've cleared him out and we'll wait to see if he improves.'

'When will you get the results of the test?'

'Hopefully by tomorrow afternoon.'

Her father put his arm round her.

'Is there nothing we can do?' she asked.

'We'll take good care of him and we'll ring you if there's any change.'

She checked that the surgery had her contact details before they drove home in silence. So many things were running through her mind, including whether Earl had found the pesticide at David's farm. It wasn't his fault, of course, but it could explain why he had acted so swiftly. She would have to try to sound grateful when she rang him that evening but it might be difficult. She accepted the offer of something to eat from Fiona but was unable to manage more than a few mouthfuls. It was a sombre meal and she soon excused herself to get back to the cottage where she wouldn't have to maintain a brave face. There was a message from David to say he'd spoken to the vet and hoped for better news on the following day.

Half the night spent on the internet convinced her that Earl was too ill to recover if it was metaldehyde. She'd hardly slept and by morning she felt too sick for breakfast. She'd no idea how she would manage to get through the day. She slowly made sandwiches for Nige's lunch, filling the kettle for a cup of tea. Before it had boiled she heard the minibus outside.

'D'you mind if I follow in the car?'

When she explained why, Nige was more than politely sympathetic. He offered to take the class for her but she refused, saying that she probably wouldn't hear from the vet until later in the day.

'Have you got a signal at the site?' he asked, concerned.

'No. I'll pop into Settle at lunch-time.'

'Don't worry,' he said. 'I've got a brilliant geophysics competition I use on the first years; I can do that with the groups this afternoon so you can hop off back here.'

Mills squeezed his arm and smiled with a nod.

The morning dragged but as soon as it was mid-day she announced lunch. Nige ordered her to go and she agreed gratefully, travelling as fast as she could back to the main road. As soon as her mobile peeped to indicate a signal, she stopped the car to read the text message from her father: the poison is carbofuran they are treating with atropine. She called up the internet. *Carbofuran: a pesticide used on crops, banned in the European Union, illegally used to intentionally poison wildlife including golden eagles and buzzards.* And red kite? wondered Mills.

Chapter 8

'Did you get a carrier for Flora?' Mills asked.

They'd been sitting in silence too long. No-one could keep up the pretence of enjoying their evening together. The news from the vet's was no better, no worse. Only time would tell if the treatment was effective. Mills wanted to be with Earl but they said there was no point at this stage. She'd agreed to eat with them because Fiona had gone to a lot of trouble to make her spaghetti carbonara despite having difficulty finding her usual exotic ingredients. Mills played with the food, apologising for eating only a little. Fiona was clearing the dishes, refusing her offer of help.

'Yes, we did. I went to the outdoor shop in Reeth and, guess what, I was able to hire one for the week!' her father replied.

'And did you visit Gunnerside Gill?'

'No.' He lowered his voice. 'Fi doesn't have anything sensible to wear on her feet.'

'What size is she?' Mills asked.

'I've no idea.' He turned towards the door and shouted, 'Fi! What size are your feet?'

She came into the sitting room, teatowel in hand.

'What?'

'Your feet? What size?'

'Six, why?'

'I can lend you some boots, if you like,' Mills offered.

'Fine.'

Hugh raised his eyebrows and shrugged as she returned to the kitchen without further comment.

Mills had to smile. The thought of Fiona in her walking boots was enough to cheer anyone up.

'I'd better go and get them,' she offered.

'Don't worry now, love.'

'I should go, anyway. I'll drop them in tomorrow before I go off for the day.' She gave her father a hug before popping her head round the kitchen door. Fiona was surrounded by pans and dishes.

'I'm going now – are you sure you don't want a hand?'

Fiona gave her a wan smile. 'I'm fine, really.'

Hugh was waiting for her by the front door.

'Let me know if there's any news. We'll be around.'

For once, Mills was grateful that they were.

It was getting dark as she left Ivy Cottage but the path was flooded with light from the windows at the Manor. Music drifting through the open windows was loud but not so intrusive that it would bother Fiona tonight. Only as she was letting herself into Laurel Cottage did she hear gunshots. Bursts of two at a time – coming from back up the lane. She retraced her steps quietly until she was level with the windows of the big house. The curtains were drawn back, giving her a perfect view of the scene inside. Gareth was leaning out of the window overlooking the back garden; she could hear him firing out into the darkness. Each time he fired he would shout, 'Yes!' or 'No!' He appeared to be alone. Mills stood for a few minutes, undecided whether to confront him. It was late... she was tired... she'd speak to him tomorrow.

The cottage seemed empty as she mechanically switched on the answer machine: *Hi, it's Nina. Nige told me about your dog. Just wanted to say how sorry we are – give us a buzz sometime.* The message had been left at nine-thirty-two.

She waited while it rang, hoping it wasn't too late to call. It was so nice to hear her friend's voice.

'Nina? I thought you might be in bed.'

'Don't be silly. I only just got home an hour ago. Just finished my tea.'

'Working too hard?'

'It's this murder case. I had to sort out something for Crimewatch tomorrow.'

'Oh... I'll look out for it.'

'Nige said you'd been doing some forensic work on the case?'

Mills told her how the soil samples had shown that the body had been moved.

'That was a really important turning point in the case, Mills. What we need now is for someone to identify the woman. Hopefully the papers or the telly will give us a breakthrough. Anyway, that's not why I rang you – tell me what happened to your dog.'

Mills had difficulty getting through the account of how Earl had been poisoned with a banned substance that could be used on birds of prey. Nina was sympathetic but also, as always, practical.

'If that's the case, you should contact the authorities.'

'You're right. I hadn't thought about it but I should ring George.'

'George who?'

'George Herbert. He's the police wildlife officer for the area.'

'Well, there you are then. This George, is he fit?'

'Fit? What d'you mean?'

'I mean is he young, good-looking and single.'

'No he must be nearly as old as Dad. Not my type, Nina. Sorry to disappoint you.'

'Oh well, I'll have to keep looking, I suppose.'

It was Mills who kept Nige and Gareth waiting the next morning. She'd woken late to the sound of heavy rain on the window. She dressed hurriedly, wanting to call the vet and ring George before leaving for the day. There was no change in Earl, which made her yet more determined to report the incident to the police. Even if the poison had not been meant for Earl, someone was trying to kill birds or animals in the area. However, she had to be satisfied with leaving a voicemail for George before stuffing some food in her bag for lunch.

'Would it be ok if Stu and Jay come back in the van tonight?' Gareth asked when they had set off.

'I suppose,' said Nige.

Mills wanted to know why but thought better of it. She'd probably find out on the way back anyway.

'Damn,' she said. 'I meant to give my boots to Fiona.'

It was a miserable day at the site but the students would need to appreciate what was involved in archaeology – whatever the weather. She insisted they did some excavating in the rain but when the trenches became too waterlogged she let them under the tarpaulin that Nige had rigged up, where there was a display of their finds. Gareth had spent the morning working hard to arrange the flints in rows and she wondered whether she should tell him that his mascara was running.

The students were a subdued group during the lunch break. There was hardly room for everyone under the makeshift shelter. Mills could feel the water running down her neck and Emily was complaining that her top was ruined. Mike looked ridiculous with the plastic carrier bag on his head that had once contained his lunch. Mills talked to them about flint tools during the break, using their finds as models although there was only one piece that was a decent example. Finally the rain eased off, giving them a chance to apply what they had learned the day before about photographing a site. Each of them had brought a camera, as requested, and spent the rest of the afternoon taking pictures. The students who were taking "A level" archaeology appreciated that these images might be valuable and were taking their work that afternoon quite seriously.

It wasn't until they were packing up that Mills realised that the best flint artefact was missing from the collection. She took Gareth aside to question him about it since he'd been responsible for setting the display out and collecting the flints up afterwards but he denied any knowledge of the theft, taking it rather badly and accusing her of being "on his case". He sat in the back with Jay and Stu on the way back while she chatted to Nige about his plans for the final day of the course.

When she climbed out of the van at Mossy bank, Mills felt compelled to speak to warn Gareth about keeping the noise down.

'I heard you shooting again last night,' she called as he set off towards the Manor.

'It wasn't me' he called over his shoulder.

She could hardly say she saw him. 'Well, keep the music down. My dad needs his beauty sleep!'

She felt uncomfortable as the three boys walked up the lane laughing. She'd tried not to be heavy but she was supposed to be keeping an eye on him.

The red light on the answer machine was flashing beside a number three. George had left a message to say he'd be over on Sunday morning if that was all right with her. Just let him know if it wasn't. Mills hesitated, but only for a second. She needed to talk to someone official about the poison; she also wanted some advice about Gareth and his shooting activities. The nurse from the veterinary practice was pleased to say that the atropine appeared to be having a small but positive effect. Mills rang back immediately but learned very little more information than the message had given her. No, there was no point in coming down; he was still a very poorly dog and it would be at least another day or two before he would be sufficiently well for that. The last message was from Dad, repeating the news about Earl and telling her to come over if she wanted to. Of course she wanted to. They would be going home at the weekend and she'd hardly seen them.

She could hear the music as soon as she stepped outside her cottage. Inevitably it was coming from the top of the village. Muriel was standing in her front garden with her arms folded across her matronly chest.

'Have you heard that din?' she asked. 'Is it them folks at the Manor having another party d'you reckon?'

'No, they're away.'

'Ooh, it's not your dad?' Muriel looked concerned.

'No.' Mills laughed. 'It's the son; he's there on his own – well, with friends.'

'Someone should tell 'em to keep it down then.'

'I think that would be me,' offered Mills, as she walked slowly up the lane.

Fiona started the moment Mills entered the cottage. She had to agree it was outrageous... inconsiderate... unacceptable... but she drew the line at calling the police.

'I told Hugh to go round and sort him out,' she muttered through gritted teeth.

'There are three of them in there...' he protested.

Mills sighed. 'I'll go.'

'Would you, sweetheart?'

Mills could detect, through the open door of the Manor, that the music was coming from the back of the house. She made her way into the kitchen and out into the garden, where the rock music blared from speakers perched precariously on the window ledge of the lounge. She almost choked on the smoke from a barbecue set up half way down the lawn, where the three culprits were standing with bottles of beer.

'Gareth, can I have a word?'

'Oops, here comes teacher,' Stu called. 'Go on Gareth, be a good boy.'

Gareth came over to her. 'What?' It was difficult to read whether his deadpan expression indicated belligerence or nervous embarrassment. Perhaps it was a combination of both.

'The noise, Gareth. It's deafening.'

'So?'

'There are people living next door. If nothing else, they are paying your aunt good money to stay there. You are making their stay unpleasant.'

He was looking at the ground.

'Yes?' Mills waited for a response.

'I'll turn it down.'

'Thank you.'

He made to return to his friends.

'Wait. Your parents asked me to keep an eye. Please don't let me down. I don't want to have to ring them.'

'They don't care anyway,' he threw at her as he turned and left.

She walked back into the house to the sounds of laughter from the others. When she caught sight of the gun bag in the hall, she stopped to consider whether she should do anything about it. There was a box of pellets on the hallstand, nearly full. With no particular plan in mind, she took a small handful and let them fall into her pocket. At least if she showed them to George he might recognise what sort of gun it was.

As she settled down in Ivy Cottage, there was a noticeable reduction in volume which was maintained for an hour or so. She stayed for supper, mainly to keep tabs on the boys next door. Hugh cooked so it was sausage and mash with a few glasses of wine to celebrate the encouraging news about the lurcher. It was just after ten when the music was ramped up and the shooting began. This time Hugh insisted on accompanying Mills. As usual, the Manor was a blaze of light. There was a Land Rover parked outside which she hadn't seen before. It took a long time before they attracted anyone's attention. When he opened the door Gareth looked the worse for drink – or drugs, thought Mills. He said they were just having fun, there was no harm. Soon he was joined by Stu, who was just as bad. Someone in the background was encouraging them to slam the door on them.

'Listen here...' Hugh shouted, but Mills stopped him.

'There's no point trying to reason with them. I'll call Naomi tomorrow,' she said, sufficiently loudly for Gareth to hear. She could tell that it had registered with him.

'Who's Naomi?'

'She owns Ivy Cottage, Dad. She's Gareth's aunt. She'll know what to do.'

'Shouldn't you tell his parents?'

'To be honest, Dad, I don't think they care.'

Nina was feeling smug. The pathologist had got back to her with the answer: there was noteworthy hardening of the skin on the middle finger of the left hand. "Noteworthy". She considered the word. It was not one she ever used but it sounded significant. Definitely significant. She told Hazel as soon as she arrived.

'So this hard skin, this callus, is due to shooting?'

'Not just shooting – pistol shooting. Apparently it's due to the trigger guard.'

'Which hand is it on?'

'The left hand.'

'Just to play devil's advocate – is there any other sport or activity that would cause it?'

'I've thought about that. It's possible but the reason for looking at shooting was it's one of the sports where beta blockers are used to steady the hand, like archery or snooker.'

'Makes sense,' conceded Hazel. 'It would tie in with the services angle. What if he was in some special service corps or something, similar to the SAS but in America?'

'I was thinking more about a professional shooter, like in the Olympics.'

'Will that be part of the Crimewatch appeal?' Hazel asked, just as Mitch came in.

'What's that?' he asked, dumping a large file on his desk.

Nina gave him her news about the pistol shooting connection while he listened.

'I suppose it's possible,' he said but sounded sceptical. 'I suggest you just stick to the picture of the woman for now.'

'Have you seen the papers this morning?' Hazel asked. 'The picture's on the front page of some of them.'

'Well, let's hope it gets us the result we need.'

'Feeling the pressure, guv?' Hazel asked.

'Just a bit.'

When he'd gone, Hazel turned to Nina. 'I was thinking. If I did go out with the Major again, I could check whether he's got a callus on his finger this time.'

Nina couldn't help teasing her friend. 'Holding hands on your second date? What d'you mean "if"?'

'I was thinking of cancelling – but if it helps the case...'

Nina put on a serious expression. 'I think it's your duty as a police officer to have dinner with him.'

'Seriously?'

'Seriously.' Then she burst into fits of giggles.

Mills sprinted up to Ivy Cottage clutching her old boots hanging by their laces. The soles were still muddy from when she'd last worn them but Fiona would have to put up with that. Although she'd deliberately woken early there was just twenty minutes left and she wanted to be sure that all three lads were ready when Nige arrived. She knocked gently and soon her father, still in his dressing gown, was peering out from the partly open door.

'Those lads need talking to, sweetheart,' he said, taking the boots. 'I don't imagine they've been to bed. It seemed to go on all night.'

'I rang Naomi this morning and left a message. Hopefully she'll be able to speak to Gareth this evening.'

'Fi wants me to speak to them today. Just thought I'd warn you.'

'They'll be on site all day – if I can get them onto the minibus in time.' She looked at her watch. 'Speaking of which... I'd better sort them out fast.'

She hurried on to the Manor, hammering on the front door and ringing the bell. Finally there were footsteps and Gareth appeared, dishevelled, half-dressed looking strangely young without makeup.

'The bus goes in fifteen minutes. Hurry.'

He nodded, disappearing back inside, leaving the door ajar. When she returned twenty minutes later to tell them the bus would go without them unless they appeared *now*, three figures emerged, squinting into the sunlight.

'Don't forget to shut the door behind you,' she called.

'It's ok,' replied Gareth, 'Gus is still inside.'

'The last day of the course today,' Mills muttered to Nige as they sped through the lanes.

'I know. Isn't it a shame? Still it's the treasure hunt today.'

'A shame? I'll be so relieved when it's all over. It's been much harder to keep everyone occupied than I expected.'

'It's been fine – except for the rain. And the forecast is for a real scorcher today.'

As it turned out the students were on good form for the remaining part of the course, partly because Stu and Jay were particularly subdued but mainly because Emily was too busy applying sunscreen to irritate Amy. Gareth was taciturn, still avoiding Mills whenever he could. No-one was surprised when the team led by Piers won the competition and everyone seemed genuinely pleased for them.

'So what is the hidden artefact?' Mills asked Zak, curious to know what Nige had used.

'That really good flint tool we found.'

She looked across at Nige but he was in a circle of students with his back to her.

Gareth was glaring at her. 'Satisfied?' he growled, turning away to join his friends.

She wondered if Gareth would have known about the flint when she accused him of taking it but there was no opportunity to ask Nige. They were finishing early and soon parents began to arrive. There were farewells and promises from some of the students to keep in touch. When it was time for Mills to leave just Nige and Gareth were left in the field. The teenager sat with his headset on, ignoring them on the journey home. Mills told Nige to drop them both at the Manor so she could have a quick word with Gareth but he darted towards the house without a word, turning to shout, 'Don't worry, I'm not here tonight, so your precious parents won't be disturbed.'

Mills dragged her rucksack out of the minibus, thanking Nige for his help. 'By the way, how did you pinch that flint for the treasure hunt?'

'I asked Gareth to get it for me,' Nige said.

She waved him off, making her way to Ivy Cottage where her father was feeding the baby.

'Fiona's having a bath.'

'Will she be long? I wanted to ask about the boots.'

'Don't,' Hugh replied. 'She's been up there an hour; her legs are aching and she's got blisters on both feet.'

'You went to Gunnerside Gill, then?'

'Some of the way. We got to Gunnerside.'

'And?'

'We went a little way up the Gill but Fi's feet were hurting and the carrier was getting very heavy. She weighs a ton now, don't you Flora?'

He jiggled the bundle on his knees and a tiny spot of milk shot out onto the front of his shirt. Mills watched with amusement as he nonchalantly wiped it away. This was a new side to her father.

'I thought you'd like to know that they'll be out next door tonight,' she said.

'That's a relief. We thought we'd have an early night after our strenuous day.'

Mills laughed. 'You do realise you probably walked a maximum of three kilometres.'

'Ah, you forget – we rarely walk more than a few yards when we're in town.'

'True. You must come round tomorrow. I'm going to show you some of the other dales and prepare a picnic as it's your last day.'

'That would be nice but Fi wants to do a bit of shopping before we go. Apparently these tweedy jackets are very "in" at the moment and she has her eye on a suit to take home.'

Typical, thought Mills but she smiled, suggesting she gave them supper instead.

'Must go,' she said, looking at her watch. 'I'm seeing Earl this evening. They said he might be ready to come home soon.'

It was an emotional reunion. Mills had to kneel down to see him properly. There was a drip attached to his front paw as he lay flat in the cage at floor level. At first she thought he was asleep but he lifted his head as she spoke gently to him and she was sure he recognised her voice.

'He's still sedated,' the nurse said, 'to help preserve what strength he has in his muscles.'

Mills put her fingers through the bars to touch his rough hair. 'Hello old boy. You get better soon won't you? I've got a big bone waiting in your basket when you come back.'

She wiped away evidence of her tears before standing up. 'When can he come home?' she asked.

'That will be the vet's decision,' the nurse replied.

She had a chat with the vet, who wanted to keep Earl in over the weekend, just to help build his strength. 'He's been through a bad time. He'll need a lot of TLC to build up his muscle strength again. It'll be a long haul and he may never be a hundred percent again.'

She was interested to know if he'd seen any cases of carbofuran poisoning before.

'Once, years ago in Cumbria, before it was banned. At the time it was being used as an insecticide and a cat got hold of some. Unfortunately it didn't survive. Now, of course, it's illegal and I'll be contacting the appropriate authorities. I understand David found him on his farm but he says he doesn't have any himself.'

'No.'

They stood looking down at the cage where the dog was lying, inert. Mills managed to hold back the tears until she was through the waiting room and outside in the road.

Chapter 9

The publication of the artist's impression resulted in furious activity at Headquarters. Hazel and Nina were working at full stretch even with the additional staff allocated for the follow-up work. Many of the fifty-seven calls related to sightings at campsites on the Coast to Coast path but there were a number of names that occurred more than once.

'Are any of these women living in the area?' Mitch asked.

'Three all together. The rest are miles away.'

'We can't rule any of them out, can we?' Hazel was still of the opinion that the mystery woman was involved in the murder and that the killers were not local.

'We'd better get on with it then,' said Mitch grimly. 'Nina, you follow up the most likely names and give the rest to the team.'

Hazel was disappointed. 'What about me, guv?'

'Get over to the campsites we've not covered yet.'

'All of them?'

'Yes.'

She'd have to get a move on, if she was going to get back in time for dinner. 'Might not get them all done today, guv.'

'As long as they're finished tomorrow.'

That was Saturday out then, she thought and began planning how to get Liam to martial arts and back in her absence.

'I'll see you then,' she called to Nina as she was leaving.

'Have a good time tonight!' her friend called back.

It was a frustrating day. Most of the people she spoke to had little recollection of the woman beyond her face. They recognised her straight away but after that it was a blur. She appeared to be a quiet, even shy person, who said little; quite different from her partner. Were they married? Someone remembered her wearing a wedding ring but not him... definitely not him. They all agreed she was of slim build. By mid-afternoon she had very little additional intelligence – they'd bought Yorkshire tea and he was partial to sausage rolls, judging by the number purchased *en route*. No-one suggested the man might be in the military but when asked, several agreed he could well have been.

The journey back was equally exasperating. The weekend traffic to the Filey coast was already building up and the queues became longer as she got closer to home. Consequently she arrived at her mother's much later than planned.

'You can stay for tea if you like,' she offered.

'No, Mum, it's fine. I've got Liam some chops.'

'Lovely.'

'How's he been?'

'He's all right. He's just being a teenager. Your brother was exactly the same at thirteen.'

'Where is he. Anyway?'

'Up in his bedroom getting packed.'

Hazel sat in the garden having a cigarette while her mother made a cup of tea.

'Doing anything this weekend?' she asked, putting the tray down on the rickety table.

'I've got to work tomorrow.' She wasn't going to tell mother about her "date" with Robert.

'Why didn't you say – d'you want Liam to stay here, pet?'

'No, Mum. I see little enough of him. He's been here most of the week.'

'You know I don't mind. He likes staying with his Nan. He knows it's difficult in the holidays.'

'That's what worries me. I think he prefers it.'

'Don't be silly, pet.'

Eventually Liam appeared – tall, independent, and moody. He didn't realise that he was the spitting image of the father he couldn't remember. Niall had left when his son was only a year old; a young soldier who wanted to see the world not the inside of a flat, with a teenage wife and a baby. At the time it was devastating but with hindsight it was for the best.

'I've called Sanjay's mum and she'll take you to your class and back tomorrow.'

'Why?'

'I've got to work.'

'Is it that murder? Nan and me saw it on "Crimewatch" last night, the face. Is she the murderer?'

'...and I'm out tonight. I wouldn't go but it's connected with work. A colleague... we need to discuss something...'

There was no reply. Liam had put his headset on and was fiddling with his phone.

Robert had said he would pick her up at seven. It was after six when they reached the flat. She flung the chops under the grill, asking Liam to keep an eye on them.

'Stick some oven chips on, Liam!' she shouted as she went through to change.

When she was dressed she salvaged the meat before it was completely black, turning on the extractor fan to remove the blue smoke that was filling the kitchen.

She switched the oven on, warning her son that the chips had yet to cook.

'No problem,' he replied without taking his eyes from the TV.

'Call me if there's anything!' she shouted. 'I won't be late.'

'No problem.'

She'd worn an old dress but the shoes were new. The way they clicked on the stairs put her in a positive mood. She'd deliberately come down early so she could wait on the corner – Liam would ask questions if he spotted the convertible. But she'd not reached the end of the road before she heard a car horn and turned to see Robert waving. He was wearing an open neck shirt in a blue that matched his eyes and was smiling. He had a really nice smile.

'Hey, you look great!' he yelled.

She looked round, hoping none of her neighbours were watching as she climbed in, sinking low into the leather seat until they were out of town.

"The Star" had a Friday evening atmosphere; full of happy couples enjoying each other's company at the beginning of the weekend. Hazel enjoyed her meal, a guilty pleasure since she felt she was there under false pretences.

'You know, this is really very nice indeed,' he was saying. 'Good food, good company.'

She smiled reassuringly. He'd not mentioned the case at all during the meal. Surely he would say something soon.

'We had a slot on Crimewatch this week,' she offered. 'Did you see it?'

'No, I was down in London at a meeting all week. I've only just got back from there this afternoon. You should have seen the traffic.'

She tried again. 'We think we might have a lead from the artist's impression.'

'That's good. Now, shall we order coffee?'

It was obviously a ruse to put her off the scent.

'So what kept you in London all week?' she asked sweetly.

'Boring meetings. Admin. You know.'

Some detective, thought Hazel. She tried to remember the list of tactics they'd gone through on the course.

'Hazel.'

He'd taken hold of her hand across the table. Taken by surprise, she looked up at him. Was her mouth still open? He was saying something but she wasn't listening. She was feeling the middle finger of each hand. Did he notice? She thought not. The trouble was, it was actually quite difficult to feel for hard skin on someone's finger.

'Sorry, I didn't catch what you said.'

He'd let go of her hand.

'Sunday? Would you like to go for a picnic on Sunday?'

She hesitated for a few seconds then took his right hand in both of hers for a final feel.

'That would be lovely...'

'Excellent!'

'No... it would have been lovely but I can't. I'm sorry.'

Their coffee arrived, she let go of his hands and he looked disappointed. Fortunately he didn't ask for an excuse or explanation. She wasn't ready to tell him she had a teenage son.

She asked him to drop her at the corner but he insisted on stopping outside the flats. He leant over to kiss her as she opened the passenger door and she ducked away laughing, making a joke of it. She looked up as the car drove off to see the curtains closing quickly at Liam's bedroom window.

Mills had waited until mid-morning before contacting Naomi. It was an embarrassing call to make, so she'd put it off as long as she could.

'I'm so sorry to disturb you at the weekend...' she began.

'Don't worry. I was surprised not to hear from you before this; what's he done?'

Mills told her about the noise, adding that it wasn't just the music but the pot shots at rabbits late at night. Naomi listened without comment until Mills had run out of steam. '...and anyway I thought it would sound better coming from you.'

'I'll come straight over,' Naomi said briskly.

'I didn't... I mean, you don't...'

'Yes I do. It's my tenants that are being disturbed by his adolescent behaviour – and he shouldn't be using firearms at his age, I've seen too many victims of that sort of misuse.'

She planned to be in Mossy Bank by early afternoon and Mills promised to be around when she arrived; after all, her family wouldn't be back until five.

It suited her to have a free day to catch up after the hectic week she'd had. She tidied and cleaned in anticipation as if she was expecting visitors rather than preparing for the return of a dog. She washed his blanket, collecting his toys in an old wicker basket which she placed beside his bed. She vacuumed the sitting room, opening the windows to let the fresh air in. There was a strong breeze and soon the sashes were rattling, doors banging. So at first she didn't notice there was someone at the front door.

'Hi, I'm early. Hope you don't mind but there's no-one in at the Manor!'

Mills didn't mind at all. It meant she could chat with Naomi over the picnic lunch she'd planned to give Dad and Fiona. They sat in the tiny garden, sheltered from the wind, enjoying the sun when it appeared from between the clouds.

'I hope this business with Gareth hasn't spoilt your father's holiday,' Naomi said between mouthfuls of sausage roll.

'I don't think so,' Mills lied.

'He's not such a difficult lad to understand, you know. He lacks attention that's all. Everything with Dan and Penny is about Lucy. They dote on her. Drool over her. It's quite nauseating.'

'He worked really well this week, really well. It was only the noise – which wasn't helped by the boys who he brought back from the course... also I accused him of pinching an artefact which turned out not to be missing at all. He really resented that.'

'Don't worry. I'm sure we can sort it out. To be honest the only thing that worries me is the air rifle.'

Since the subject had come up, Mills took the opportunity to mention the red kite.

'... it had been shot with a high velocity rifle, the wildlife officer said.'

'You contacted the police?'

'Of course.'

'You didn't mention Gareth?' Naomi looked concerned.

'No.'

'But you think he was involved?'

'No I didn't... then.'

'But you do now?'

'I don't know.'

Her friend continued to take small bites from her apple.

'I took some pellets from a box in the hall,' Mills said and waited to see what her reaction would be.

'What for?'

'I thought I could show George – the wildlife officer. He might say they're the wrong sort.'

'What if they're the right sort? Please don't do anything. Not yet. Not until I've spoken to him.'

'But George is coming over tomorrow. I told him I'd found some pellets.'

Mills was wondering what the pellets might tell them. Suppose they did match the ones that killed the red kite? That wouldn't be proof, would it? Other people might use the same supplier. On the other hand, they could prove they weren't the same.

By the time Naomi went to look for her nephew again, they'd worked out how they could prove whether the pellets were a match – without implicating Gareth.

'But if they do match, the police will have to be told,' warned Mills.

'I know, I just want him to have a fair chance to be cleared,' Naomi said as she left.

Mills reached for the recipe book to make a start on supper. She'd only just placed the lamb casserole in the oven when Naomi returned to report on her meeting with Gareth.

'I can't understand him. He says he's not using the rifle to shoot rabbits. He seems quite genuine but when I tell him that people have heard him he just says it's not him. His parents are back on Tuesday. I told him, if there's any more trouble I'll be on the phone to them straightaway.'

'Did that make any difference to his attitude?'

'I think so. As a youngster growing up he would confide in me. Although he's not opening up with me now, I don't think he'd like me to end up on his parent's side.'

'Where was he last night?'

'With a friend, he said. That young Scottish lad we met with the gamekeeper last week.'

Mills agreed to contact Naomi after the wildlife officer had visited on the following day. Mills waved her off before returning to the kitchen to start on the rhubarb fool.

The evening went better than expected, although Fiona was still complaining about her blisters. She had purchased a ladies shoot coat and matching skirt in Hulme tweed that she declared would be an ideal autumn outfit for London. Hugh gave a smile that said, if you are happy then I am happy. It was a look she remembered from when she was a child. Although Mills could only take her father's new wife in small doses, the birth of Flora had quietened her down a bit. However, she could still be irritating, especially when she started quizzing Mills about boyfriends.

'What about the guy who went to Colombia?' she asked. 'The one who left you the dog? I suppose you've had to get in touch with him about the poisoning?'

'No. It's difficult. He's not often able to e-mail. It's best not to worry him.'

Her father, appearing to sense an impending clash of opinions, suggested that Flora needed to get to bed and they still had to pack for an early start in the morning.

'We're going back home via York,' he explained. 'Fi wants to do a bit of shopping.'

It was a chaotic parting with Fiona insisting that Mills kiss Flora goodbye. The baby woke up and howled, resulting in a scramble to get her back to the cottage for a feed. Mills stood in the doorway watching Fiona hobbling up the lane followed by Hugh clutching the screaming bundle. With a smile she went back inside to tackle the washing-up.

It wasn't unusual for Nina to work at weekends and usually she didn't mind too much. Nige was always happy to spend time with Rosie, especially now she was past the tiny baby stage. Nina joked that soon he'd want to take his daughter to football matches with him.

'Are you sure you'll be all right?' she checked as she made for the door.

'No problem.'

The good thing about Sunday mornings, she thought, was that the traffic was virtually non-existent. The office was equally silent and she settled down, undisturbed, to collate all the intelligence she'd obtained on Friday relating to the list of names she'd compiled following the appeal on "Crimewatch". Currently, she was only looking at names that cropped up more than once. She'd divided them into two groups, depending on whether they were local or not. She'd chosen a thirty mile radius to denote local, since it divided the women arbitrarily, but rather neatly she thought, into two equally sized groups, containing three names apiece.

She was prioritising local addresses but had left instructions for the researchers to identify places of work and family backgrounds for all the women. She was keen to see what they had discovered, particularly if any of them was missing or married to a serviceman or a professional pistol shooter who happened to be an American citizen. Unfortunately there was nothing. All six women were alive and well, living alone or with husbands or partners, all of whom were British.

It was a disappointing start but she couldn't rule them out on those facts alone. They would have to speak to them all to find out what they had been doing in the week beginning the eleventh of July. It wouldn't be difficult for them to provide an alibi for such a recent period if they were unconnected to the crime.

Nina put the process in motion by calling the numbers on the list to arrange appointments, deciding to start with any local ones she was able to contact immediately. As a result she was soon driving out to Catterick to meet a Sandra Cogan. Her name had been suggested by a couple of workmates who, independently, had said the picture was a remarkable resemblance. When Nina met her, she wondered whether they had connived to get their colleague into trouble. As soon as she opened the door Nina could see the woman was enormous. There was no way she could have attempted the Coast to Coast walk. Anyway, she had been at work for the entire week in question.

'It's those cows Marie and Tina, ain't it?' the woman asked without any particular hostility in her voice. They've always got it in for me, them two.'

'I don't have that sort of information with me,' Nina lied.

'I'll give 'em the sharp end of my tongue when I see 'em tomorrow,' she threatened.

Nina crossed Sandra Cogan off her list as soon as she left and focussed on the next name. Isobel Fleming. She lived alone in a small cottage outside Thirsk. It had been a pleasant drive and Nina was anticipating a potential offer of at least a cup of tea when she knocked on the door. Miss Fleming was upset. It took some time before she calmed down and only once Nina had made tea for them both. She reassured the middle-aged spinster that no-one was accusing her of anything – she just happened to have a strong resemblance to the drawing of the woman they wanted to question. With a sigh of relief she left the cottage and drove straight home. There was nothing more she could do that day.

'I found these pellets on the moor.' Mills hoped she sounded convincing; it was important that George believed her story.

'Oh, aye?'

He took the six pellets, scrutinising them on his large open palm.

'I wondered if they might be the ones used to shoot the kite?'

'They're a similar type.'

Mills had assumed from their previous conversation that he had little understanding of the powers of forensic science. She immediately launched into a detailed description of the matching of lead bullets and gunshot pellets. While he listened, he shuffled his feet and stared out of the window.

'But we couldn't prove they were the same make,' he muttered.

Mills was in with her offer straight away.

'I could do it for you.'

He looked up in surprise.

'Yes, I could get the chemical composition of the lead measured at the university. Easy!' she hoped it sounded that simple to him.

He scratched his head, rubbed his chin then handed her the pellets.

'Righto then. How long does it take?'

'Not long – about a week, say?'

He still looked troubled. 'What if these pellets were used to shoot the red kite?' he asked. 'It still doesn't identify the culprit. I don't see...'

'No,' conceded Mills. 'But it's a start.'

He shrugged and turned to leave.

'So you'll send me a pellet from the red kite then? I'll ring you as soon as I've got the results,' she offered.

He shrugged. 'Ok. I'll be off then.'

'Before you go, George, may I ask you about carbofuran.'

She could see his back stiffen before he turned and walked back into the centre of the room.

'What about it?'

She explained about Earl's poisoning. This time he was looking at her as he listened attentively throughout her description of the details.

'We've had cases of birds being poisoned in the past,' he said. 'It was probably left out for the kites.'

'Really?'

'Oh, aye. Without a doubt. Has it been reported?'

'The vet said it had been.'

'I'll follow it up. In fact I'll spend a bit of time this afternoon having a look around; there's been a report of some shooting at night in this area on Friday night. We think there might be poachers about. We wouldn't want anything spoiling the start of the grouse season on Saturday would we?'

She ignored his sarcasm. At least Gareth wasn't here last Friday night, she thought. 'Can I join you?' she asked.

He shrugged, so she followed him out to the porch where she laced her boots and observed George releasing three dogs from his truck.

'Stay!' he ordered as they raced about. They responded immediately, sitting submissively until he had locked up. Then he set off, calling them to heel and Mills followed obediently.

She hadn't been up on the moor since Earl had gone missing and she was content to walk along quietly, watching the dogs enjoying their freedom.

'Did your lurcher eat raw meat?' George asked after a long silence.

'Not normally but he'd eat anything he could find. Why?'

'Usually these people put the bait in some meat – to attract the kite. They're carrion eaters.'

'So we're looking for meat left out here?'

'Not if your dog ate it all but there's a chance we might find traces.'

'What if your dogs find it?' she asked. The three figures were dots in the distance.

'They won't eat anything unless I give permission,' he replied. 'But they'll find it if it's still there.'

They were standing at the top of the track where the path went off in three directions.

'David found Earl down on his farm, that way, towards Keld.' She pointed west.

'Close to the Coast to Coast path here,' George remarked before whistling his dogs, and moving off without further comment. They must have walked another mile when it happened. The dogs were barking excitably and circling a patch of heather. He shouted for them to leave while galloping dramatically across the clumps of heather. When he reached the spot the dogs drew back and he sank to his knees. By the time Mills caught up he was struggling to his feet.

'Meat. Probably rabbit.'

She looked down at the patch of brown stained with blue.

'Whoever left this poisoned meat out deliberately,' he said, 'deserves to be shot.'

Chapter 10

Mills knew that lead shot carried a fingerprint of metals that could identify the origin. In the past she'd studied the composition of shotgun pellets and discovered that the arsenic, antimony, tin, copper and cadmium content of lead provided a signature that would identify the origin of the lead shot. The six pellets she'd shown George had come from a green box labelled "Bisley Premier Pointed". She decided to give three of them to the laboratory in case there were small differences between the metals in them. It was important to know that, if she was going to try to match them with the pellet George was going to send her. She'd placed the bag carefully on the passenger seat beside her as she set off to Harrogate.

'You wanted to see me?'

The office was a mess. Brenda was almost hidden by a pile of files on her desk.

'Don't come in – we'll go for a coffee,' she came round to greet Mills. 'Can't stand all this...' she waved her hand at the paperwork with a theatrical gesture.

She led Mills out into the sunshine and round the corner to where a van was serving food and drink. She bought them both a cappuccino and a muffin then motioned Mills to sit on the low wall outside the laboratory.

'This is better,' she remarked. 'I miss being outside. It's all paperwork now.' She took a large bite of her muffin. 'In fact that's why I called you. I wondered if you would like to help me out with some admin to cover the summer holidays?'

Mills would rather have helped in the lab but work was work. 'Yes, that would be great. Is your PA going away for long?'

Brenda laughed loudly, nearly choking on her coffee. 'No, love. It's to cover *my* holiday.'

'Are you serious?'

'Of course. What d'you say?'

'When are you going?'

'Next week. And don't worry; it's only to keep things ticking over.'

'How long are you going for?'

'A fortnight. What can go wrong in two weeks, eh?'

Mills knew she'd be a fool to refuse such an offer. They finished their coffees and made their way back to the laboratory.

'... so if you come into the office a couple of days this week, I can show you the ropes. Everyone is very helpful and Glyn knows how to run the place without me anyway – I just don't want to leave him with the responsibility for any important decisions.' She smiled. 'Not that there'll be any, of course.'

As she was leaving Brenda asked Mills what is was she had wanted to ask *her*. She felt her pocket containing the bag with the three air rifle pellets.

'Could I get a bit of work done while I'm here?' she asked cautiously. 'It's just that I've got these pellets...'

Brenda was already settled behind the pile of paper. 'Whatever you want to do. It'll be up to you to arrange, provided the main work gets done. We'll go through the work plan when you come in on Wednesday, all right?'

'Yes, fine.'

Mills couldn't resist asking Brenda if she was going away somewhere.

'I've booked myself on one of those activity holidays,' she said without lifting her head.

'Oh yes?'

'Yes. Salsa dancing. I thought it would be good exercise.'

Mills was still smiling when she unlocked the car and reached for her phone. She wanted to call the vet before she headed off, in case Earl was ready to be collected.

'Yes. You can pick him up any time. He's weak but he's taking notice and it'll be good for him to be in familiar surroundings again.'

She was there in less than an hour and with help from the veterinary nurse she was able to settle the lurcher into the back of the car. He made no sound during the journey home, apparently sleeping, but when they drew up outside Laurel Cottage, his head popped up in the back. No amount of coaxing would get the dog out of the back seat without some additional help. Mills looked up and down the lane.

'Sorry, Earl, but I'm going to have to find assistance.'

She considered for a moment then made her way up to the Manor. Gareth would help if he was in. Encouraged by the loud music emanating from the open windows, she leant on the bell and counted to ten.

Eventually Gareth appeared at an upstairs window and Mills shouted to him above the noise. Someone opened the front door, standing in the hallway, observing Mills as she carried on her stilted conversation. She glanced across and recognised the

Scottish lad she'd seen at the drinks party when she was chatting to Naomi. The door closed again.

A few minutes later Gareth came down to the car and helped Mills carry Earl inside the cottage. The dog seemed grateful to be home, wagging his tail weakly as his head dropped, his eyes closing.

'Is he going to be all right?' Gareth sounded genuinely concerned.

'I hope so. He'll need lots of rest to build up his muscles again.'

It was an ideal moment to talk to Gareth. Mills told him about the poison, how it was probably put out as bait for the red kite.

'Someone shot the kite, Gareth, and I know you've been using that air rifle.'

He reddened, looking at the ground. 'I haven't,' he said sullenly.

'Well there's been a lot of shooting going on in that house. Someone's been doing it. Who, if not you?'

He pulled a face, as if trying to decide whether to speak up or not.

'Just tell me, Gareth, if it's someone else.' Then it dawned on her: it was the Scottish lad, the trainee gamekeeper. Of course. Who else?

'I'm coming back up to the Manor,' she said. 'I want to speak to your friend Fergus.'

Gareth wasn't able to keep up with her in his high boots. Her thumb was still on the bell push when he arrived, breathing heavily as he fumbled in his pocket and produced a key. Mills followed him inside and pushed past him in the hall.

'Fergus!' she shouted. 'Fergus, are you there?'

'Who's asking?'

She followed his voice to the sitting room, where he was lounging on the sofa in his boots, which were covered in dried mud.

She stood over him with her hands on her hips. 'You've been using an air rifle here. Have you been shooting up on the moor as well?'

'What's it to you?'

'I'll tell you – a red kite was killed up there.' As she pointed in the direction of the open moorland, she sensed that the gesture was rather melodramatic.

'So what?'

'They're a protected species, that's what!'

'It's the grouse that should be protected. I'm a gamekeeper and I've seen the damage they do to the game birds.'

Mills was taken aback by his reaction and looked to Gareth for support but he'd disappeared.

'Are you saying that you would shoot a red kite?'

'I didn't say that, did I?'

'Not exactly but... What about baiting them with poisoned meat? Is that another of the ploys you learnt in Scotland?'

He swung his legs round and jumped up from the sofa. He stood in front of her, looking down with a sneer. 'It's not your business what I did at home or what I do down here. And if you poke your nose into my affairs you'll likely end up the same way as your wee doggie.'

He pushed her aside and marched out of the room, leaving Mills motionless with the shock of his outburst. Her instinct was to race after him; to challenge him with using carbofuran but she was also frightened by his aggression. As she walked to the front door she could hear voices in the kitchen. She was tempted to stay and listen but was propelled forward by her desire to get away from Fergus – now she was certain he was responsible for poisoning Earl.

It had been a difficult day for Nina. She'd finished speaking to all the women on the list and taken the precaution of checking the size of the women before bothering to visit them personally and had established that three of the them were at least size sixteen and so were far too big to be a match. Several had alibis for the period when the woman had been seen at the campsites, including a lady with a broken leg who had been in hospital and another who'd been on holiday in Egypt at the time. She had finally come to the conclusion that none of them could be the mysterious companion to the dead man.

Hazel had finished her tour of the campsites on Saturday, reporting that there was no new intelligence to report.

'So nothing fresh to go on, again,' said Mitch, screwing up his paper coffee cup and aiming at the wastepaper basket. He sighed, closing his eyes for a moment while Nina and Hazel exchanged glances.

'Ok,' he continued, 'let's start again. Nina, I want you to go through all the intelligence on the victim one more time. Make sure everything is up to date and nothing's been overlooked. Hazel, I want you to concentrate on the woman. Check all the interviews, see if there's any information we've missed... and contact missing persons again.'

As soon as Mitch had gone, Nina asked Hazel how her date had gone.

'Don't ask. I should never have gone. Liam's been acting all weird ever since.'

'What d'you mean?'

'First of all he didn't believe I was working on Saturday, so he insisted on coming with me, even though his mates were going swimming.'

'What? Keeping an eye on you?'

'No. He kept asking when I was going to see Robert again.'

'That's good, isn't it?'

'Only because he thought his car was "cool". He wants a ride in it.'

'So when *are* you seeing him again?'

'I don't know. I don't think I should. It doesn't seem right somehow.'

She began tapping on her computer keyboard.

'I did check his finger though,' she confided, without looking up.

'Oh yes? And how did that happen?'

'Don't ask!'

'And?'

'I didn't feel any calluses. Now, I must get on.'

They worked in silence until lunch-time when they went out into the sunshine to eat their sandwiches.

'I don't know why Mitch had to swap us over to review the intelligence,' said Hazel. 'It's like he's checking up on us.'

'I don't mind,' Nina replied. 'In fact it's a good way to make sure nothing is missing.'

'There won't be anything missing from your files but I bet you find something I've forgotten, Miss Meticulous.'

'Nonsense,' said Nina. 'Anyway, tell me about your meal with Robert. You did have a nice evening?'

'Yes, the meal was very good.'

'So why won't you be seeing him again?'

Hazel took another bite of her sandwich, chewing it slowly and brushing crumbs from her jeans. 'You won't say anything to Mitch if I tell you?'

Nina shook her head.

'I've been trying to trace him in the US Army records. It's taken ages but finally this morning I got a call. It wasn't very helpful but it confirmed that he's in Special Operations Command.'

'I thought he was in the airforce.'

'It's got "Airborne" in brackets apparently.'

'So what does "Special Ops" do?'

'It sounds like the SAS.'

'Is that why you don't want to see him?'

'It's too much like déjà vu.'

Nina understood. Liam's father was in the "Paras" and that relationship hadn't lasted long.

'Oh well, it's time to get back to work,' announced Hazel, jumping up and grabbing her bag.

Nina ran to keep up with her friend as she strode towards the office. Her mind was racing. If Major Henderson was in the American equivalent of the SAS, why was he sent to discuss the stabbing victim with Hazel? Did it mean that the victim was of interest to them? She searched for details of the Special Operations Command to find that most of their work was concerned with the threat of terrorism. Was it possible that their unidentified body was the victim of an attack related to that work? Suddenly their job had got a whole lot harder, she told herself.

Chapter 11

The early morning sun was almost blinding as Jeremy Singleton drove slowly through Catterick. It was his day off, the one day of the week when he could enjoy a day's fishing. His wife had decided to visit their daughter and grandchildren in Halifax so he wouldn't have to be back until teatime. It was a journey he always looked forward to, particularly the drive over the moor, past the ranges to the river. It reminded him of happier days, training as a young soldier before he met his first wife. When he reached the junction with the Leyburn road, he turned the car towards Grinton, climbing gradually, admiring the view, envisioning the time when he was retired and could spend every day by the river. It was too early for firing practice but something caught his eye. Almost hidden at the edge of the range was a small yellow Renault Clio – definitely a woman's car, he thought. His wife said it was his redcap training that caused him to analyse everything. She was probably right because although it was his day off, he felt compelled to have a look.

He drove down slowly, veering off the road and up to the first building, where he stopped before approaching the car. His first reaction, when he saw a woman asleep in the back, was to tiptoe away. Her blonde hair strewn across the seat was rather attractive, he thought, although her face was turned away from him. He felt it was his duty to remind her of the dangers of sleeping in a car in the open country – especially on her own – and tapped gently on the window. Perhaps the vehicle had broken down and he could be of some assistance. When vigorous tapping elicited no answer he opened the door and shook her gently. He agreed that in hindsight he should have been more careful and that he could have affected the investigation by putting his hands all over the car and disturbing the body. It was all right for them but he hadn't known she was dead until he saw all the blood on the seat and the knife on the floor. He'd had to wait for a motorist to pass by until he was able to alert the civilian police. It was obviously disappointing to miss his day's fishing but, as he'd told his missus that evening, it was pretty exciting to find a dead body – and he knew he'd be involved in the investigation, even if it was a suicide, since she'd been found on MOD land.

The pathologist was a young woman, hardly out of school. He tried to explain to her about the knife falling off the seat when he opened the door but she said she had her doubts about suicide – the wounds weren't commensurate with that theory. By then the local police were in attendance as well as more senior officers from the garrison. He was told to get himself over to HQ to give a full statement to CID because it was likely to turn into a murder investigation. But he'd had to wait several hours before he was allowed to take his car away. Meanwhile he helped secure the scene, liaising with the civilian police officers. As he told his wife, it was good he'd taken a packed lunch because it was early afternoon before he was able to drive across to Newby Wiske.

The woman who interviewed him made him feel most uncomfortable. He'd asked her name and rank but she told him to call her Hazel. We don't mess about with surnames between ranks in civvy street, she'd said – sarcastic like. She acted as if he was under suspicion, asking him why he was there so early in the morning. He'd had to explain to her how important he felt it was to make an early start when fishing in the summer, while it was still cool. He'd started to list the statistics he'd collected over the years but she obviously wasn't interested. In the end he'd dictated his statement slowly while she typed it up on her computer. She didn't even offer him a cup of tea while he waited for her to make a copy for the MOD.

'Did you see him?' Hazel asked Nina as soon as Jeremy Singleton had left. 'That boring man from the Military Police. He wouldn't stop talking about his bloody fishing!'

'You just don't like army personnel.'

'Well, that's true.'

Mills hadn't told Naomi or George about what Fergus had said to her. He'd virtually admitted that he'd left the poisoned meat out on the moor but his manner had frightened her. She needed time to think before acting. Gareth's parents would be back now so hopefully his unpleasant friend would have retreated back to his own accommodation again. And at least it was unlikely that their outrageous behaviour would continue with Daniel and Penny back in control.

She was also becoming concerned about whether she'd made the right decision to help Brenda. She'd been up several times in the night to check on Earl and now, at five-thirty, it hardly seemed worth going back to bed. The dog watched her as she wandered aimlessly round the kitchen with her coffee. She knew it was a brilliant opportunity to work at the lab but her nerves were getting the better of her.

'D'you think I'm being silly?' she asked him. 'Perhaps I should have told Brenda that I couldn't spare the time.'

Already the sun was sending long shadows across the room and Mills longed to take the dog for a run on the moor. Instead she fed him some rice and chicken left over from the evening before. He seemed more interested in the food, lifting his head to lick the bowl clean. She was able to coax him the few steps into the garden where he relieved himself gratefully before returning to his bed.

The next hour was spent washing her hair and deciding what to wear. Although Brenda was not interested in fashion, generally appearing in a flowery skirt and baggy top, Mills felt she should make an effort which meant exchanging her jeans for the black trousers she reserved for interviews and funerals. She could get away with it if she wore a shirt over the top. She surveyed herself in the mirror by standing on tiptoes – it would do.

'Now, Auntie Muriel will come in to look after you at lunch time,' she told Earl.

The dog's tail was wagging feebly as she left, which made her feel even worse for leaving him in such a weak state. When she reached Harrogate she rang Muriel once more to make sure she would remember to check on him.

Brenda was already in the office when Mills arrived. She took her for a tour of the laboratory, introducing her to the scientists, explaining that Mills would be "keeping her seat warm". Most of them smiled politely but she sensed a couple of them exchanging glances as she left the room.

'Now, I need to go through the work file with you, Mills. It lists all the ongoing jobs we have on the books at the present. Of course new things may come in while I'm away.'

'That's what worries me,' admitted Mills.

'Don't you fret. The analysts know exactly what to do. All you need to do is ask them.'

'Really?'

'Of course.'

Brenda went through the job numbers systematically, explaining what each one entailed.

'It's very simple,' she concluded. 'The analyst will give you a report containing the results and all the necessary information. It will have been checked thoroughly before you receive it. You just have to read it through and sign it off before it goes to the customer.'

'What am I looking for?'

'Just any inconsistencies. Don't worry, I never find any mistakes. My lot know more about the science than I do.'

Mills was about to ask her what to do if she did find a mistake when the phone rang. Brenda answered it, speaking for a few minutes to someone she apparently knew well.

'No problem, love. Send them along. We'll have a look.' She put the phone down. 'A woman found out near Catterick. They want her clothes examined for traces of fibres, hair and DNA.'

Mills was obviously not hiding her anxiety very well.

'Don't worry, dear. They're sending the samples down this afternoon so I'll be able to talk you through the procedure. Meanwhile we'll have a look at this report which is about to go out. It's the body that was found on the North York Moors a couple of weeks ago. We did an initial analysis which gave us some interesting results, including your soil measurements, and the police wanted us to check again, particularly for any traces of DNA from a female companion they think was with him up to his death.'

'Was that the walker on the Coast to Coast path?' Mills had seen something on "Crimewatch" about it.

'Yes. It's been quite a mystery... especially this woman companion. Anyway we think we have a hair that will help. At least, it's a woman's hair: blonde. So we're sending off the results today. Perhaps you'd better have a look at the report so you can see what to expect in future.'

The package containing several evidence bags arrived after lunch. Brenda watched Mills as she signed her first chain of custody form to show that the packages were now her responsibility. Then they went down to hand the parcel over to the laboratory manager, Glyn, who distributed the contents between the analysts who would be looking for evidence on individual items of clothing. Glyn was one of the people who Mills felt might have resented her presence. He was helpful but remained aloof and Mills expressed her concern to Brenda.

'Don't worry about Glyn,' she said as they walked back to the office. 'He'll come round when he gets to know you.' Mills was not reassured.

They spent the rest of the afternoon entering the information about the new samples into the computer system. The garments belonged to a Tanya Stewart who was found dead in her car at Black Beck ranges. Because her body was found on MOD property and she lived at Catterick Camp, the report was to be sent to Newby Wiske – as usual – but also to the Military Police at the garrison. The police wanted a full analysis of anything found, including any blood, semen or saliva, which was why there were several people working on the clothes. One would look for hair and fibres, another for fluids. There was even an expert who could be called on if they found any pollen, which gave Mills some confidence. By the time she left Harrogate at the end of the day, she was thinking that she might just manage to hold things together – for a couple of weeks.

When she got home Earl greeted her by climbing gingerly out of his basket. She let him out into the garden while she prepared a tasty meal of rice and chicken. It was encouraging to see him tucking into his food again – he was still weak and needed as much nourishment as possible. Once he was settled in, Mills turned to the answer machine: there was a message from Penny Banford, her superior tone unmistakeable as she thanked Mills for keeping an eye on Gareth, inviting her round for drinks the following day. It was more of a summons, with the assumption that she would be free. Although she was not enthusiastic about spending another evening with Penny and Daniel, there was a small chance that Naomi might be there once again. She waited until evening before calling Naomi's number, on the pretext of asking her whether she'd also been invited to the Banfords.

'Why? Are you going?' her friend asked.

'I felt I should but...'

'I know how you feel. Tell you what – I'll come over if you promise to be there.'

'Ok. I'll be able to tell you about Fergus.'

'Fergus? Who's Fergus?'

'The Scottish lad who was there last time. Friend of Gareth's.'

'What's he been up to?'

'I think he might be responsible for putting out poisoned bait... and maybe for shooting the red kite.'

'Have you told George Herbert?'

'Not yet. I wanted to be sure. I wanted to get the pellets analysed first.'

There was silence at the other end. 'This is a serious matter, Mills. You should inform the police.'

'I will but I want to be sure. Don't you see? Gareth might get involved. I don't want to be mistaken.'

'It gets worse,' moaned Mitch as he skimmed through the report. 'Now we've got DNA for the mystery woman but it gets us no nearer to identifying either of them.'

'It means we can easily check if a suspect is identified,' offered Nina.

'If.'

'Medium length blonde hair fits the description we have for her.' Nina was irritated by his negative attitude to their discovery.

'Fat use that is,' he muttered, slapping the file down on his desk. 'We might as well consider the investigation on hold for now... unless there's anything you'd like to propose?' His tone suggested he did not expect a response. 'Anyway,' he went on, 'we've got a new investigation to concentrate on, haven't we Hazel? This woman from Catterick, Tanya Stewart, died of stab wounds. Found in her own car on the ranges near her home.' Mitch was already sounding more cheerful. He always did when a new investigation started.

'What've we got?' asked Nina.

'Pathologist's initial view was that it wasn't suicide. People don't normally stab themselves several times in the chest – they slit their wrists or go for the throat. And why climb into the back of the car?'

'We're still waiting for her report,' added Hazel.

'The husband is away in Iraq. No kids. Thames Valley's talking to her parents. Hazel, I need you to liaise with the MOD on this – we can save time by sharing intelligence from neighbours. See if there's a boyfriend.' He opened a file on his desk. 'There's an officer over there by the name of Singleton you can speak to.'

'That's if he's not gone fishing,' Hazel remarked, ignoring their quizzical looks.

When she finally spoke to him on the phone, Sergeant Singleton informed her that he only went fishing on his day off so he was at the Garrison but planned to talk to the neighbours in the afternoon.

'Good,' she remarked, 'I'll join you.'

'Oh I don't think that'll be possible young lady.'

'I'm sure it will be, Sergeant Singleton,' Hazel said before replacing the receiver.

It took some time to find the right contact but a call from Mitch to the Military Police at the garrison produced the required result and she arranged to be over there by one.

The sergeant stood stiffly at the entrance to the administration building where they'd arranged to meet. She was deliberately a few minutes late and he looked satisfyingly irritated. Commenting that he'd expected her to appear in uniform, he indicated where his car was parked, marching towards it stiffly.

'Get in, we're not going far. She lived on camp so we'll be talking to the wives.'

'Good.' In that case it'll be helpful to have a woman with you, thought Hazel.

They spoke to four women individually, all of whom seemed in awe of the sergeant, giving monosyllabic answers to his questions. When Hazel spoke to them they opened up a little, glancing at the military policeman every so often with a nervous expression. The general impression they gave of Tanya Stewart was of a typical army wife. She was a local girl who'd met her husband in Richmond when he was training. She had no children so was able to take a full-time job in the garrison, supporting service families. Her neighbours seemed envious of her freedom, surrounded as they were by babies and toddlers. Tanya had obviously not been part of the tight-knit group of young mothers she lived among, Hazel observed.

'Well, it's past four o'clock. I'll be going off shortly,' announced Sergeant Singleton as he drove her to where she had parked her car. 'I don't suppose we'll be meeting again.'

'No,' she agreed.

She waited until he was out of sight before locking her car again and making her way into the administration building to locate the "Overseas Family Support Team".

'You're lucky to have caught me.' The woman had her own office, which indicated her senior status. 'I come in early and leave early.' She indicated for Hazel to take the seat opposite her. 'Of course we were shocked to hear about Tanya. She seemed pretty grounded, although of course her husband is overseas, but she has a sister locally.'

'Did she seem to be concerned about anything recently?'

'I hadn't seen her for a couple of weeks. She was on leave.'

'Did she go away, do you know?'

'She was visiting her sister, I think.'

Hazel made a note to find out where the sister lived and continued with the usual list of questions. Apparently Tanya was a pleasant, outgoing girl with a wicked sense of humour, a loud dress sense and would stand no nonsense. Her boss didn't rule out that she might be seeing other men while her husband was away. Hazel thanked her and left with a sense that she'd moved forward more in the last thirty minutes than she had all afternoon with the redcap.

She called Nina before setting off so, by the time she was back at Newby Wiske, Nina had the information ready for her.

'I've written her name and address on this card with the phone number. She's called Rachel. I rang her and she's in now but she's off to Reading early tomorrow morning to be with her parents.'

'Another late night then,' muttered Hazel.

Liam wasn't concerned when she rang to say she'd be late. His grandmother was making shepherd's pie, which was his favourite, and his friend was coming over for supper.

'What friend, Mum?'

'I don't know, pet. Don't you want him to have his friends round?'

'I didn't know he had any!' she commented, putting the phone down.

She gave Nina a quick report of what had occurred at the camp, explaining that Tanya may have confided in her sister while she was staying there. Then she drove as fast as she dared across to Kirkby Stephen. It was getting on for seven by the time she arrived at the cottage and the family were eating their evening meal.

'I'm sorry to disturb your tea.' Hazel began.

'We've nearly finished. I can leave them to it now. Let's go into the garden.'

'I can see why your sister liked to visit you here.' Hazel was admiring the view across fields and out onto the hills. 'I'm sorry for your loss,' she added.

'Well, she was brought up here. The cottage used to belong to my parents. She lived here until she got married.'

'Did she seem happy when she was here last?'

'Of course it's difficult with Mike in Iraq but she's used to it... I mean she was.' Her face contorted as she tried to prevent herself from crying.

'I'm sorry. I'll try to keep this short. Was there anything that might make you think she would take her own life?'

'Nothing.' She blew her nose and wiped her eyes. 'I don't believe she would ever do that. She had a great time. We even went on a few of our old walks while she was here.'

'Would she have told you if there was anything worrying her?'

The woman paused. 'I think so. With Tanya what you saw was what you got. She also spoke her mind. She didn't store things up, if you understand me.'

'So you would know if there was anything wrong?'

'I think so. Why? What do you think was wrong? What happened to her? They told me they thought it was suicide.'

'They?'

'The family liaison people from the camp.'

'They may be right... but the pathologist had her doubts. I should warn you that it could have been murder. That's why it's important to know if there was anything at all that she might have said that would indicate...'

The sister shook her head. 'Nothing to make me think that something was wrong. In fact she seemed very... well, content, I suppose.'

'I have to ask – did she go out much? Might she have had any men friends?'

Her sister looked puzzled. 'You mean like... with Mike away... No! She wouldn't. They're soul-mates, she's always saying.'

'Well, if anything occurs to you later, please call me,' Hazel said, handing over a card as she stood to go.

'What shall I tell my parents? They're bound to ask.'

'Tell them that we're still investigating the cause of death. There's no point in upsetting them further at this stage.'

She gave Rachel a sympathetic smile and a reassuring pat on the arm as she left.

The smell of food wafting from Rachel's kitchen had made her hungry and she hoped that there would be some leftovers when she reached her mother's house. She was in luck.

'I kept you some, pet. I knew you wouldn't have had anything.'

Hazel ate in silence, savouring the first decent meal she'd had for days. She cleared the plate, leaning back in her chair comfortably until she noticed how quiet it was in the house.

'Did Liam bring his friend back?' she asked.

'Oh aye. She's a lovely thing isn't she?'

'She?'

'Yes. Lily she calls herself, although I think her full name is Lilibet. Very polite and well spoken like, isn't she?'

'Don't keep saying isn't she. I don't know, do I? I've not had the privilege.' Suddenly a thought occurred to Hazel. 'Is she here now?'

'No, she had to be home by nine.'

Hazel relaxed. For a second she'd thought they were alone together in Liam's room.

'Now don't you start teasing him, Hazel. I know what you're like. Leave the poor lad alone – he's obviously smitten.'

'Don't worry, Mum, I wouldn't know where to start with that conversation.'

In the car it was her son who was asking her the questions. 'Are you going to see that man with the BMW Z4 again?'

'Why?'

'Just wondered.'

'Would it worry you if I did?'

'No, it's none of my business, is it?'

Hazel considered for a moment but before she could answer, he continued, 'I just wondered when I'm going to get to go in the Z4.'

'...and apparently the fish and chips are good there too.'

Next morning Hazel was describing her visit to the cottage where Tanya's sister lived when Nina began her own recollections of Kirkby Stephen.

'So how come you know so much about it?' Hazel asked.

'Because I had to visit the campsite there – where the mystery couple stayed. It's on the Coast to Coast path, if you remember.'

'Oh right.'

Hazel settled down to write up the visits she'd made to Tanya's friends and place of work, as well as to her sister. Two cups of coffee later, with half the report written, she had a visitor. It was the pathologist.

'I just wanted to let you know that the knife they found at the scene was the weapon that was used to kill Tanya Stewart.'

'To kill her? Not suicide?'

'No. The angles are all wrong. It's virtually impossible to stab yourself straight in the chest when sitting or lying in the back of a Clio. Also there are defence wounds and bruising on the wrists.'

'Any tissue or fluids other than the victim's?'

'We're waiting for forensics.' She paused. 'There was another thing. Probably just a coincidence, after all it's quite a common sort of hunting knife.'

'What's the coincidence?'

'The knife wounds are almost identical to those found on the man stabbed on the North York Moors. They could be the same weapon. I don't suppose the crimes are connected?'

'Not that we know of but I'll bear it in mind. Thanks, Diane.'

When the pathologist had gone, Hazel turned to Nina. 'Did you hear that?'

'I did. It could just be a coincidence but the weapon from the first murder was never found.'

'That's two coincidences in one morning then.'

'The other being?'

'That both victims were in Kirkby Stephen at the same time.'

Chapter 12

Mills was back at the forensic laboratory in Harrogate for a second day of training before Brenda went on holiday. She had the air-rifle pellets with her again, but this time she'd included the one George had sent her, hoping to get them all analysed quickly. She felt under pressure from Naomi and wanted to have something she could tell her that evening if possible.

She spent the entire morning familiarising herself with the company computer system which was so secure that even Brenda had to consult her notebook to access some files. Mills hoped she wouldn't need to find the more confidential parts of the system. At lunch-time she asked Brenda if she could see Timothy for a minute, with a small request for analysis.

'No problem. He'll be glad to help.'

Mills wandered along the corridor to the mass spectrometry laboratory. She could see Timothy through the glass in the door and signalled to him that she would like to speak to him. Inside the door was a barrier to keep the laboratory free of dust and dirt and anyone going in had to put on a white coat and plastic overshoes. Timothy came as far as the barrier and removed a protective cap from his head. They carried out their conversation across the barrier.

'Hi. Brenda said you'd do a few analyses for me?' She offered the two plastic bags containing the pellets. 'I'd like to get a compositional analysis of metals in the two sets to see if they're a match.'

The young man took the bags, examining the contents through the plastic. He counted the pellets, held the bags up to the light and peered at them individually again. Then he looked up and smiled.

'No problem. I've done it before.'

'Great. How long will it take?'

'When d'you want the results?'

'This afternoon if that's....' She felt awkward asking for what she thought was the impossible.

'Ok. I've got the laser on. I can do them by five. Are you happy with just numbers?'

'Yes of course.'

He walked back through the laboratory, swinging a sample bag in each hand. When Mills opened the door into the corridor, she was confronted by the laboratory manager, Glyn.

'Good afternoon, Dr Sanderson. I didn't know you were visiting the laboratories this afternoon.'

'I w.... I was just talking to... to Timothy,' she mumbled.

'Oh yes?' He stood in front of her in the doorway so she couldn't move in either direction along the corridor.

'Yes. I asked him to do some work for me. Brenda said it was ok.'

'Did she?'

As he went to open the door Mills ducked under his arm and made her escape. 'I hope it's not a problem,' she shouted as she made her way quickly back to the office.

Later in the afternoon, when Mills was in the outer office looking at the filing system with Brenda's PA, Glyn marched through saying he had to speak to Brenda. The door shut behind him and raised voices drifted from the room for several minutes. Finally the door burst open, Glyn re-appeared red-faced, and left without acknowledging their presence. From what Brenda said later, he was unhappy when he was not consulted about his team's workload.

'I just thought I'd warn you that he doesn't like change. He may be a little difficult at times but don't worry. He knows that you have the last word.'

So Mills felt rather uncomfortable when Glyn knocked on Brenda's door towards the end of the day to report that the pellet results were ready. He handed her a sheet with the data for each metal found in the pellets together with the plastic bags and chain of custody forms completed in neat handwriting.

'I think you'll find they are a match,' he said before leaving.

'There you are,' said Brenda, beaming, 'putty in your hands.'

When Mills got home and had shared a meal of fish and rice with Earl, she settled down to study the sheet that Glyn had given her. Without the electronic version it took some time but once all the numbers were entered onto her computer it was easy to manipulate the data to test the significance of the match – it was perfect. There was absolutely no difference between the pellets found in the red kite and those she'd taken from the Manor.

Naomi had arranged to call in at Laurel Cottage before they went to the Manor for drinks so they could discuss the analyses. When Mills told her the pellets were a match she screwed up her face.

'Technically it means nothing,' she said. 'Probably half the pellets sold round here are a match. All it tells us is that Fergus could be guilty or he could be innocent.'

'I know,' admitted Mills. 'And I wouldn't want to go to the police with such flimsy evidence – especially since it could implicate Gareth.'

'Heaven forbid. Honestly it would kill Penny. The shame! I know it's not funny but...' she giggled.

'What shall I do if George asks me what the tests showed, Naomi?'

'Tell him the truth – that the pellets "you found on the moor" match the ones that killed the red kite. It doesn't help does it?' She looked at her watch. 'I'd better be going. Don't worry – I'm staying at Ivy Cottage tonight so I'll have a chat with Gareth later this evening; he might open up a bit if I talk to him after he's had a few ginger beers.' She winked. 'I'll let myself out.'

Mills had planned to spend the next hour getting herself ready but Fiona rang to ask how the lurcher was recovering and then she had a call from Nina.

'Brenda Yardley told me you're holding the fort for her while she's on holiday!' she said. 'I had to call to congratulate you.'

'She told you that?'

'She's doing all the forensics on our latest stabbing victim. We've sent the knife over to the lab now as well.'

'It should be very interesting, seeing how the laboratory works.' She didn't want to show her lack of experience by getting involved in technical discussions. 'Anyway, how's Rosie? Still enjoying nursery?'

Nina insisted they made time in their busy schedules to meet up very soon then they said goodbye and Mills rushed upstairs to get changed before leaving for the Manor.

'Mills, how nice to see you!' Daniel was in ebullient mood, opening the door wide with a bottle in his hand. 'Come in, come in. Penny's dying to thank you properly for looking after our wayward son. She is delighted with his transformation.'

Mills was about to ask him to explain when she caught sight of Gareth crossing the hall and disappearing upstairs with a can in each hand. He was wearing an army jersey and tweed breeches, a perfect copy of his new best friend, Fergus. Gone was the white face and mascara, his hair looked shorter and rougher as if he'd hacked his fringe away himself. Although the result was a very normal looking teenager, Mills rather missed the Goth that was Gareth.

'Isn't it a transformation?' his father remarked.

Penny appeared in the doorway and smiled at Mills. 'Such an improvement. He's been out beating today and is going to work on the shoot until the end of the holiday. He's even talking about joining the cadets when he's back at school.'

'Really?' Mills could only assume that Fergus was having an enormous influence on him.

'Naomi's here,' offered Penny, leading her into the lounge. 'I'll get you a drink. White wine all right?'

Mills nodded and smiled at Naomi. 'Fancy seeing you here.'

'Penny was just telling me about their stay in Scotland. Apparently it was heaven. Shooting every day, rubbing shoulders with knights and barons.'

'Lords, Naomi, lords,' Daniel corrected her.

'So is Penny a good shot?' Naomi asked him.

'Better than I am,' admitted her brother.

Penny returned with drinks and fancy snacks on sticks which she passed amongst the small number of guests. Clearly there weren't many suitable locals so they seemed to be pretty much the same group as on the previous occasion. Fergus's mentor, the gamekeeper, was on good form and was the centre of attention. His stories of amateurs out shooting grouse were quite amusing but after about ten minutes Naomi signalled to Mills to follow her into the kitchen, where they entertained themselves until Penny arrived to take yet more titbits out of the oven and asked Naomi what she thought of Gareth's conversion to the shooting fraternity.

'To be perfectly honest I would prefer a son of mine to be a peace-loving Goth rather than a teenager obsessed with firearms.'

Penny picked up her tray of sausage rolls without comment and walked out.

'That was a bit harsh, Naomi.'

'I know. I can't help it. Every time I speak to her I say something I regret afterwards.'

When Mills left at just after nine, Naomi promised to speak to Gareth about the red kite and the poisoned meat. She was sure that he would tell her if Fergus had anything to do with it. As he saw her out, Daniel thanked her once again for looking after his son.

'We feel so grateful that he's finally growing up and is someone we can be proud of. I'm sure his time working with you helped him mature.'

Mills smiled. 'I'm not sure it was anything I did,' she said.

It had been a long day so once she'd let Earl into the garden and steered him gently back into his basket for the night, she had a bath and climbed gratefully into bed. She wasn't sure how long she'd been asleep when she was woken by barking and the sound of banging on the door. Without thinking, she ran downstairs, nearly falling over Earl who continued to bark as she fumbled with the light switch. She opened the front door, expecting to see Muriel or one of the other neighbours but was pushed backwards by Fergus who was shouting at her. Mills almost tripped over the dog as she reversed down the hall.

'You need to mind your own business, bitch!'

She could smell the alcohol on his breath as he pressed his face close to hers. She had backed into the wall at the end of the hall and there was nowhere to go. The tiny hallway seemed to be filled with his fury.

'What've you been saying to that copper friend of yours, eh? What business is it of yours or hers? Eh? Eh?'

She could feel his spit on her face.

'I don't know what you mean,' she offered, recognising immediately it was a stupid thing to say. She felt horribly vulnerable standing in her pyjamas – the target of his alcohol-fuelled rage. He grabbed her face in one large hand, pressing on her cheek-bones.

'If you don't keep your nose out of it, it won't be just the wee doggie that'll get it. Do you understand?'

He pushed her head back against the wall. Mills considered for a second whether to retaliate but remained where she was, passively taking his verbal abuse. She could hear Earl's incessant barking somewhere in the background. He called her a range of abusive names before thumping her head once more. Then he turned, staggering down the hall and out into the lane. Mills ran to shut the door, pulling the bolts across, top and bottom. Her heart was pounding, she was shaking and the adrenalin had left a taste of iron in her mouth. Earl was standing by his basket looking anxiously at her. It was a long time before she turned out the lights and made her way upstairs. Her bedside lamp remained on all night.

She was up and dressed soon after dawn, her mind still going over the confrontation with Fergus. Earl came out of his basket to greet her so she walked him slowly out of the cottage and up the lane. He was happy to keep going, moving slowly and stopping frequently to sniff at the heather and watch the curlews circling above the fields. Mills didn't let him go too far, turning after ten minutes to retrace their steps. He collapsed gratefully into his basket after his breakfast, allowing Mills to consider what to do while she made herself a bacon sandwich. Finally at seven-thirty she walked up to Ivy Cottage, hoping that Naomi was awake.

'Hi there, what d'you want at this time?' Naomi greeted her, bleary-eyed. She was dressed but Mills suspected her clothes had been pulled on quickly when she knocked on the door.

'I need to talk to you about Fergus,' she began.

Naomi listened as she made a pot of tea. At first she appeared annoyed for her friend but then she began apologising.

'I'm so sorry, Mills. I never thought it would result in Fergus kicking off. I simply spoke to Gareth, when he was on his own, and explained what a predicament we were in. He seemed to understand the seriousness of what I was saying. He even offered the fact that it was Fergus who was the one shooting out of the windows. I told him about the kite of course but I said that the pellets could have come from anywhere. He's a good lad at heart, Mills.'

'Either he spoke to Fergus after your conversation or he overheard you. Whatever it was, it certainly touched a nerve. I'm sure he's responsible for killing the bird and for the poisoned bait. I'm going to ring George Herbert this morning and tell him what we know. Ok?'

Naomi sipped her tea for a minute before making up her mind. 'Yes but I'll speak to Gareth before I go this morning. He needs to understand what the consequences are if it becomes a police matter.'

'That's fine. I don't want him getting into trouble if he's not involved. What about your brother? Will you tell him what's happening?'

'Now that *is* a difficult one. But I suppose I should. Penny will go ballistic.'

Mills left Ivy Cottage contemplating her call to George. She rehearsed what she would say but it sounded odd, particularly when she realised she didn't even know Fergus's surname. She was tempted to turn back to ask Naomi if she would handle it but pride prevented her. It was her call, she told herself – she'd made the accusation and so she should have the confidence to follow it up.

She forced herself to ring George's number the moment she walked through the door. It was a relief when there was no answer.

'I just wanted to let you know what was happening about the air rifle pellets... I'll call again later.'

Grateful for the delay in having to face George, she wandered into the garden, calling Earl to follow her. It was unusual not to have work to do but until she started her post at the forensic lab she was free to do what she wanted.

'We'll go for a little walk down to the beck later,' she promised the dog.

He looked up at the word "walk" then lowered his head again, quite content to watch the blackbird hopping across the stones as he lay on his side in the sunshine. Her reverie was interrupted by the telephone. Mills walked up to it with trepidation, hoping it wouldn't be George and knowing it would be.

'Is that Mills?'

She recognised his voice immediately. 'George?' she asked, playing for time.

'Aye. You've got some news like?'

'Yes. I have.'

She went on to explain the comparison between the pellets found in the kite and those she had discovered "on the moor." He listened in silence.

'...so, you see, it doesn't prove anything one way or the other.' She hoped he appreciated her argument.

'No. Right.'

Mills took a deep breath. 'But there is something else I wanted to tell you. It concerns a young man from Scotland who's been here in the village for a few weeks...' She told him about Fergus shooting rabbits with an air rifle. There was no response from George. 'Are you still there?'

'Aye.'

She described the conversation she'd had with him about Earl being poisoned; how he'd virtually implied it was her problem if the dog ate poisoned bait. 'He said the grouse needed to be protected.'

'Did he? Well... there have been cases of carbofuran poisoning in Scotland.'

'Where does this guy live?'

Mills admitted how little she knew about Fergus. 'But I could find out,' she offered.

'Could you get him round so I could have a chat with him d'you think?'

'Yes... yes of course.'

When they'd finished speaking Mills grasped the significance of what she'd agreed to do. Not only had she said she would get Fergus *in her home* so George could talk to him but that meant he would know that she'd arranged it. He'd already threatened her and her dog. She'd have to seek Naomi's help once more.

Hazel had some difficulty finding Robert's rented cottage. The postcode brought her into the village, leaving her no choice but to ring him. Of course, she had no signal. She left the car and wandered down the lane, hoping to meet someone she could ask but at six on a Saturday evening it was unsurprising that the place was deserted. Once she was surrounded by fields, she turned to walk back in the other direction – it hadn't occurred to her it would be so difficult in a village of just a few houses. She tried the other way but gave up when she passed the last cottage. Back in the car she was pointlessly trying her mobile again when there was a tap on the window. Robert opened the passenger door and climbed in.

'You passed it. It's just behind you. You can reverse down to the corner. It's the turning on the left.'

They crawled down a narrow lane, stone walls on either side, with a green strip down the middle. His car blocked the way outside a small stone cottage almost hidden by foliage. The gate brushed against shrubs and nettles, the path was covered in moss, and windows were almost invisible under the sheet of ivy reaching beyond the guttering. She followed Robert inside, noting that he had to duck to get through the doorway. Standing to become accustomed to the dark interior, she stared round the room. It was sparsely furnished in dark wood, the carpet worn into a track from the doorway across to a door on the opposite wall.

'Come through.' Robert indicated for her to follow as he negotiated the beams.

There was hardly room for both of them in the tiny galley kitchen. Robert opened a further door leading to what Hazel guessed had once been a nice little garden. It was a small area of knee-high grass and thistles enclosed by a dry stone wall. The only feature was a shiny barbecue that looked brand new, standing in the corner.

'I'd mow the lawn but there's nothing but a rusty old scythe,' he declared. They stood surveying the field over the wall. Suddenly a large bird emerged from the stone barn in the distance and disappeared into a stand of trees.

'Was that a barn owl?' Hazel asked.

'I have no idea. What's a barn owl?'

Then they both laughed out loud.

'*Is* that a barn?' Robert asked incredulous.

'It's a very old stone barn. I suppose your barns are much bigger over there.'

'Yep. I guess that's what I'd call a screech owl.'

'I didn't put you down as a twitcher.'

'Twitcher? I'm afraid I don't talk Yorkshire, lady.'

'It's not Yorkshire. It's English.'

'Pardon me, I didn't mean to upset you.' He sounded hurt.

'Don't be silly. It's just my way. I'm too blunt.'

'I like someone who speaks their mind.'

'Do you? In that case I could murder a drink.'

He went inside, returning with a bottle of merlot and two very large glasses. She felt more relaxed with a glass of wine in her hand and as they chatted she found they had quite a lot in common. Robert had joined the military as soon as he was old enough and had eventually done his officer training at Fort Benning. She could empathise with that, having made the same decision at an early age to join the force.

The barbecue was glowing red hot when the first drop of rain fell.

'You've got to be kidding.' Robert was cursing under his breath.

'It might not be much,' suggested Hazel.

'Oh yeah?'

It was falling heavily now, large drops hissing on the hot coals.

'You go inside, Hazel. I'll cook the meat quickly with the lid on.'

She wandered through the kitchen, noting the pile of dishes in the sink, and settled on the lumpy sofa in the sitting room. The room was bare except for the dining table and chairs, and a television that looked so old she wondered if it was black and white. The only ornament was a framed photograph on the mantelpiece – one of those professional affairs that rich families might send as a Christmas card. She got up to inspect it more closely: a mother and father with two children. The girl was about thirteen, maybe fourteen, her smile so broad that her braces glinted. The grinning lad, who was perhaps eight, looked so like his father. He was the image of Robert.

Her first reaction was to walk out to the car and drive home but she could hear the clatter of plates in the kitchen and it wasn't her way to run. There could be an explanation – she hoped there was – he hadn't hidden the picture. She was certainly going to find out before she left.

'More wine?'

'Why not.'

She'd been eating her food in silence. She knew it tasted good but she was no longer hungry. Robert kept apologising for the fact their dinner was burnt and smoky but wasn't that the point of a barbecue, she thought. She glanced at the mantelpiece and when Robert caught her looking he shuffled uneasily in his chair.

'I think we have an elephant in the room,' he said at last.

In other circumstances she would have laughed but she continued to chew her steak.

'I expect you're curious about my family?'

She didn't look up from her plate. 'It's not my business.'

'Those are my kids. It's an old picture. Hilda's sixteen now and Henry is nearly eleven. It's his birthday next month.'

'Will you be there for his party?' She asked, remembering all the parties Liam's father missed.

'I guess not. Don't get me wrong – I'd like to but I'll be back out...' he broke off abruptly.

'Afghanistan?' she suggested.

He seemed taken aback. 'What makes you say that?' he asked sharply.

'I *am* a detective,' she answered coldly, picking up her handbag and searching for her keys. 'It's been very nice Robert but I think I should be going.'

'At least stay for coffee. Let me explain the set up. Please?'

It was easier to stay seated than make a dramatic exit. Her Mum always said her bark was worse than her bite. He disappeared into the kitchen, leaving her to stare at the happy family group. Leaning forward she could see that his wife looked pretty – well manicured with every hair in place. But it was taken several years ago, so did he not have a more recent photograph or did he prefer to remember them playing happy families. She wasn't sure she wanted to find out but if he was going to "open up" to her it would be an opportunity to discover why he'd shown an interest in her and, more importantly, her investigation. He returned with a jug and two mugs on a tray and she leant back on the sofa, deciding she would take the lead.

'Are you still married?'

'Not any more, no.'

'But you were when that was taken,' she indicated the photograph.

'Not really. I'd been away mostly for a whole year.'

'You all look happy enough.'

'I guess we were good at covering for the kids.'

'So you were separated then?'

'Yep.'

'Do you see them much – the children?'

'No.' He sighed. 'She's back in Germany with her family. I'm not welcome.'

If any of it were true, Hazel was going to test him by asking her next question. 'Why did you ask me out?'

He stood up to pour more coffee into his mug, making time to compile his answer. 'To be frank... you know why... I liked you... I thought...'

'What did you think, Robert?' Please give me a proper answer, she thought.

'I thought it would be nice to see you again.'

'Is that the only reason? Honestly?'

'Oh that... yeah, well... and they wanted me to keep in touch over the missing guy...'

At last. 'Why?'

'Pardon me?'

'Why are "they" interested in the missing American?'

'Because he's American, that's all,' he replied tersely.

'Not good enough.' She stood up, an automatic reaction to increase her height, she realised – she had no intention of leaving. 'I need a proper explanation, Robert.' Before I go for good, she thought.

His shoulders crumpled as he sat down, as if admitting defeat. Then a smile crossed his face. 'You don't miss much do you?'

The tense atmosphere relaxed a little.

'I just want to know where I stand, Robert. I know you're Special Ops and now I know your people are interested in my murder victim. So what do you know about him?'

His relaxed features became tense then relaxed again, as if he was arguing with himself about what to give away. Hazel picked up her bag and turned to go but he stopped her with a raised hand.

'Here goes then,' he said. 'We have a man missing. He was due to leave for the Middle East last week but he hasn't reported in for duty. But...' he emphasised the word, 'there is no reason to believe it's the same man because he sent a text message a week ago saying he was delayed.'

'Delayed?'

'That's what the message said – delayed. These guys, you know they're under a lot of pressure. We do what we can to accommodate them.' He drained his coffee. 'I'm sure we'll find he's just a bit strung out. More coffee?'

Hazel looked at her watch. 'I really must be going. I told Liam...' she stopped, looking across at him.

'Liam?'

'My son. My thirteen year old son.'

'I see.'

'No you don't. His father left soon after he was born and I haven't seen him since.'

'Ok, ok.' He was holding up his hands in mock submission. 'I'll see you to your car.'

He guided her as she carefully reversed back to the village street. There was no attempt to kiss her before she drove off this time.

The arrangement with her mother had been for Liam to spend the night "in case she was back late". It was only just after ten when she reached town but she decided to go straight home. If she picked him up Sunday morning Mum might ask them to stay for lunch. Anyway, she wanted to look up a few things, including more information about Fort Benning. She wasn't able to find specific reference to Major Robert Henderson but another name caught her attention – Eisenhower. But this reference was not to the mystery man but to General Dwight Eisenhower, President of the United States, who apparently trained at Fort Benning in the twenties. Probably a coincidence, she thought.

She turned off the computer and lit a cigarette – a guilty pleasure since Liam wouldn't be in until the next day and by then the smell would have gone. She considered how the case would be affected if they knew the victim *was* an American Special Operations soldier. Was it just another coincidence that the woman found in the car was an army wife from Catterick? Was there a connection? If so, what was it? Then a thought struck her. Was it possible that Tanya Stewart was the mystery woman accompanying the American on his walking holiday?

Chapter 13

Hazel didn't want Mitch to know her theory that Tanya Stewart was the missing companion of the murdered man until she'd had a chance to test it out.

'She doesn't even look like her from the drawing,' offered Nina.

'What about the hair? This Tanya has long blonde hair.'

'Curly? The woman's hair was a bit curly.'

'It's easy to curl your hair, Nina.'

She looked at her friend's glossy black locks hanging heavily down her back. She doubted Nina had ever experimented, whereas she had coloured, permed and ironed her hair until it had to be kept short for its own health.

'Do we have any DNA for the companion? Wasn't there a hair on the man's clothing?'

'Yes, blonde. We're waiting for the DNA results. The only thing we have at the moment is the artist's impression, which witnesses say is a good likeness.'

'Yeah, right. And we know how well that usually works in practice.'

Nina sighed. 'We could take a picture of Tanya Stewart round to the campsites but Mitch won't be keen.'

'I've got a better idea. Why don't we take the artist's impression to her sister in Kirkby Stephen?'

'Her neighbours are nearer. Why not take this drawing over to Catterick and get it done with. I guarantee they're not the same person.'

'I can do better than that – I'll take it in to the "Overseas Family Support Unit", where she worked. They can ID it.'

'Why are you so keen to go over to the garrison?' Nina giggled. 'If you're hoping to meet your favourite redcap over there you'd better hurry up before Mitch gets back.' She paused. 'Oh no, sorry, it's Major Henderson you'll be wanting to bump into, isn't it?'

Quite the opposite, thought Hazel as she set off towards Catterick. The revelation that Robert had a family had set her thinking about whether she wanted to continue the relationship, particularly if he was going to be in action again soon. Life in the services was hard, even harder than in the force and she'd vowed never again. The effect on Liam had been unexpected – when she'd indicated to her Mum that it was probably not going anywhere, Liam seemed really disappointed, and not just because of the car. Was he beginning to miss the father he never had and saw another man in the military as a surrogate?

She was so deep in thought she nearly missed the turning that would take her to the administration block. They took her straight to the boss, seating her in a meeting room and offering her a coffee. After a few minutes the woman she'd seen before appeared and greeted her like a long lost friend. Hazel took the photocopy of the artist's impression from her pocket and smoothed it out on the table between them.

'Jan, just one question. Do you recognise this woman?' she asked.

'Of course,' she replied and Hazel held her breath. 'It's Bea, I mean Beatrice Egglington.'

'Are you sure?'

'Of course.'

'Not Tanya Stewart.'

'No, of course not.' The woman seemed amused by her mistake.

Hazel sat quietly drinking her coffee.

'Is that all?' asked Jan.

'No, sorry. So who is Beatrice?' She couldn't remember the surname, it had been such a surprise.

'Beatrice Egglington? She works here. She's one of our support workers.'

'Are you sure it's her?'

'Positive. It's a striking likeness.'

'Is there anyone else who could confirm that?'

'Certainly.'

A young woman was summoned and asked if she knew the person in the picture. The response was the same. When they were alone again Hazel asked Jan if she could speak to Beatrice.

'I'm afraid not. She was taken ill when she heard about Tanya – they were friends. She went home sick and hasn't been in since.'

Hazel made some notes to provide her with some thinking time.

'Just one more thing, Jan. Would you know whether this Beatrice was around in July?'

'I can find out for you. May I ask, is this to do with Tanya's death?'

'I can't say at present. I don't suppose it would be possible to have another coffee?'

Jan returned after about ten minutes with another cup of coffee.

'I've written the dates down here. Bea was on leave from the eighth to the twenty-second of July but she didn't come back until the eighth of August.'

'Why was that?'

'Off sick.'

'Do we know what it was?'

'Between you and me I think she's pregnant. Several of her colleagues have told me that they suspect it, although she's not said anything.'

'Does she have family?'

'Just her husband. He works on the garrison as well. I can give you his number.'

She disappeared for a minute, returning with another scrap of paper.

'There's a phone on the side there if you want to ring the extension.'

'Thank you. And thanks for the coffee. I'll see myself out when I've made the call.'

She let the phone ring for a long time and eventually a harassed voice answered. When she asked for Mr Egglington the man responded sharply, saying he wasn't in. When pressed he admitted that no-one knew where he was.

Mills spent her first morning at Yardley Forensic Services browsing Brenda's computer and playing with paperclips. When finally the phone rang, her response was efficient, advising the caller to send the blood samples via courier – she'd have to call back with a price.

'Price list,' she said aloud. 'Where is the price list?'

Eventually she had to ask the PA who took her straight to it on the company intranet.

'Brenda sometimes gives a special price to regular customers,' she advised. 'But we haven't dealt with these people before.' As an afterthought she added, 'I'd best do a credit check on them first.'

Once the customer had received the PA's approval, Mills was able to tell them the overall cost of the work and when they might expect their results. She was feeling rather pleased with herself when there was a gentle tap on the door. It was Glyn. He walked quietly into the centre of the room and looked across the desk at her.

'You've settled in all right then I see.' His tone was disapproving.

'Yes thank you.' Mills smiled, hoping her manner came across as open and friendly.

She waited while he shuffled through a sheaf of papers in his hand.

'I've got some results here,' he said at last, pulling two sheets from the pile. 'Here are the data for job 103 – a male stabbing victim – which have already been reported.' He handed her a page full of columns, each containing handwritten numbers and comments. She couldn't make sense of it and she suspected he knew it.

'Please talk me through it.'

He spent several minutes explaining every section, most of which was routine examination procedure leading to a nil result. At last he came to the matter he wanted to discuss.

'...and here is the one interesting artefact – a curly fair hair. We were asked to DNA it and I've got the results ready for transmission.'

'Good.' An appropriate response, Mills thought.

'Wrong. It's not good because...' He waved the second sheet at her. 'Here are the data for job 107 – a female stabbing victim.' He pointed towards the bottom of the page. 'See this short black hair found on the woman's jacket. Her own hair is long and blonde. We got a DNA on that one too – the police were bound to ask and we were doing the other one.'

'Very good.'

'No, Dr Sanderson, it is *not* good. Both the hairs have the same DNA. They are unrelated crimes and distinctly different types of hair. Something has gone wrong!'

He was leaning across the desk in a threatening posture.

'Please sit down, Glyn,' she suggested.

When he was seated she asked him what he would suggest had happened.

'Someone has messed up. The sample has obviously got contaminated.'

'Can we repeat it?'

'Not unless we really have to. We've kept a tiny piece back for records but if that goes we have nothing.'

He sat back with his arms folded watching her and waiting.

'Who did the work?'

'Esther. She's worked here for years – long before Dr Yardley took over.'

She sensed that he also had been around in those earlier days, possibly preferring his original boss to the more recent incumbent.

'So she's competent?'

'Very. She's done thousands of tests.'

'In that case we should report the results as they are.'

He looked horrified. 'But they're obviously wrong. We can't report them.' He jumped to his feet, waving his papers at her. 'I refuse to let you do it – it will damage the reputation of the entire laboratory!'

'Ok, ok. If you can show where a mistake has been made we'll discuss how to handle it... but I need to make a decision by tomorrow, at the latest.'

He shut the door quietly behind him and Mills relaxed back into the large leather chair. He knew what he was doing; he was far more experienced than she was. Let's hope he comes up with an explanation in time, she thought.

The confrontation prompted her to read the last few reports sent out by the laboratory, so she could understand how the jobs were written up. The reports were concise with tables of results prepared by the analyst making up most of the paperwork. The text simply recorded what had been done and a summary of the findings, if necessary. She noted that the descriptions of the methodology were standard, and Brenda had shown her where all the necessary files were stored on the computer. Don't worry, she'd said. Glyn will deal with it all – you just need to sign it and send it off. Yeah right, Brenda.

At five o'clock Mills wandered down the corridor before she left the building. Glyn was hunched over his desk in the corner of a large open plan office while two women worked at the other end of the room.

'How's it going?' she asked him.

He looked up and then across at the women. 'I'll discuss it with you in the morning,' he replied, his eyes still focussed on the women. Mills assumed that one of them was Esther.

'Ok, no problem,' she kept her tone light. 'I'm off now.' She raised her voice to include the others. 'See you in the morning.' They responded with a friendly goodnight; Glyn grunted.

It was nearly seven when she reached Mossy Bank. Earl climbed out of his bed more easily than before, walking over quite quickly. He badgered her for his food, becoming excitable as she prepared it and eating greedily as soon as his bowl touched the floor. She could hear the dish clanking on the stone slabs as he licked it clean.

'You *were* hungry. Are you feeling better now?' Mills asked. She was struggling to open a handwritten envelope addressed simply to "Mills" that she'd found on the mat when she arrived home. Naomi had written with a blunt pencil and her typical doctor's scrawl made it difficult to decipher. She read it through twice before she'd understood it fully: *Gareth and Fergus are free tomorrow night. Can you ask George – for 7.30 and let me know? We can meet in Ivy Cottage if you like.* She rang George, who was happy to come over. She told him to come to her and they could walk up together. For convenience, she had said, but she hadn't relished arriving alone.

She'd just finished eating when there was a knock at the door which made her jump. Telling herself it was unlikely to be Fergus she opened it gingerly to find Muriel beaming at her. As usual she was in her slippers.

'I thought I'd catch you before you took Earl out. He's already had a good run today.'

'Thanks, Muriel. You didn't need to. It's ok just to pop in and take him in the garden.'

'Oh no, love, it weren't me. That nice young Scottish lad came. He were knocking so I told him you were out all day. He said he'd come to take Earl for a good run so I said "go ahead!" Such a nice lad.'

'You let him in?'

'Oh yes. Any time, love.' She was already halfway down the garden path when Mills called her back. She tried, politely, to let Muriel know she didn't want Fergus coming in again. She made out that Earl wasn't to have much exercise as she wanted to walk him herself in the evening, so could Muriel just let Earl in the garden in future. Her neighbour nodded as if she thought Mills was unappreciative of the "nice lad".

She went back to look at the lurcher. He seemed content, lying in his basket. If Fergus had done anything to the animal it wasn't obvious so far. She hoped he was simply demonstrating that he could hurt him if he wanted to. Hopefully after the following evening, with the police involved, he would be properly warned off such threats again.

Nina had the job of putting together every bit of intelligence they had on Beatrice Egglington. So far she'd received very little apart from her age, national insurance number and next of kin. The woman was thirty-one and lived in Ripon. She was a support worker at the Overseas Family Unit, just like Tanya Stewart. Her husband did something in procurement, also at Catterick Garrison. Neither she nor her husband appeared to be at home and the neighbours didn't really know them. Her friends seemed to be her work acquaintances, principally Tanya Stewart. The dates of her absence from work did tie up with the time the American was doing the Coast to Coast walk. Her own GP was not available but Nina learned that Mrs Egglington had a repeat prescription for a mild anti-depressant. The husband, who was also on his list, had not been seen recently.

Nina reported all this to Mitch, who sighed heavily and told her to carry on the good work.

'Have they checked the knife for any other blood types yet?' he asked.

'I've asked for it to be treated as urgent,' she replied. 'I'll chase it up.'

It was an opportunity to call Mills to see how she was getting on in her new, although temporary, role.

Her friend sounded stressed. 'You mean it should have been completed by now?' she asked.

'No, no, calm down, Mills. I just asked if it could be fast-tracked. It has been tested once already for fingerprints and DNA but we just want to check whether there is the smallest trace of any other DNA, particularly any old, dried blood trapped in the handle or grooves in the blade.'

There was a pause. 'I'm just writing all this down,' her friend explained.

'No problem, take your time.'

'I'll get on to it straight away, Nina.'

'And what about the DNA on the blonde hair found on the clothing of the man who was stabbed?'

'Would that be Job 103 or 107?'

'The earliest one.'

'They'll both be ready tomorrow.'

'I need it today, Mills.'

'Really?' she pleaded.

'Yes, really, Mills. This is a murder case. We have to crack on.'

'I'll do my best.'

Hazel arrived back from another visit to the garrison as Nina replaced the receiver.

'Any luck?'

'Nope. Mr Egglington is definitely not at work or at home. No-one knows where he is and it's out of character for him to disappear without trace. He's usually a bit of a workaholic actually.'

'What is procurement, anyway?' asked Nina

'Buying stuff. I think it used to be called purchasing.'

'I've got some family info here,' offered Nina. 'Parents live in Scotland, haven't seen him for a couple of years but receive cards and presents on appropriate occasions. They've met the wife a few times at family weddings and funerals but couldn't tell as anything we didn't know about her.'

'What family does she have?'

'A mother. Father died when she was ten. One older brother – emigrated to Australia years ago.' She visits Mum two or three times a year down in Dorset.'

'Someone paying her a visit?'

'Yes but she's away on a cruise at the present. Back at the end of the month.'

'Has anyone checked her house for the missing pair?'

'Yes and no. They're not there. A neighbour is watering the plants. He's certain no-one has been near. He's been asked to let Dorset Police know if they appear.'

'So what does Mitch want us to do now?'

'When the warrant comes through we're to go over to search their house.'

The laboratory manager had stormed into her office as soon as Mills was seated behind Brenda's large desk. He stood over her with his arms folded looking at her accusingly.

'You said you'd make a decision by today.'

'Yes, if you showed me where a mistake had occurred,' said Mills, playing for time. 'I said today but it's early yet. Why don't you come back at, say, eleven?'

She was desperate for a coffee and went down to the kitchen as soon as Glyn had gone. Brenda's PA was boiling the kettle.

'I'll bring it for you. We can't have you making your own coffee.'

Another time Mills would have argued but she was glad to hide back in the office until the coffee arrived.

'Is Glyn giving you a hard time?' the PA asked kindly.

'Yep. I'm afraid he doesn't have much faith in me.'

'Oh don't worry; he doesn't think much of Brenda either. He's seen so many bosses come and go.'

'It's good to know it's not personal – but it feels like it.'

'Don't let him bother you. I don't!'

She left Mills alone to plan her next move. It was quite possible that the hair samples could have become contaminated and she'd had a sleepless night considering what to do about it. The chances of the two hairs being from the same person were pretty unlikely – they were a different colour for a start! What would Brenda do, she wondered. The coffee was dark and strong but it touched the spot, giving her confidence to finally make a decision. She reached for the phone.

'Mills! How are you getting on? Enjoying your new job?'

'That's why I've rung, Nina. I need to talk to you – off the record.' She wasn't convinced she was using was the right jargon and even less sure that she could have an informal chat about evidence but she continued anyway. 'It's about the hair we found on the stabbing victim.'

'Male or female?'

'Well, that's the point really...' She went on to explain what had happened. 'So the DNA matches both samples.'

'I see.' Her friend sounded confused.

'I know it can't be the same but the analyst is convinced it's right. I can't think what to do.' Mills hoped she didn't sound too pathetic.

'Can't you repeat the DNA test?'

'No, there's not enough material left. We can't do any more in our laboratory.'

'Then you'd better put it in the report. That's all you can do.'

'But that means we're admitting a mistake – there's no way the hair can be from the same person.'

'I'm sorry but I can't suggest any other way of dealing with the situation.'

Mills scribbled on the pad beside the phone while she thought of something to say.

'Anyway how's Rosie?' she asked eventually.

'She's fine. When are you going to come and see us?'

'Soon.' She was distracted by the thought of explaining her actions to Glyn. 'Anyway, I must go. I'll send you the report.'

The rest of the coffee was cold and bitter. She took her mug to the kitchen and poured it away before she continued down the corridor to find Glyn. The conversation was awkward but there were other members of staff within earshot so he confined his responses to low mutterings. He registered his disapproval of her actions later in a long e-mail which was copied to Brenda "so she could see how things were being managed in her absence". Mills noted that he'd used the work address for Brenda and hoped she wasn't accessing her e-mails while on holiday.

Nina hated searching people's houses. It seemed such an intrusion, looking through letters and diaries, sorting through their wardrobes and rummaging in rubbish bins. The Egglingtons were particularly tidy folk, she concluded, and so it seemed even more invasive when they opened cupboards and drawers. There were four of them going through the semi-detached house on the outskirts of Ripon but after several hours they had found nothing to connect them to the murder on the moors.

Hazel was building a picture of Beatrice Egglington as she went round the immaculate rooms. They were all beautifully decorated in pastel shades, with silk curtains and pale cream carpet. The kitchen was a junk-free zone with cupboards free of chocolaty breakfast cereals and snacks. Instead there were tasty cheesy snacks, muesli, olives and breadsticks; jars of pasta in neat rows on the shelf and a variety of herbal teas arranged artistically on the windowsill. Clearly there were no children to mess up this residence and nowhere was there anything to indicate they were looking forward to a new arrival.

Nina was sitting at a pretty little desk which overlooked the garden. The drawers were stuffed with paperwork relating to the house but she was looking for something more personal – a diary, passports, photographs of family. The middle drawer was locked and she didn't want to damage it so she was scanning all the other drawers, just in case there was a key.

'Hazel!'

Nina knew of her friend's prowess when it came to breaking in and soon the drawer was open without a scratch on it. Neither spoke as they stared down at the contents. It held a file marked "Recipes".

'Strange thing to keep locked away,' commented Nina, removing it carefully and turning the pages slowly. It was a lever arch file with transparent sleeves to hold the cuttings taken from magazines and newspapers. Some pages were yellowing with age. Nina reached the end and was about to close the file as she turned the last page.

'Aha,' she said triumphantly, placing the file down on the desk.

Smiling up at them was a photograph of a soldier and next to it was an ID tag with a name, number, blood group and religion: Larry Wright was A-negative and a catholic.

Chapter 14

Mills was relieved to leave the laboratory behind. It had been a difficult day, even after she'd made the decision to report the potential contamination of the two hair samples. The test results had to be compiled by Glyn, who was resistant to any of the data leaving the laboratory. At one stage he virtually handed her his resignation. It had been a close call. Eventually she'd got his agreement on the wording of the report and the results went off indicating that "an unfortunate contamination appeared to have occurred which could not be confirmed – all attempts to identify the source having failed".

Despite having dealt with the problem, she was not looking forward to the evening ahead. The meeting with Fergus was unlikely to be amicable and since he'd demonstrated he could get at Earl very easily, she was concerned at the outcome. It was a relief to find the lurcher safely in his basket when she finally arrived home. It was already seven o'clock so it was all she could do to give him a quick walk and his dinner before George arrived.

As they walked up to Ivy Cottage, Mills described how Fergus had threatened her, and how he'd taken Earl for a walk without her permission.

'He sounds a bit of a wayward lad,' commented George.

Naomi had already explained to Gareth the purpose of the visit. He was sitting with a half pint glass looking uncomfortable in the camouflage clothes that had replaced his Goth look.

Naomi served wine or beer and the four of them made polite conversation until the bell rang. Each looked even more uncomfortable as Naomi rose to answer the door. She brought Fergus through and made the introductions, including George "an acquaintance" of hers, who he regarded suspiciously before accepting a beer.

'So you'll be in the police like Naomi then?'

He was quick, Mills had to concede.

'Yes. I'm a wildlife officer.'

'Oh aye? Looking after the wee birdies eh? Same line of work as mine then.'

George expressed interest in gamekeeping, asking him about the estate back in Scotland.

'So what are you doing in Yorkshire, Fergus?' he asked politely.

'Training, learning the ropes. When I go back I'll be taking over from my father – in time.'

The conversation continued in the same cordial manner until George asked the question that changed the atmosphere in a second. 'So where d'you keep your gun?'

Fergus's eyelids lowered, his lips twisted. 'What business is it of yours?'

'I'm just curious.'

'I've got a licence.'

'I'm sure. I was just interested.'

Naomi jumped up, announcing she'd put some sausage rolls in the oven and would fetch them right away. She indicated for Mills to follow her into the kitchen.

'Has he got a plan or is he going to hedge round it all night?' she asked as soon as they were alone.

Mills shrugged. 'I don't know. He has to tread carefully.'

The atmosphere had changed when they returned to the sitting room. There was a heated debate in progress between Fergus, who was advocating control of birds of prey, and George who was repeating that it was illegal whatever he thought.

'So you think it's perfectly acceptable for golden eagles to be killed to preserve smaller birds so they can be shot during the season?' George was asking, his face reddening.

'I didn't say that but I agree with those that do.' Fergus calmly helped himself to a sausage roll as Naomi passed the plate across to George.

Mills watched Gareth, who was looking increasingly uncomfortable as the debate became heated.

'... anyway, I believe people like that should be locked away.' George's voice was composed but he was clearly rattled.

'That's your opinion. Professional managers like my old man's keeper know best how to preserve the countryside. If he went out to kill a few predators I'd go wi' him.' He rose and left the room.

'Is he leaving?' Naomi asked, putting down the plate of food and going to the door.

'He's just gone upstairs,' said Gareth quietly.

They chatted politely until the sound of footsteps descending the stairs stopped the conversation. But he did not return to the sitting room; the front door slammed and the gravel crunched under his feet.

'I'd better go,' announced Gareth.

Naomi followed him to the door. 'Be careful,' she warned. 'He's a dark horse, that one.'

Back inside she commented what a waste of time that had been.

'Not necessarily,' said George. 'He's clearly not averse to taking a pop at a bird of prey. It's never easy to prove anything but it means we need to keep an eye on him. He's already made threats against the dog, hasn't he?'

'Yes,' confirmed Mills, for Naomi's benefit. 'He blagged his way into the cottage and took Earl onto the moor.'

Naomi looked alarmed. 'If you think he's dangerous I should warn Dan.'

'It would be worth making it clear to your nephew that he's a dangerous friend to be involved with,' said George. 'I intend to catch him red-handed and when I do...' he left the sentence unfinished. 'Meanwhile, thank you for your hospitality.'

When they were outside Ivy Cottage, Mills asked George whether he'd be able to do anything about Fergus.

'While he's in my area, he's my problem and I'll do what I can to prove he was responsible for what happened to that kite – and your dog. Once he goes back to Scotland I'll be able to do nowt.'

'So we must hope you can do something soon.'

'Yes. There might be something you can help me with. I can't search his property without a warrant and I won't be able to get one on the evidence so far. Would you be able to have a quick look next door to see if he's hiding anything there?'

'Such as?'

'Well if he laid the poisoned meat, he must have some carbofuran. It's not something you leave lying around.'

'Ok,' Mills said. 'I'll have a look for it.'

'Let me know if anything develops,' George said, as he climbed into his vehicle. 'I'm going to record the details of what's occurred but without evidence...'

'I'll see what I can find.'

Mills bolted the front door and checked the windows on the ground floor before she went to bed. It was a hot night and she woke suddenly several times before dawn, at odd sounds through her open bedroom window. But everything was as it should be when she went down in the morning and she left for work hoping that Fergus had been sufficiently cautioned to leave Earl alone.

'So you think this bloke is the dead American?'

'It could be, don't you think?' Hazel placed a photograph of the corpse down on Mitch's desk beside the one of the soldier. 'He's definitely an American, you can tell by the uniform and the ID tag.'

'Ok. So why hasn't anyone noticed he's missing?'

'I think I know the reason for that, guv. Is it all right if I go over to the garrison to check it out?'

'Yes, if you tell me what you think the reason is.'

Hazel explained what Robert had told her about the missing Special Ops soldier not turning up. 'He just thought the guy wanted a bit more time off.'

'Furlough. That's what they call it... furlough.'

'I'll remember that when I speak to Major Henderson,' she called as she dialled his number.

Just over half an hour later she drew up outside the office block where Robert had his temporary office. She was glad of the excuse to see him and he'd sounded pleased to hear from her.

'Hi there, Hazel!' he was calling from the open window. 'I'll come out.'

He took her arm as soon as they met. 'I'm so glad you came. I really missed you. Did you get my calls?'

She had. She wished she'd returned them now. He was so solid, so competent. He would be such a good influence on Liam... 'Sorry, I've been so busy. That's why I'm here.'

'You said you may have found our soldier that went awol?'

'Does the name Larry Wright mean anything to you?'

He paused. Was it her imagination or did he straighten up a little, become a tiny bit more formal?

'Yes it does, as a matter of fact.'

'Would he be your missing man?'

'You know I can't answer that, Hazel.'

'No?'

'I have to make some calls first.'

'I can wait.' She sat back in her chair.

'Coffee?'

'Thank you.'

He disappeared. About ten minutes later a lad in uniform brought a tray. Amused, Hazel poured the coffee from a china pot and added milk from the matching jug. She called Nina to report what was happening and sat back to wait. The building was silent and she seemed quite alone so she wandered casually round the desk to glance over the papers lying there. Intriguing as the messages looked, they meant nothing to her. She scanned the pages for a familiar name but there was no mention of Larry Wright. The desk drawers were empty. At the side of the chair was a briefcase – the sort with a combination lock. She tried it and cringed as it opened with a loud snap. Inside she found a blackberry, which was password protected, she discovered, and a brown paper file. The cover was marked "restricted" with various code numbers printed in a neat hand – inside was the personal file of Larry Wright. Her handbag was large enough to hide the A4 file, as she sauntered down the corridor to find a photocopier. She'd reached the end of a row of locked doors when she saw Robert coming towards her.

'Sorry, Hazel, it took longer than I planned. Do you have to go?'

She hesitated. Back in the office was the open briefcase. 'I was looking for the ladies,' she lied.

'I guess there's one somewhere in the building.' He thought for a second then, taking her arm, said, 'Come with me.'

They went to the entrance hall, where there was a small office.

'Pardon me, miss?' he asked, leaning round the doorframe. 'Is there a bathroom round here?'

The girl looked bemused.

'He means a "ladies"... a cloakroom,' offered Hazel.

'The girl laughed and came out into the hallway. 'I'll show you, it's a bit of a maze down there.'

'I'll wait here,' offered Robert.

Hazel followed her downstairs and along a corridor with offices on either side. 'Is there a photocopier down here?' she asked, casually.

'Yes, in the room at the end. You need a code for it though.'

'Could I use it, please?'

'Certainly. I'll turn it on and put the code in for you.'

With her help, Hazel copied the contents of the file: one, two, three, four pages. It seemed to take forever.

She was thinking hard while she waited. She'd seen stairs just past the room at the end of the corridor and with luck they would bring her back up to the ground floor close to Robert's office.

'Thanks for that,' she said as she packed the file and copies back in her bag. 'Would you do me a favour and tell the Major that I'll find my way back to his office?'

Her helper looked puzzled but nodded, shutting the door behind them and turning back the way they'd come. Hazel dashed off in the opposite direction and took the stairs two at a time. As she'd thought, she was back at the far end of the corridor and slipped into the office to replace the file. When Robert returned she was sitting waiting on the right side of the desk, his briefcase undisturbed behind the desk.

'I've spoken to my colleagues further up the ladder and I can't give you any information at present. I'm sorry.'

'What is the reason they give?'

'I can't say.'

'But this is a murder investigation!'

'You'll have to make a formal request. It's a formal matter, Hazel. I can't help you however much I'd like to.'

'Ok, we'll make a formal application. Is there a form for that?' She knew she sounded testy, which wasn't professional.

'Hazel, sweetie. I'm sorry. Can I buy you lunch?'

'Not now, I'm busy investigating a murder.' She picked up her bag with its illicit contents.

'So when? When can I take you out again?'

'I'll ring you.' She was in a hurry to get outside to see what information the file had contained on Mr Larry Wright.

In the car she learned that Larry Wright was a "pararescueman" in Special Operations. His training record covered three pages and included parachute training, combat diving, underwater egress training, basic survival, and paramedic training. He'd spent time in Iraq and Afghanistan and had been commended for his bravery. Nothing in the paperwork helped identify him as the dead American but the fact that his file was in Robert's briefcase certainly suggested a connection. Hazel looked at her watch; she'd be back by lunch-time – and she was going to enjoy showing this to Mitch.

'You're right – he is the victim. Apparently he was due on a highly secret mission, working with the British forces on a project in Pakistan. That's highly confidential and mustn't leave this room.' Mitch gave her a meaningful look.

'D'you think that has anything to do with his murder?' Hazel asked.

'*They* do. Very jittery about the whole thing. They want no publicity, especially no identification of the victim in case it was politically motivated.'

'You're kidding!'

'No.'

'So they think it was the Taliban or Al-Qaeda?'

'Not necessarily but we can't rule it out.'

Hazel was about to comment on men being hysterical creatures but Mitch's expression warned her off. 'So what happens now?' she asked.

'We need to get them up to speed – share intelligence. Which means you can go and give Major Henderson all the intel we have.'

'And will they share theirs?'

'No.'

'Seems a bit one-sided, guv.'

'I don't make the rules,' he replied as he left the office.

Hazel looked across at Nina, who had been quietly working at her desk during the exchange. Her friend raised her head and grinned.

'What?' Hazel asked.

'I would have thought you'd be pleased to have an excuse to see Robert again.'

'You think?' Hazel was uncomfortable with the prospect but she smiled enigmatically as she picked up the phone to call his mobile.

The line was poor but she established he could see her that evening when his meetings were over.

'I'll come to the garrison,' she offered.

'No way! It's a nice day. Let's have a drink in the country.'

'Robert. This is official business. I'll be at the garrison at six.' She put the phone down before he could argue and looked across at Nina who was deep in thought.

'What's up, girlfriend?' she asked.

Nina looked up and smiled. 'Just going through the report of the forensic analysis for Tanya Stewart.'

'And?'

'The results are confusing. The lab has a DNA match between two hairs; one from Tanya's clothing and one from your American servicemen.'

'Well that makes sense, if the murders are connected. Are they his hairs?'

'No. One's blonde and the other's black. Neither belongs to the victims.'

'That's pretty odd. Perhaps it's yet another cock-up by forensics.'

Nina didn't answer – she didn't want to admit that her friend Mills was responsible for the results.

Hazel spent the rest of the afternoon compiling a report for Robert, containing all the intelligence they had collected on Larry Wright. Since they hadn't known his identity the details were limited to his Coast to Coast walking holiday under the false name of Eisenhower, including where he'd stayed each night, what he'd eaten and snippets of conversations he'd held with locals on the way. Hazel included the name of Beatrice Egglington as a possible companion but had nothing to confirm the relationship. All in all, she concluded, they had very little to impart to the US military and the file she carried to Robert's office was slim.

'Since you denied me the opportunity for Pimms in the pub, I got it ordered in,' he announced when she was shown into his office. The secretary giggled and left quickly.

Hazel looked down at the tray on his desk. There seemed no point in wasting it.

'Where did you get the umbrellas?' she asked as she settled down in the chair opposite him.

'I do have some influence round here, you know.'

'I'm sure.'

The ice tinkled as he filled a tall glass from a large green jug and placed it on the tray. Once he'd poured a second glass he brought them round and handed her one.

'Cheers!' he said in a comic English accent as he clinked his glass against hers.

'I have a file here for you,' she said stiffly. 'It contains everything we have on Larry Wright.'

'Everything?' he asked with a wry smile. He was perched on the desk, sipping his drink slowly and deliberately. 'I think you might have some material which you found right here in this office, young lady.'

His smile made her uncomfortable. He knew about her sleight of hand with his file on Wright.

'I don't know what you mean,' she said innocently and sipped her Pimms.

'No problem,' he said, 'since we plan to share information.'

'Share?'

'Yes, that's right. What's mine is yours and what's yours is mine. Isn't that what they say?'

She handed him the file and waited while he examined it. His expression became instantly serious as he moved behind the desk to seat himself, placing the file open in front of him, the glass forgotten. He was unaware of Hazel as she watched him absorb the information, turning the pages slowly. Eventually he spoke.

'It all seems to fit. It makes perfect sense; the timings, everything.' He leaned back in his chair.

'I asked him what he was going to do with his furlough. I thought he'd want to go back home to the family.'

'He has family?'

'Sure. Back in Illinois he's got a wife and young kid. They're going to be devastated when they hear. I thought they were pretty devoted so that was the puzzle when he said he was staying in the UK.'

'With his bit on the side.'

He smiled. 'Is that what they call it over here?'

'It looks like he was on this walking holiday with a woman who works in the garrison – with the new Overseas Family Support Unit.'

'Some support,' he commented.

'Beyond the call of duty, one might say,' agreed Hazel.

He was suddenly serious again. 'So what do we know about this woman?'

'Very little. She and her husband have disappeared.'

'You think something's happened to them also?'

'She was in work after Wright's body was found. She only went missing after they found...' Damn, thought Hazel, she hadn't meant to mention Tanya Stewart.

'Go on.'

By the time she'd explained about Tanya's murder, Robert was back on his feet. 'We're going to need time on this, Hazel. Are you ok if I speak with your senior officers?'

'For what reason, exactly?'

'To ask for you to help us with *our* investigations.'

As she agreed, she wondered whether it was the right thing to do. After all it could be a ploy to keep her quiet and prevent her making any further discoveries unless they wanted her to.

Mills was hurrying to complete the report on the murder weapon found in Tanya Stewart's car. It was complicated by the request to check carefully for any other blood type that might be found in the crevices of the knife handle or blade. The police wanted to know if it had been used in a previous attack.

Glyn was still touchy over the hair sample mix-up and so he had taken his time, checking everything at all stages to ensure that the results were fool-proof. The knife was covered in blood and there was much discussion about how to deal with the analysis. In the end Glyn agreed to take a number of swabs of the blood which was clearly visible on the blade, which confirmed that it was last used on Tanya Stewart. Then the knife surface was cleaned, leaving only the tiny indentations in the handle and in the manufacturer's name on the blade. These samples were picked out and placed into tiny individual bottles for DNA testing.

As soon as the results were available, Mills contacted Nina.

'We've examined the knife,' she began.

'And?' Her friend sounded interested.

Mills could hardly keep the excitement from her voice. 'There's a second blood type in the groove between the handle and the blade.'

'Right. I want you to compare it with the pattern for Larry Wright. We think it might be the same weapon.'

'Will do. And I promise there won't be any mix ups this time.'

'Don't worry, Mills. I'm sure everything will be done properly,' her friend reassured her.

It didn't take Glyn long to compare the DNA profiles – he was soon back looking pleased. It was a positive match. When Mills rang with the news, Nina sounded really excited.

'That's the break we need, Mills. You've done a grand job. Now we're getting somewhere.'

Mills passed on the news to Glyn before going home. He received her thanks graciously, without any of the animosity he'd expressed previously. Perhaps we can put it behind us, thought Mills as she left the building. She left work early for the first time that week, reaching Mossy Bank in record time.

'Earl, I'm home.'

She expected the sound of his overlong claws scurrying across flagstones or at least a disturbance as he woke up suddenly and struggled to get to his feet but there was silence. She rushed round the house, thinking he might have collapsed somewhere, even looking upstairs where he never usually ventured. But the house was deserted. She checked the back door – it was locked, she even looked into the garden before acknowledging to herself that he had disappeared.

Logic finally prevailed and she went next door to ask Muriel what had happened, assuming the dog had been taken ill or got lost when she was walking him.

'No, pet, I didn't take him today on account of your note.'

'My note? What note?'

'About your friend coming to take him a walk.'

'My friend?'

'He came around lunch time. I'd left the key under the mat as you'd said so I didn't go to speak to him, like.'

'This man, this friend, Muriel, did you get a good look at him?'

She looked puzzled. 'No but is he in the army, pet?'

'Why d'you ask that?'

'Well, it was the camouflage jacket that made me think, like.'

Chapter 15

Mills fell into a chair when she was back in the cottage. Her legs were shaking and she felt sick. Uncertain what to do next, she rang Nina.

'Mills? What can we do for you?' Nige's soft Welsh accent was comforting but she was not reassured and asked if her friend was there.

'Hold on.' His cheerful tone had changed and she knew he sensed there was something wrong.

Nina must have felt it too because she immediately asked what was wrong. Mills explained what had happened, adding, 'I know it's him, Nina. He threatened me before George came to see him. Now he's taken Earl and I don't know...' She could no longer control her feelings, sobbing into the phone.

'Mills, you must call George now. He'll know how to handle it. He's met the guy and will have already made a report. D'you want me to come over?' she added.

Mills had regained enough composure to thank her friend, telling her she'd be fine.

'I'd better ring George straightaway,' Mills said. 'I'll ring you later to let you know what's happened.'

She ended the call, redialling immediately and waiting impatiently for George to pick up. It seemed to take an age until finally there was a crackling at the other end. The signal was poor; consequently it took several minutes before he fully comprehended what Mills was trying to tell him.

'I'm sure it's him because Muriel said he was in camouflage gear. What d'you think I should do?'

'Look, don't do anything too reckless. Let me see... it will be an hour or so before I can get over there. Could you find out where this character is likely to be? I'll come over as soon as possible. We can tackle him together. I might bring a colleague.'

Now the initial shock of Earl's disappearance was wearing off, Mills was feeling increasingly angry. She marched up to the Manor determined to tackle Gareth about his unpleasant friend and it was probably fortunate that it was Daniel who opened the door. His welcome was friendly as he ushered her inside, offering her a drink.

'No, no I can't stop. I've got to find my dog.' She was close to tears and he must have sensed it because he insisted she take a seat while he fetched Penny, and when he returned with her he was holding a glass.

'Drink this, Mills.'

She took a few gulps before realising it was not water but a gin and tonic.

'Whatever is the matter?' Penny asked, sitting herself beside Mills and taking her hand.

On any other occasion Mills would have got out of there as soon as possible but she needed to find Fergus so she explained that she'd lost Earl and thought the boys might have seen him; it all came out in a muddle.

'... so I need to find Fergus right away.'

The pair looked at each other before Daniel appeared to come to a decision.

'The thing is, Mills, Gareth went up to the lodge to stay with Gus while they're working with the shoot.'

'He's helping with the beating,' Penny explained.

'The lodge?' Mills asked. 'D'you mean the old shooting lodge up the track?' She thought the place was derelict.

'That's right. You know it?' Penny was smiling politely.

She nodded and stood up. 'Thanks for the drink,' she said, putting her glass down carefully on the mantelpiece. 'I should be going.'

'I'm sure you'll find your dog,' Daniel assured her. 'I expect he'll be back at home when you get there.'

'Yes, probably.' There was no point explaining to him why that was very unlikely.

Anywhere else she would have gone straight over to tackle Fergus but the lodge held bad memories for her. In her teens when she was staying at Mossy Bank with her grandmother she'd watched the building burn while her friend only escaped in the nick of time. She'd kept clear ever since and assumed it was still just a shell. Best wait for George to arrive, she thought.

It was an anxious hour and a half but eventually she heard a vehicle and opened the door as George and another man were climbing out of a Land Rover.

'This is Harry,' George said. 'He's come to give us a hand.'

'Hi.' His deep voice was reassuring, as was the broad smile that wrinkled his brown eyes. 'George has explained what's happened. You must be very anxious.'

'I am...'

'Have you found out where this Fergus is?' George asked. 'We need to crack on.'

'Up there.' She pointed up the track. 'D'you see the stone building on the ridge? It's an old lodge.

Apparently he and Gareth are staying up there while the shooting is on.'

'Get in,' George ordered, jumping back into the driver's seat.

Harry opened the passenger door and Mills climbed in. There was nowhere else for him to sit and he squeezed in beside her. The lane petered out and they were joggled together as they slowly climbed the rough track towards the lodge. As they drew closer Mills was surprised to see how the building had been restored. It was in a much better state than it was before the fire and had obviously been completely renovated with new windows and front door. .

'No vehicles up here,' commented George as he pulled the Land Rover onto the piece of land adjacent to the building.

Harry jumped out, offering Mills a hand as she scrambled down. They followed George who had marched ahead and was banging on the door. While they waited in silence Mills wondered what was going to happen next. George knocked impatiently until there was a movement inside. The door opened slowly and Gareth stood surveying them with a puzzled expression. Mills noticed he was wearing khaki trousers tucked into thick woollen socks and looked much shorter without his boots on. The boy was saying that Fergus wasn't there but George continued to raise his voice, demanding to know where he was.

Mills intervened, in an attempt to defuse the situation. 'Gareth, I've lost Earl. Have you seen him?'

The boy looked nervously at the floor, his face reddening as she spoke. He hadn't seen the dog he said but was sorry if he was missing. He even offered to help search for him.

'I think you know a lot more than you're letting on.' George said. 'Are you going to invite us in?'

Gareth looked confused. 'What for?'

They stood in silence for a few seconds.

'I can get a warrant,' threatened George.

Mills looked at Harry who, like her, was shuffling uncomfortably at the confrontation.

Gareth opened the door, stepping back to let them pass, waiting until they were inside the hallway before closing the door behind them. Mills was struck by the transformation that had taken place inside. It was not the dirty and uncared for dwelling she'd visited before the fire. It had been transformed from a cold damp lodge into a modern house with brightly painted walls and carpets throughout. The three of them followed Gareth into the sitting room and stood awkwardly while George explained that he was searching the premises with Gareth's permission. Mills knew Earl would have been making a noise unless he was incapable so she waited anxiously while George and Harry searched the property. She could hear them upstairs moving from room to room.

'Don't worry, Gareth,' Mills said, taking a seat on the leather sofa. 'They don't think you've got anything to do with it. It's Fergus they want to talk to.'

'Why? Why do they want him?' he mumbled, dropping into the chair opposite.

'Someone took Earl from the cottage today. I know Fergus has done it to threaten me. Have you seen him with my dog?'

'No.' He sounded indignant, like an obstinate child.

'It's serious, Gareth. He's in real trouble.'

He didn't respond. They sat in silence until the search was complete.

'There's nothing here,' George announced.

Mills turned to Gareth. 'Do you know where Fergus is?'

'I told you, I don't know,' he replied sulkily.

'When he comes back, tell him we need to speak to him urgently.' George passed him a card. 'My number's on there. I want him to call in the next twenty-four hours or he'll be in even more trouble.'

When they were outside, Mills broke down. 'I can't wait for another day before we find Earl. He could be ill, he might be...' To her embarrassment she began to sob.

George gave a hollow laugh. 'Don't worry, we'll be watching out for him. We won't let him get away with it.'

Harry had put his arm round her shoulder. 'We'll find your dog. We're not going to give up, so you mustn't either,' he said awkwardly.

Mills couldn't speak.

'I need to make some calls – there's no signal here,' George complained.

They drove back down to Mossy Bank in silence and Mills made a pot of tea while George spoke on the phone to his superior. She caught only a few snatches of conversation as she carried mugs into the sitting room but it sounded as though he was planning to watch the lodge overnight.

'Harry's going to help me keep an eye on that youngster and his mate. It's my impression that the boy knows more than he's letting on. He's in camouflage gear himself. We don't know it wasn't him that took the dog.'

Mills started to protest but he carried on, ignoring her objections.

'He probably knows where his mate has gone and isn't letting on, so we'll watch the house to see if he comes back. If the dog's not up there, they must have him somewhere else unless...' He stopped abruptly but Mills knew what he meant.

'D'you think he might have, you know, done something to him already?' Mills asked Harry as George finished his conversation.

'It's difficult to say, isn't it?' His voice was calm, reassuring. 'If he was using it as a threat, it would be logical to keep him alive and well, don't you think?'

'Then why hasn't he left a message or contacted Mills to say so?' George asked.

Harry shook his head. 'Perhaps he doesn't want to incriminate himself. There's no evidence to connect him with it so far, except his verbal threats.'

The phone rang and Mills answered it.

'Is George still there?'

She handed him the receiver.

'Yes, sir. I won't do owt without referring back, sir. We're just going to observe.'

Mills wasn't hungry but guessed the others would need to eat if they really were staying to watch the lodge. It was eight o'clock and they could have a long night ahead. After some discussion they settled for sandwiches and while they were eating, she made up a flask. They set off back up the lane half an hour later, after Harry had once again reassured her that they would do everything they could to bring Earl back home. As Mills watched them go, she wondered absently whether her new acquaintance had a 'significant other'.

She didn't go to bed that night but dozed on the sofa with the television softly flickering in the background. She was alert at every sound, hoping it was George or Harry coming to give her some good news. At dawn she got up, drawing back the curtains to reveal a dull day. It was already five thirty. She splashed her face with cold water and made instant coffee before opening the front door to look for the Land Rover. There was no sign of it on the track above the village so she assumed they'd either gone home or were hidden up on the moor. She went back inside for a jacket before setting off up the lane. The lodge was only a few hundred metres away when she spotted the Land Rover tucked up a small valley made by a tiny rivulet running off the hill. At first she thought it was empty but as she approached she saw two figures in the front seats, heads back, fast asleep. She knocked gently on the passenger window, watching in amused silence as Harry gradually woke up, clearly unable to take in where he was and why. He knocked George on the side of his head as he yawned and the pair of them jostled to stretch their limbs and clamber down onto the damp grass.

'Hello.' Harry smiled as he scratched his head and beard.

'Have you seen him?' she asked.

'No. He hasn't been near the place.'

Mills wondered whether they'd been asleep for long, suspecting they may have missed Fergus arriving back if it had been late.

'So what happens now?' she asked.

'He's got another twelve hours or so and then he goes on our wanted list.'

When they accepted her invitation to have breakfast, Harry announced that he needed fresh air, suggesting that they walk down the hill together while George drove.

'Is this part of your normal work?' Mills was curious about what his role was.

'Sort of. I'm training to become a wildlife officer.'

It confirmed that he was in the police force but still didn't tell Mills much about him. Like George, he was not a man of many words.

'So you're usually on the beat in the town?' she tried.

'Traffic.'

'Zooming up and down motorways then?'

'Pretty much.'

She put his lack of words down to being awake half the night and was happy to walk the rest of the way in silence. But as they reached the lane, and the Land Rover was overtaking them, he stopped and turned.

'Would you like to go for a drink? I sometimes come over to the "Farmers' Arms". Do you know it?'

'In Muker? Of course. I'd love to.' She hoped she didn't sound too desperate.

'Saturday? We could get something to eat.'

He went over to the Land Rover, which was parked outside Laurel Cottage, leaving Mills to consider whether she'd made the right choice.

After a brief conversation with his colleague, Harry returned to say they had to leave. Something urgent had called them to base. He was at pains to explain that it was unrelated to their wildlife work and therefore it unfortunately took priority over her case. They would be back as soon as they could but it might not be until the next day.

'But I'll see you on Saturday whatever happens?' Harry said.

'That would be nice.' Nice? That sounds feeble, thought Mills.

'About seven-thirty?'

'Great.' Did that mean she would see him there? 'I'll see you there then.'

'Ok.'

She watched them go then sat on the tiny wall at the front of the cottage. If they weren't able to pursue Fergus, she would have to do it herself.

Before she left for work, she called her friend.

'Naomi, calm down. I only rang because I thought you'd want to know what had happened.'

'Does Daniel know?'

'No. Should I tell him?'

'No! If Gareth's not involved it's best to keep quiet. I'll come over this afternoon – will you be there?'

She wasn't due any time off while Brenda was away.

'Don't worry, Mills. I'll come over and talk to Gareth. I'll catch up with you when you get back from work.'

'I wondered if you'd like to stay with Granny until the weekend?' Hazel asked Liam as he helped himself to cereal.

'Why?'

'Because we're finally getting moving on the case I've been working on.'

'What, the murder on the moors?'

'Yep.'

There was a pause. 'Ok.'

'Not a problem then?'

'Nope.'

Hazel was puzzled by the ease with which her predicament had been solved but knew better than to extend the discussion.

When she was telling Nina about it, her friend suggested it could have something to do with Liam's girlfriend.

'She's been round to your mother's hasn't she? Perhaps he prefers to meet up with her there, away from Mum's prying eyes!'

'Now you've got me worried.'

'Your Mum says she's all right, doesn't she?'

'Yes, but...'

'And you said she was fussy about your boyfriends?'

'Yes but that's different.'

'I shouldn't knock it – it'll leave you free to work with your major, won't it?'

'Yes. But it's the work that I'm interested in.'

'Yeah, right.'

Nina went back to her report on Tanya Stewart. It was becoming more complicated because Larry Wright's murder, which was Hazel's responsibility, was so mixed up with it. The two victims were connected now the results of the DNA on the blood samples proved they had been killed by the same weapon. It appeared to be a very ordinary hunting knife; they'd not been able to identify its origin and any prints had been wiped clean.

'Do we assume that they were both killed by the same person?' she asked Hazel.

'Seems very likely,' she replied. 'Same MO, same weapon.'

'So we're looking for Mrs Egglington for a double murder?'

'Possibly. We won't know until we find her. How are *you* getting on?'

Nina pulled a face. 'Nothing. They've done a very good disappearing act. No-one has heard from them since the husband left the office last week, not even his family.'

'Mobile phones?' asked Hazel.

'Not switched on and not used since they disappeared.'

'What about tracing their cars?'

'There is only one.'

'In that case we can put it on the ANPR hotlist. That'll tell us if the number plate is picked up on any of the cameras in the region.'

'Good point.'

Hazel left her friend entering the car registration number onto the system which would automatically alert them if a number plate recognition camera spotted the car. She headed for the garrison to begin her joint investigation with Major Henderson. She was thinking about the connection between Mrs Egglington and Larry Wright as she drove. If the woman was pregnant, was the child his? Did her husband know? It would certainly be useful to speak to her GP. If she was in hiding, was she alone or with her husband? More importantly, how could they find her and her husband without any leads? She was looking forward to seeing how the military tackled such an investigation – perhaps it would be an interesting collaboration in several ways.

Robert was waiting for her in the entrance hall when she arrived.

'Good timing,' he said. 'We'll take my car.'

He took her arm and steered her toward the BMW.

'Where are we going?' she asked.

'To talk to a colleague of Pararescueman Wright.'

This was a new avenue that she hadn't considered – a friend of the victim could really help the investigation.

'Who is it?'

'He prefers that his name remains confidential.'

Great, thought Hazel but said nothing.

They were soon on the A1 speeding towards RAF Leeming. The car was waved through security and they were ushered into a large office to meet a very senior officer, as Robert described him. Coffee was served while they made polite conversation until the Wing Commander coughed nervously as if to make an announcement.

'I'm afraid it won't be possible for you to speak directly to our American colleague,' he said, looking at Hazel. 'He will speak to Major Henderson, who can give you a full de-brief.'

Hazel would have cracked a joke had the situation not been so formal and had she not felt totally sidelined. She looked at Robert, who was avoiding her gaze.

'So what shall I do while Robert... the Major is speaking to this witness?' She hoped her tone transmitted the annoyance she was experiencing.

'You are welcome to stay in my office if you wish, or you can stretch your legs around the grounds. It's a nice day,' he added.

'Fine,' she said, picking up her bag. 'I can have a smoke while I wait.'

Robert caught up with her at the bottom of the stairs. 'Hey, wait for me,' he called. 'I hope you don't think...'

'Don't think what?' she asked, rummaging through her bag for a packet of cigarettes.

'I hope you're not thinking I support you being excluded from the interview.'

'Par for the course,' she said, lighting the cigarette and inhaling deeply. 'Exactly what I expected from your lot.'

'Hazel, they're not "my lot" which is why I've gotten zero influence. Look, I'll tape everything and feed back when I'm done.'

Hazel found a seat outside the building, enjoying the sunshine. Although she might have been the first to complain about being shut out of such an important interview, she'd been in the Force long enough to know that there was no point in making a fuss. She used the time to consider the intelligence she had, to ponder and then finally come to a conclusion about how to take the investigation forward.

When Robert finally emerged from the building, he was quickly followed by a young man in baggy shorts who turned off in the opposite direction. Hazel guessed this was the friend of Larry Wright.

'Quiet kinda guy,' Robert said. 'He wasn't giving much away. Not a close acquaintance; just one of the boys.'

'Is that it?'

She hardly listened to his response; she was busy with her new line of investigation.

'... so the bottom line is that this guy suspected Wright was seeing someone but didn't know who.'

'Did you ask about Beatrice Egglington?'

'Yep, but he didn't know the name or recognise the picture.'

Hazel had to take his answers at face value. He could be lying but she had no way of knowing.

'I've been thinking,' she said.

'And?'

'And I think we should be contacting Mrs Egglington's doctor again.'

'Why?'

'Because she was pregnant and no woman would risk the health of her baby – even if she's on the run.'

'Well I thought, since we have the time and it's a nice day, we might run over to where the body was found.'

'Why? The whole area has been searched thoroughly weeks ago.'

'I know you've seen it, Hazel, but I've not. And they tell me there's a real typical Yorkshire pub right by the crime scene.'

Hazel wanted to pursue her own enquiries but didn't necessarily want to miss the opportunity of a drink with Robert, so she followed him to the car. While he drove, she rang the surgery and asked for Dr Trent.

'Sergeant Singleton! Over here! Can I buy you a drink?'

It took him a few seconds to locate where the voice was coming from. Mr Egglington was seated at the bar with a half empty pint in front of him. Jerry made his way over and seated himself on the adjacent bar stool with some difficulty.

'Thank you, sir. I'll just have a half.'

'A half of best!' His voice was too loud and Jerry suspected that the man had been at the bar for some time. 'I'm having a whisky chaser – d'you want one?'

'No thank you, sir. I'm working this evening.'

'Of course, you are. Keeping the old place safe are you?'

Jerry didn't know Steven Egglington well but his reputation was that of a ruthless, ambitious business man. When he'd gone missing there was a rumour that he'd absconded with funds. He'd even heard that the local police were looking for him.

'This is your local, isn't it, sergeant?'

'Aye, it is.'

When the barman pushed the drinks across the bar, they sat in silence. The place was nearly empty and only the fruit machine made intermittent sounds despite the absence of a punter. Jerry was formulating how to begin when Egglington spoke.

'I expect you know I've taken extended leave.'

'Hadn't seen you about, sir.'

'It's the wife – she's not been well.'

'Sorry to hear that, sir.'

'Yes.' Jerry watched him swallow the whisky in a single mouthful and pick up the pint glass. 'She became very depressed a few weeks ago, after she came back from holiday.'

Jerry waited.

'Doctor gave her something for it but it didn't help.'

'Perhaps it's... you know... women's trouble, sir.' He didn't know why he said that. His own wife had gone through it all but Mrs Egglington couldn't have been more than forty, perhaps in her thirties.

'I think it's deeper than that, sergeant.'

They drank their beer together, in a companionable way. Jerry counted the spirit bottles lined up along the shelf behind the bar, wondering how long he needed to stay before it would not appear impolite to leave. He refused Egglington's offer to join him in another drink, wondering whether he should buy another round himself. But there was a rule about alcohol before going on duty and he'd already had a half. He looked at his watch in an exaggerated manner and declared that he had to run. Egglington grabbed his arm, pulling him closer and speaking directly into his ear.

'I can't find her. I've been looking for her but she's disappeared.'

'Have you reported it to the police?'

'Not yet but I'm worried she might be in trouble. I think she might have been murdered.'

Chapter 16

Hazel had finally won the argument and instead of turning east towards Thirsk, Robert drove west to Ripon. She insisted he remained in the car while she went into the surgery to speak to Dr Trent, not because of any confidentiality reasons but simply because he'd not involved her in his interview with the pararescueman.

'Is there a particular reason you want to talk about Mrs Egglington?' the doctor asked once the surgery door was firmly closed and Hazel had shown him her identification.

'There is, Dr Trent. We want to speak to her about an incident we're investigating. She's left her home and hasn't been seen since last Wednesday – just over a week ago.'

The GP pulled a record card from its envelope and studied it. 'She came to see me on the fourth of August. She hadn't been prior to that for nearly a year. Just the usual checks otherwise.'

'May I ask why she saw you then?'

'She was feeling rather low. She asked me for something to help.'

'Did you prescribe medication?'

'I gave her a mild anti-depressant... but I stopped them again on the tenth.' The young man was staring at the card.

'And that was because... ?'

He straightened up, putting the card down in front of him. 'It's a bit delicate.'

'It's a murder enquiry, Dr Trent. She may be in danger herself. We need to know what we're dealing with.'

'Well, she didn't want her husband to know – not at this early stage. She'd tried to conceive before – for years actually. Probably didn't want to raise their hopes.'

'She was pregnant. We know.' It confirmed their identification of Wright's companion.

'In that case I suppose it's all right to discuss it with you. She rang me to say she'd done a test. She wanted to be sure it meant she was definitely pregnant. I offered for her to come in – to reassure her?'

'Has she been in?'

'No. She said they're on holiday so she couldn't come over.'

'Over?'

Somewhere near Leyburn. She didn't say exactly but I suggested she visited the health centre if she felt she needed to.'

Hazel stood up and gave him her card. 'Please let me know if she contacts you again.'

'Should I ask her to come into the surgery?'

'If she is coming to see you do let me know. Otherwise just keep in touch, please.'

At last she had something to go on. She almost ran back to where Robert was waiting.

'Can we eat now, sugar?'

The sugar thing annoyed her. 'Not yet. I want to pop into Leyburn before we eat. You can pick up a sandwich while I visit the medical centre there.'

'You don't take prisoners, do you?' Robert was beginning to sound a little irritable.

'You don't know the half of it, sunshine.'

She left him listening to the radio and returned after just a few minutes. They had no record of a Beatrice Egglington visiting or registering at the centre.

'Perhaps she used a pseudonym,' Robert suggested.

'No holiday makers fitting her description and definitely no-one in the early stages of pregnancy.'

'In that case we can have a nice pub lunch.'

'No. I need to get back to Newby Wiske to brief Nina. Then we can go to the crime scene if you really want to.'

Robert left the radio on, singing along to a variety of hits from the seventies and eighties. Hazel joined in when they played songs she recognised. She was conscious of admiring glances when they stopped at junctions, and hoped it wasn't just for the car. Did they make an attractive couple? Now she wanted her friend to meet "the Major" and have her honest opinion. So when they arrived at headquarters, she insisted Robert accompanied her.

'I don't want to be in the way, sugar,' he said as they went upstairs to the office.

She was already regretting the offer – if he called her "sugar" in front of Nina she'd never let her live it down.

'Robert – would you mind not calling me that?'

'Calling you what?'

She couldn't bear to say it.

'You mean "sugar", sugar?' His voice was loud, they were almost outside the door.

She shook her head and frowned at him before turning the handle.

'Hazel! We've had a breakthrough!' Nina jumped to her feet as they entered, then stopped when she spotted Robert.

She looked at Hazel, who introduced him. Her friend was clearly unsure whether to continue.

'Does it concern Larry Wright?'

'Not sure. It's the husband – Mr Egglington.'

'In that case it's related,' said Robert, seating himself beside Nina's desk. For the first time he seemed to be taking the investigation seriously.

'We haven't eaten yet. Can it wait until we get something to eat?'

Nina shrugged. 'Go ahead.'

'Robert, there's a canteen downstairs. Could you be a love and get us a cheese or egg sandwich and a coke?'

'But...'

'I need to type up my report for this morning – it won't take long.'

He rose and sauntered to the door. 'Don't start without me,' he called but not in a light-hearted way.

They looked at each other.

'He's fit,' said Nina with a giggle.

'He's ok, isn't he?'

'He's really nice, Hazel. You should hang onto him.'

Hazel sat down in the chair Robert had vacated. 'So what's the news?'

'Don't you want to wait for Robert?'

'No way – quick before he gets back.'

'There was a call from your creepy friend... the one called a red berry or something like that.'

'Not the redcap from Catterick? Sergeant something.'

Nina consulted her notepad. 'Sergeant Jerry Singleton.'

'That's him.'

'He met Mr Steven Egglington in a pub in Catterick yesterday afternoon. He'd had a bit too much to drink and told Jerry, Sergeant Singleton, that his wife had disappeared.'

'Interesting.'

'There's more. He also intimated that he thought she might be in trouble.'

'Right.'

'That he was concerned she may have been murdered.'

'So why hasn't he contacted us?'

'Because he thought it wouldn't be taken seriously, he said.'

Hazel considered for a moment. 'D'you believe that?'

'I'm not sure but I told him to ask Mr Egglington to contact us.'

'Has anyone tried his address to see if he's back home?'

'No.'

By the time Hazel had related the gist of her visit to Dr Trent, Robert had returned with a selection of sandwiches, crisps, cakes and drinks enough for them all. They persuaded Nina to join them, decamping to the lawn for an impromptu picnic while they exchanged information, until Robert eventually conceded that he'd been properly brought "up to speed".

'Now can we go to the site on the North York Moors where Pararescueman Wright was found murdered?' he asked.

'No,' said Hazel, 'we're going to Ripon to see if Mr Egglington is at home.'

It was a long shot and she hoped it wouldn't be a wild goose chase. But to Hazel's surprise, Steven Egglington opened the door to them as if nothing was amiss. She showed him her ID before stepping inside, motioning to Robert to join them.

'I'm glad you called,' Egglington said, smiling politely and offering them a seat. 'When I spoke to Sergeant Singleton about my wife, he said I should contact you.'

Hazel pulled a notebook from her bag. 'And why is that, sir?'

'Because she's gone missing.'

'When did you last see her, sir?'

'A week ago. It was just after her friend died.'

'Would that be Tanya – Tanya Stewart?'

'Yes. They weren't close but they'd worked together for a long time. It affected her badly. She said she wanted time to get over it. She was here when I went to work but when I got back, she'd gone.'

'I presume you saw the paperwork we left here after we came to search the house on Tuesday?'

'Yes. I wondered what... I was going to ring... I've only just got back.'

'Where have you been since Monday, sir?'

'Looking for my wife, sergeant. Trying to find my wife.' He looked strained and Hazel wondered if he knew that his wife had been on holiday with another man.

'This is rather delicate, Mr Egglington, but I have to ask you – was your wife on holiday in the middle of July?'

'Yes. She walked the Coast to Coast Path with some friends.'

'You didn't go?'

'No. Not my idea of a holiday. I planned to go sailing later in the year.'

'Would you be able to give me the details of the friends she was on holiday with?'

'Of course. It was Lynn and Angie.'

He walked over to the desk where she and Nina had discovered Larry Wright's ID tag. He scribbled on a sheet of paper and returned with two names and their telephone numbers.

As soon as they were in the car, Robert turned to her.

'You're not going to arrest him?'

'Why?'

'For killing his wife's boyfriend!'

'Don't be silly Robert, the man's distraught. Couldn't you see how cut up he was by his wife disappearing like that? There's no motive to murder Tanya Stewart and we know it was the same person who did that.'

Naomi was on shifts so finished promptly at two in the afternoon. She did not relish meeting up with her brother again so soon but if her nephew was in trouble she owed it to him to help out where she could. When her sister-in-law opened the door, Naomi could tell it was not a good time to call. Her face said it all.

'Don't worry, Penny, I'm not stopping. I just wanted a quick chat with Gareth.'

'What about?'

'Just wanted to know what he wanted for his birthday.'

Penny glared at her. 'I may not be in the police, Naomi, but I'm not stupid. Kindly do me that courtesy.'

'I just need to speak to him about that Scottish friend of his.'

'You mean Gus? What about him. If he's in trouble we need to know. We're close friends of his parents... we're almost *in loco parentis* when he's down here.'

'In that case you need to keep a better eye on him. The wildlife officers have him in their sights.'

'Daniel!' Penny was turning her back to summon her husband.

There was no reply.

'Stay there!' she commanded.

'I just need to know where he is!' Naomi shouted at her disappearing figure.

She wandered into the hall and waited while raised voices drifted from the direction of the kitchen. A door slammed and Daniel appeared looking flustered.

'Hi Dan, how's tricks?'

'How d'you think? What's this nonsense? We're having a dinner party tonight and Penny is very busy.'

'Just want to know where Gareth and Fergus are hanging out. I need to talk to them.'

'They're beating again today.'

'How do I reach Gareth?'

'You could try calling his mobile. He's never parted from it.'

Naomi put the number into her phone, even though her mobile had no signal in the dale, and went to leave.

'D'you know where they're shooting today?'

'Up on the top here I believe. You're not going up there?'

'If I have to. Can I use your phone?'

She didn't expect a response when she tried Gareth's number, certain there was no reception on the fells. But to her surprise there was a crackling followed by the unmistakable voice of her nephew.

'Gareth, it's Naomi.'

'Hi.'

'Are you busy beating?'

'No.'

'I thought you were beating today.'

'I am but we're waiting for the others to catch up.'

'I need to talk to you about Fergus.'

Silence.

'He's in big trouble Gareth. Tell me you're not involved.'

'I don't know what you're talking about.'

'Yes you do. Is Fergus with you?'

No answer.

'I take that as a yes. Whereabouts are you?'

Either they'd lost signal or Gareth had cut her off.

'Have a good dinner party.' She shouted as she slammed the door behind her.

When she went to the end of the drive and looked up the track, she could see several Land Rovers parked by the shooting lodge. Guessing that the shooters had taken lunch at the lodge, she assumed they were not too far away for the afternoon's sport. She changed into her walking boots and was locking the car when the front door of the Manor opened and Daniel emerged.

'I'd better come with you,' he said. 'After all, he is my son.'

Naomi was too irritated to point out to him that deck shoes might not be the best footwear for crossing the moors.

The vehicles by the lodge were empty except for a couple of spaniels that barked intermittently. The sound of gunfire came from over the top of the fell and Naomi left the track, heading due north towards the sound. She had to admit that Daniel was keeping up well. When they reached the highest point she could distinguish the line of beaters making their way slowly across the slope towards the butts. Occasionally a bird rose up from the heather and two shots were fired, only for the bird to make a quick exit to the side.

'We'll have to wait here until the line reaches us,' Daniel stated, firmly remaining where he was.

Naomi stopped, surveying the scene. A line of men and boys in khaki moving slowly through the heather waving white flags. It seemed an age until she could make out their features.

'Gareth's the third from the end.' Daniel was talking quietly as if they could be heard if he spoke louder.

'Where's Fergus?'

'Gus? I can't see him.'

'Would Gareth be up here if his friend wasn't working today?'

'I doubt it. He's a lazy lad.'

Naomi waited until the line broke up, and then went down to join Gareth, thinking Dan was following her, but when she turned round he was gone.

'If you're looking for Gus, he's over there,' Gareth said, throwing himself on the ground and tossing the flag to one side.

'You look knackered.'

'I am.' He was pointing to the right of where Daniel was speaking to an elderly man in tweed. The Scottish lad was sharing a joke with a couple of young men.

'Who's your dad talking to?'

'He's one of the shooting party.'

'Does he know him?'

'Probably, he likes to think he's one of the toffs.'

Naomi could see that Fergus had spotted her but he carried on chatting with his friends as if he was indifferent to her presence. She walked towards him but veered off at the last moment to join her brother.

'Naomi. I've spoken to Roger, here, and he's happy for Gareth and Gus to leave the party. I've told him that we need to speak to them both.'

'Ok.'

They hung around until the group was ready to move off again. It seemed an interminable wait but eventually Naomi saw first Gareth, then Fergus, being issued with their instructions. Gareth looked resigned as he joined his father but Fergus was still remonstrating with his boss as the rest of the group moved on.

'What's going on?' demanded the irate lad when he reached Naomi.

'Hello Fergus, or may I call you Gus?'

'Who the hell d'you think you are?'

'Actually I'm a police officer and you are wanted in relation to an enquiry regarding a missing dog.'

He laughed loudly and uttered some coarse expletives.

Daniel stepped over and suggested he watch his language. 'I won't have my sister spoken to in that manner,' he added.

'Will you come into the station to give a statement?' she asked politely.

'No, I won't.'

'Then you'll answer a few questions here.'

'I'll do no such thing.'

He swung round and set off down the slope. Daniel rushed forward, felling him to the ground, and with a triumphant yell pinned him down. Naomi quickly followed and from her superior standing position fired a series of questions at him. The responses were muffled as they came from below Daniel's armpit.

At first he denied having even seen Earl but eventually he admitted breaking in and taking him for a walk before returning the dog to the cottage.

'But you came back again, didn't you? This time you took him away and didn't bring him back.'

Denials at first again but Daniel stayed put until the lad squeaked for him to get off.

'You're breaking my ribs.'

'Just answer the question,' insisted Naomi. 'Where is the dog now?'

'I don't know, I don't know. I haven't seen him. I don't know.'

Gareth had been silent throughout the exchange until now. 'He had Earl at the lodge until yesterday.'

'I told you to keep quiet,' shouted Fergus. 'You are dead, Gareth.'

As he started wriggling violently, Daniel was thrown to one side and Fergus jumped up, making off down the hill while Daniel struggled to his feet.

'Leave him, Dan,' advised Naomi. 'You've done enough this afternoon. Look at the state of your trousers.'

'Come on, Gareth,' Daniel said, putting his arm round his son's shoulder. 'Let's get back home before Mum sees my chinos.'

'Naomi,' said Gareth as they reached the track and began the descent into Mossy Bank, 'You shouldn't have said you were a police officer, should you? I mean a police surgeon isn't allowed to arrest people are they?'

'No, Gareth. You're right. That was a porky pie. Listen, do you have any idea where Earl is? Mills is going mad.'

'He was all right when he was at the lodge yesterday but Gus took him away in the afternoon. Said he would be safer somewhere else.'

'Was he walking?'

'Yep.'

'And how long was he gone?'

'A couple of hours.'

'And which way did he go?'

'Don't know. I was watching the telly.'

Naomi left Gareth and his father at the entrance to the Manor. She'd spotted the red mini outside Laurel Cottage, indicating Mills was back from work.

While her friend made tea, Naomi described her confrontation with Fergus and the news that Earl had been alive until the previous day.

'But where is he now?'

Naomi patted her friend's arm. 'Don't worry, we'll find him. He's within walking distance, an hour max. We'll look at the map and decide the best places to look.'

'Anywhere in a four mile radius? You must be kidding. It's impossible.' Mills flung herself down on the sofa.

'It's not hopeless though. We can ask George...'

'He can't come until tomorrow.'

'Oh, well. Just us then. Never mind, we'll manage.'

'Please Naomi, don't. It's hopeless.'

'At least lend us a map.'

Mills went to her desk, producing a large scale map of the area, handed it to her friend and resumed her seat. Naomi spread the map on the floor, kneeling over it for several minutes before standing.

'Right. He set off in a westerly direction, which suggests he was staying on this side of the river, otherwise it would have been quicker to come down the lane.'

'He might not have wanted to be seen in the village.'

'True, but at least we know to look west – that reduces the area by fifty percent and there's nothing on the tops so that's another half...'

She was interrupted by gentle knocking on the door. Mills was looking alarmed, so Naomi opened it to find Daniel on the doorstep. Gareth was behind him.

'I... that is, we felt we should offer to help Mills find her dog. I've been grilling Gareth here and he knows some spots where that Fergus might have put him.'

'You'd better come in.'

Daniel had changed into walking trousers and boots; Gareth was still dressed in his tweeds.

Mills remained on the sofa while the three of them studied the map and Gareth pointed to several places where there were buildings he'd visited with Fergus.

'He said they were good vantage points for spotting birds.'

'You mean for shooting them,' his father corrected him angrily.

'I didn't know that then, did I? I just thought they were like hides. Mainly they're barns but there's another lodge, just there.' He pointed to a small building marked on the map.

In total Naomi counted five potential hiding places, three on the north of the Swale and two to the south.

'Would you take the barns on the other side of the river?' she asked them.

Her brother looked at his watch then nodded. 'All right.'

'Don't worry, Dan, you'll be back in time for the dinner party.'

'Naomi, I am supposed to be making the starter. I told Penny she might have to do it herself.'

Once they'd left, Mills seemed to come to life. 'So we're taking the other three buildings?'

'I don't see why not, if you're up for it?'

'Just try to stop me.'

The first barn was just half a mile along the track beyond the lodge. Naomi had passed it many times while walking across the moor as a kid. It was tucked away in the corner of a field used as pasture, behind the stone wall that defined the end of the enclosed farms and the beginning of the open moorland. The doorway and windows were open to the elements and it was clearly no longer used to store hay. As they approached, a ewe ran out of the barn, followed by her lamb now grown almost as large as its mother.

'Doesn't look likely,' observed Naomi, stepping gingerly through the layer of sheep droppings that carpeted the inside. It only took a second to confirm it was empty.

'No,' agreed Mills, studying the map and making her way back to open the gate.

Naomi shut the gate behind them and ran to catch up with her friend who was walking very fast. They continued in the same direction, not speaking until the next barn was in sight. They had to leave the path, moving downhill across the open pasture and into meadows surrounded by dry stone walls until they were within sight of the river. Naomi thought she would have been enjoying their evening walk if it had not such a dismal purpose.

The second barn was larger than the previous one, in the middle of a meadow that was ready for mowing. The windows were shuttered and the door was fastened with wire. Mills fought with it until they could pull the door ajar a little. Through the small slit Naomi could only see darkness.

'We'll have to get it open wider,' she told her friend.

Together they pushed and shoved until the gap was big enough to squeeze through.

'I wish I'd thought to bring a torch,' said Mills.

'It's ok I can use my phone.'

As soon as Naomi illuminated the building, she confirmed there was no sign of the dog ever having been there. She sighed. Although she dreaded finding the inert body of the lurcher, she had half-hoped that it would be the right place. Her phone showed it was already eight o'clock and she prayed that Dan hadn't given up on them.

'Right Mills. Let's get out of here,' she said, quickly making a few turns of the wire to prevent the door blowing open.

The last location was close to the Swale which meant they walked due west keeping to the same contour until they could see the building below them. Stopping to rest, Naomi tried to console Mills that they hadn't found anything terrible and she must retain a positive attitude. Her words of comfort were interrupted by shouting from across the river.

'It's Daniel, look!' Mills was pointing to the bridge where a figure was calling and gesticulating. 'He's found something!'

Naomi ran through bracken and boggy ground, thrashing back the butterbur aware of Mills close behind her. Dan was still on the bridge, calm now as he waited for them to reach him. He looked grave.

'Just up here,' he said.

'What is it?' Naomi whispered to her brother, not wanting Mills to hear.

But Dan just indicated for them to follow without a word. They turned up a rough track that took them through a farmyard and onto meadowland. The path joined a wide straight track that led to a stone building, the lodge that Gareth had mentioned. It was much smaller than the lodge above Mossy Bank, in fact it was little more than a hut.

'Where's Gareth?' Naomi asked as they approached the building.

'He's inside... he's... well, you'll see.'

Naomi followed Dan towards the door but was pushed aside by Mills.

'Is he there?' she cried as she rushed inside.

Dan grabbed Naomi's arm and held her back. 'It doesn't look good. I've rung the vet and he's on his way over. I don't think we should move him. He seems very weak.'

'Is he injured?'

'I don't think so but the water bowl had been knocked over so I don't know how long he's been... he's probably very dehydrated.'

Naomi stopped at the doorway. Her friend was holding the dog's head in her lap, tears streaming down her face. Gareth was wiping his eyes with the back of his hand as he brushed past her and stomped outside to lean against the stone wall. She watched his father attempt to comfort him but he pushed him aside and walked further away from the lodge.

'We can manage if you need to get back, Dan.' Naomi offered.

He argued but eventually agreed that he really ought to be with Penny. He asked Gareth if he wanted to leave but the boy shook his head and turned away. Dan shrugged.

'Don't worry, I'll keep an eye,' Naomi reassured him.

She checked on Mills who was quietly stroking the dog's head whilst murmuring reassuring words to him. His eyes were closed and the head lolled lifelessly on her knees. Outside Gareth was still slumped against the wall.

'I didn't know – Gus said he'd be safe.'

Naomi touched his arm but he pulled away from her. 'I do understand,' she said.

'But he's going to die, isn't he?'

'We don't know anything until the vet arrives. Why don't you go down to the road to tell him where we are?'

She watched her nephew, head bowed, walking slowly in the direction of the farm. Naomi sat watching the light fade, a lump forming in her throat as she listened to Mills gently comforting the dog.

Chapter 17

Nina was up long before Nige was awake. By the time he wandered downstairs in his boxers, Nina had dressed Rosie and given her breakfast. Her daughter was sitting quietly on her lap while she combed her hair.

'What are you doing up so early – and why are you wearing that suit?'

'Good morning, sweetie. Did you sleep well?'

'Yes but what's going on? It's only ten past eight.'

'Nothing, Nige. I have to go to a funeral in Lancaster today.'

'Lancaster?'

'She was murdered. It's my case.'

'But that doesn't mean you have to...'

'Yes, Nige, actually I do.' She handed Rosie over to him. 'I'm hoping that a friend of hers will come to the funeral.'

Rosie was not going to let Nige ignore her any longer and Nina was able to leave him to get her ready for nursery while she found her black handbag.

'By the way,' she called, 'I won't be back on time today – Mitch wants to have a meeting this afternoon. It'll take a couple of hours to get back from Lancaster so we won't start 'til three.'

'All right. What's for tea?'

'Look in the fridge. They'll be something.'

'I could get fish and chips.' It was Nige's usual way of avoiding cooking.

'Whatever!'

She slammed the door behind her, grateful that Nige had arranged a place for Rosie in the university nursery. Somehow, magically, it transferred all responsibility for her daughter during the day to her husband.

Once she was in the car she was able to concentrate on the job in hand. Tanya's sister, Rachel, had rung to say that the funeral was to be at eleven o'clock at Lancaster Crematorium. There was plenty of time but she wanted to be there before the mourners began arriving, to glean as much information as possible from Tanya Stewart's friends and relatives. Aware that she must maintain the necessary dignity of the occasion she'd worn her posh suit – the one she kept for interviews and occasions such as today's – with a crisp white shirt and her hair was neatly pinned back in a French plait.

The day was getting hotter and she noticed the mourners waiting for the next service were clinging to the shady parts of the gardens. It was only just after ten so she parked the car and found a quiet spot some distance from where people were beginning to congregate as a hearse appeared and slid to a silent halt. She checked her watch: it was exactly ten fifteen. Everyone disappeared and she was left to the peace of the gardens which seemed to extend off into the distance. Nina assumed that she was about to attend a Christian funeral. She'd attended a few before: Nige's grandfather had been cremated, a colleague who was stabbed a few years ago – he'd been cremated – and a friend of Nige's, who was a Catholic and had been buried. Because her only experience of the Christian religion was at weddings, christenings and funerals, she always felt a little uncertain of what was happening and how to behave. She was particularly worried about when to stand up and when to kneel down, especially as not everyone seemed to do the same thing.

It had been very peaceful for the last ten minutes but now cars began to arrive, just a single vehicle at first then a couple more until finally a queue was forming as spaces filled up. Once there were about a dozen people assembled, Nina took a deep breath, checking her hair and lipstick using the tiny mirror from her handbag, before walking slowly to join them. She stood apart from the gaggle of women who were presumably work colleagues, or members of a group Tanya had belonged to, while she decided how to introduce herself. People sometimes resented members of the Force imposing themselves in these situations and she was aware of the sensitivity of the occasion. She looked for Rachel then remembered that close family arrived with the coffin. So she surveyed the mourners, on the lookout for Tanya's friend Beatrice Egglington.

Finally she approached the group of women, who smiled sympathetically at her when she enquired whether they were work colleagues of Tanya's.

'Yes. We came over in a minibus from the camp,' said a woman in her forties or early fifties who was wearing a blue sleeveless dress that exposed her flabby upper arms. 'We wanted to show our respects.'

Nina simply said she was a friend and asked if any of them might know if Bea Egglington was coming to the funeral.

Looks were exchanged between the women before the woman in blue acted as spokesperson again. 'I don't know. We haven't seen her for a while. Not since Tanya...'

There was an awkward silence.

'I wasn't sure exactly what Tanya actually worked on,' Nina tried.

This time another colleague chipped in. 'She worked with me in the "Overseas Family Support Unit". We help families moving in from abroad who are working at the garrison, for whatever reason. It's a new initiative to help integrate communities that are here for a short time'.

'So you'd be liaising with someone who, for example, was over here from the States?' Nina asked, wondering whether she'd found the connection between Tanya and Larry Wright. 'Was that the same as Bea was doing?'

'Yes, pretty much.'

Other women joined in with descriptions of their work at the camp and Nina stood listening politely. So either of the women could have met Wright during the course of their work, Nina thought, and made a mental note to check out any files that might allude to them meeting him. Eventually she eased herself away before the group asked her about herself, not wanting them to suspect her motives for showing such an interest in their friends. She watched the new arrivals, hoping to catch a glimpse of Bea Egglington without success. The crowd of mourners had swelled to around sixty, Nina judged, by the time three long black cars swept along the drive. Everyone stood awkwardly in silence until finally the doors were opened, signalling that the service would commence. Nina watched Tanya's sister helping an elderly couple into the crematorium. Beside them was a man, tanned and muscular, head shaven, dressed in a suit that seemed too tight, presumably Tanya's husband, rushed back from Afghanistan to say goodbye to his wife.

Nina took a seat at the back of the room and observed the proceedings. She felt an interloper as family members and friends attempted to commemorate a life that had ended so tragically that no-one could maintain the façade of celebration. There were hymns and prayers then Tanya's sister read a poem, breaking down before she could finish. As soon as the service was over, Nina tried to nip out at the back but found the only exit was past the family. She nodded at Rachel, who introduced her to Tanya's parents and husband.

'This is Mike. He's come straight from Camp Bastion to be here, haven't you?'

He nodded but didn't speak.

Another man, presumably Rachel's husband, hovered behind her but was not introduced.

'You'll come for refreshments?' Rachel asked.

Nina hesitated not wishing to seem eager but was persuaded by the family who seemed genuinely pleased that she had come. She was given a map with details of a hotel in Lancaster but it was unnecessary as she followed the minibus of colleagues the entire way, parking alongside them in the yard behind the hotel. Nina counted forty people crammed into the small side room. She helped herself to sandwiches but refused the offer of wine, although she knew Hazel would not have been so disciplined in the circumstances. Three women from the minibus joined her, explaining that Rachel had told them who she was. It was obvious they had a reason for wanting to talk to her, which she put down to curiosity but eventually one of them came out with it.

'We've been wondering what's happened to Bea. It's just that she disappeared soon after Tanya was killed and if there's someone out there that's targeting women from the camp...' said one woman.

'My husband is really wound up about it. He didn't want me coming to the funeral in case it was dangerous. He thought he might be here, observing like,' added another.

The women looked around the room as if expecting to see a man with a knife lurking in a corner.

'I can assure you we're doing everything we can.' Nina hated using the same old clichés.

'Is Bea alive?' asked the first woman.

Nina paused. 'We have no reason to believe she's not.'

She knew it didn't satisfy them but she couldn't say more. She searched in her bag and gave them all a card. They each stared at her details then tucked it carefully into their handbags. It was time she was leaving. Rachel and her family were surrounded by a group of elderly people, presumably family; it was not a good time to interrupt them so she quietly made for the door.

A voice called out 'Excuse me, miss!' as she made her way through reception.

It was Tanya's husband, Mike. 'I just wanted to ask what's happening. What are you doing about finding whoever done it?'

His eyes were dark shadows and now she was close she could see he hadn't shaved.

'I'm sorry, I... We're working hard... I'm sorry. There's so little to go on.'

'She was found at the ranges, right? So it must be someone on the camp, yes? Why aren't they searching the place, taking DNA, doing door-to-door? That's what you do, isn't it – in a case like this?'

'Mr Stewart...'

'Don't Mr Stewart me! I'm Rifleman Stewart to you. I'm putting my life on the line over there for people like you.' He stopped suddenly, turned and walked away as if he needed to make space between them before his emotions got the better of him. Nina was shaken, uncertain exactly what he meant by "people like you".

She sat in the car for a minute or two until she had calmed down. He was right – they at least owed him some closure. She started the engine and set off to Newby Wiske with a plan to get the investigation moving.

Hazel had crept down the stone stairs early that morning. She wasn't used to hearing birdsong when she woke and certainly couldn't watch rabbits playing from the kitchen window in her flat. The kettle was taking ages to boil on the tiny electric ring and she couldn't find any instant coffee in the cupboard.

'Hi, sugar, couldn't you sleep?' Robert was standing at the doorway in jeans, his shirt hanging open.

Hazel gave him a hug then stepped back. 'Where's the coffee then?'

Robert laughed, taking a jug from the shelf and a tin from the cupboard. She watched him grind the beans, without mentioning she preferred instant in the morning. They took their mugs into the "yard" as he called it and chatted as they sat in the sun.

'What time is it?' Hazel asked eventually.

'Eight ten, maybe eight fifteen,' he replied.

'You are kidding!' yelled Hazel, slopping coffee on the ground as she jumped up. 'Quick! I said I'd be in early today.'

'Hold on – we haven't had breakfast yet. I thought I'd do pancakes...'

'Robert, we have to go now. Hurry up! We're meeting those friends of Mrs Egglington's in Darlington at ten.'

It was typical of a man, thought Hazel, as she waited for him to lock up then go inside again for his car keys. It was after nine by the time they'd left the village and had joined the A1.

'So why do we want to speak with them personally, instead of just calling them?' Robert asked.

'Correction. *I* want to speak to them. There are things that women will talk about in person, in a group of women, that may not be discussed under other circumstances.'

'Such as?'

'Such as did they know that Bea was going off with your pararescueman? Have they ever met him? Did they know she was pregnant?'

'I see. And you don't think they'd say if I was there?'

'I don't know. I think you might be a distraction,' she said with a grin.

Robert dropped her off close to Horsemarket where she'd arranged to meet the women in Caffe Nero. It wasn't busy and she easily spotted the only women customers sitting together. She bought a latte and went over to introduce herself. Angie looked the older of the two, although Hazel knew they were similar ages, being school friends of Bea Egglington or Bea Thornton as they had known her.

Hazel had never been good at small talk so got straight to the point, asking them when Bea had told them she was going to do the Coast to Coast walk.

'It was something we'd been planning for years really,' began Lynn. 'We always said we would do it when the time was right.'

'With kids and so on, it never seemed a good time,' added Angie.

'But Bea never had children, did she?' asked Hazel.

'No.' Angie studied her coffee cup. 'She desperately wanted them but it never happened.'

'And Steve wouldn't adopt,' added Lynn.

'So. You all planned to do the walk one day?' said Hazel getting them back on track.

'We planned to do it this year but then I had my bombshell,' Angie explained.

Hazel waited to hear what her bombshell was.

'Angie was diagnosed with breast cancer.' Lynn was whispering. 'Your treatment has been horrendous hasn't it?'

Angie nodded. 'Ruined everything.'

'We couldn't go without Angie. We said we'd rent a cottage and have a week together that way; Bea was even getting the details together. We'd decided on somewhere near that castle...'

'Bolton Castle?' Angie suggested.

'Yes, but then at the last minute Bea said she was going to do it anyway. She said she would do it on her own.'

'Did you believe her?'

'Yes.' They said together.

'Why shouldn't we?' asked Lynn.

'Because she told her husband she was with you.'

Angie laughed. 'Of course! He wouldn't have let her go if he'd known she was alone.'

'She did say for us to tell him that we were with her, if he asked.' Lynn added.

'And did he ask?'

They shook their heads in unison.

'I was glad,' said Angie. 'I didn't want to lie for her.'

'After letting us down like that.'

Hazel considered her notes. 'Did she get in touch during the walk or afterwards?'

'She sent a couple of postcards, didn't she Lynn?

'Have you spoken to her since?'

Lynn pulled a face. 'Actually we left it a while – reckoned if she wanted to see us she would get in touch. But after you rang I did try again and Steve told me she wasn't around. He sounded pretty upset actually. He implied that she'd left him. Is that true?'

'We're simply making a few enquiries for now. Do you know why she might want to leave him?'

The two women looked at each other.

Angie spoke first. 'We don't really know Steve to be honest. We meet up for a girls' night out, we don't involve partners. I haven't seen him since the wedding.'

'It wouldn't surprise me,' said Lynn. 'He always seemed pretty boring if you ask me.'

Before she left, Hazel asked one final question. 'Is there anyone else beside yourselves that Bea might have confided in, that I should talk to?'

There was a long pause.

'I don't think so,' said Lynn.

'Does the name Larry Wright mean anything?'

They both shook their heads. 'Now I come to think about it, we're probably the only real friends that Bea has,' said Lynn. There was another pause. 'Isn't that sad?'

Mills had opened the back door quietly, it was only just after four and barely light outside. She sat on the bench with a blanket pulled round her shoulders, hugging a mug of hot tea. Any other time she would have been joined by the wiry grey figure of Earl to keep her feet warm and share a biscuit or a piece of toast. The silence was painful and she couldn't stop herself from weeping silently as she recalled the events of the night before: waiting for the vet while Earl's breathing was getting shallower, his body limp and heavy on her legs. She was losing him, slowly but irrevocably. It was impossible to rouse him, despite their efforts to give him water. Finally she sat holding him while he drifted away. When the vet arrived it was too late. He'd driven them to the Manor on his way back to the surgery with Earl's body. There would be a post-mortem, he said and she remembered him asking her if she wanted the ashes. All she could think about now was how to tell Phil.

When Naomi came down she busied herself making toast, insisting Mills had breakfast. She disappeared up to the Manor, returning to report that her brother had been on to the keeper but no-one knew where Fergus was. Daniel was going to call the parents in Scotland to let them know that their son was in serious trouble.

Mills listened but felt nothing, not even anger at the young man who was responsible for the dog's death – it wouldn't change anything. She excused herself and went up to get ready for work. There was nothing she could do and they needed her in Harrogate.

'Are you sure you're ok?' Naomi was fussing as Mills made for the door.

She assured her friend she was fine and made a hasty exit. Somehow it was easier to cope with distance between her and Mossy Bank. She had to focus on her job and make sure the laboratory was in a fit state when Brenda returned. She had just one more week to keep everything on an even keel and at any other time she would be making sure she'd made a good impression – if Brenda was pleased with the way she'd run the lab, there might be more work for her or at least a reference.

The traffic was always bad on a Friday and she was late arriving in the office. Already there were reports to authorise and new requests to be juggled. Three new jobs had arrived involving DNA and a set of clothing from a rape victim. It was going to be a busy day – if only she didn't feel so exhausted.

Hazel sighed and exchanged glances with Mitch as Robert checked his watch for the umpteenth time.

'She'll be here. She's got to drive all the way from Lancaster. She said she wouldn't be here until between three and half-past,' she complained.

'It's three twenty-two,' Robert said, standing up and walking to the window.

'You won't see her from there.'

Hazel was irritated. She was trying to complete her report on the meeting with Angie and Lynn, and compile her thoughts for the meeting. Their resources were limited now the case had gone cold, so she would be fighting for any help with the investigation. She had plans, with things that needed to be followed up and she couldn't do it single-handed.

Robert had just returned to his seat when the door opened violently and Nina rushed in looking flustered.

'I am so sorry...'

'No problem,' reassured Hazel, glaring at Robert. 'We didn't expect you any sooner, honestly.'

'Are you happy to start straight away?' asked Mitch. 'Do you need a drink?'

Nina produced a bottle of water, seating herself at her desk expectantly.

'Right,' Mitch began, 'I want to go through any updates first then we'll review where we are with lines of enquiry.'

Hazel began with her meeting at Caffe Nero. Mitch listened, making notes in his large red book. It was a ritual which they were familiar with. Nina followed with a description of the funeral, including her meeting with Tanya's husband, although she didn't allude to his emotional outburst.

'Has any of this new intelligence moved us further forward, though?' Mitch scratched his head.

Hazel jumped at the opportunity to have her say. 'I think it proves that Mrs Egglington planned to take a holiday with our victim. She deliberately misled her husband, using her friends as a cover. She returned from that trip, went back to work and carried on as if nothing had happened. It proves she was involved with Larry Wright's death in some way.'

'Does it?' asked Mitch. 'Is it possible she didn't know he'd been killed? That he just disappears? She might not know what happened to him.'

'She'd report him missing,' Hazel responded quickly.

'Not if her husband didn't know she was with him.'

'I've been thinking about that, Detective Inspector.' Robert was leaning back in his chair. 'It's possible that she's no longer with him when he's murdered. I was looking at the crime scene on the map and there is a way it could happen if they arrive at the pub early, maybe in the afternoon. They have a drink, he goes off for a walk. She stays behind and he never returns.'

'I still don't believe she would just find her way home and ignore his disappearance,' argued Hazel.

'Honey, the woman is pregnant and, from what you say, it's unlikely to be the husband's. So she spills the good news to Wright but he wants nothing to do with her – he's got a family back home remember. She comes home and he goes on – then....'

'Then, what?' demanded Hazel, 'He's killed by Al-Qaeda?' She regretted it immediately, especially when she saw the change in Robert's expression.

'Can I ask about the connection with the army?' Nina spoke quietly. 'The women who worked with Tanya at the Support Unit are concerned about the fact that her body was found on the rifle range; they assume that the perpetrator was from the garrison. I wondered if Major Henderson had any comments on that.'

'Actually, Detective Sergeant, I agree with you. I'm concerned that both women were based at Catterick also. Pararescueman Wright should have flown out to Pakistan on a very sensitive mission by now. If details had gotten out he could have been under significant threat. What's more, if he'd spoken to either of these women in the Support Unit about his mission their lives could have been in jeopardy also.'

Hazel looked across at Nina and Mitch, who were staring at Robert. Everyone was waiting for Robert to expand on what he'd just revealed but it was clear that was all he was going to say on the matter.

'Is there anything we can do to reassure the women that they are safe?' Nina asked, looking from Mitch to Robert and back.

Mitch turned a page in his notebook. 'We need to find Mrs Egglington. At present we don't know whether she's alive. If she is, and she's in hiding, there's a reason and the sooner we locate her and find out what it is, the sooner we can put all this to bed.'

It was the opportunity Hazel had been waiting for. 'I believe Mr Egglington has been protecting his wife. I think he knew she was in trouble when she came home and he's helped her go to ground.'

'Then why would he ask us to help him find her?' asked Nina.

'Because he's realised she can't disappear forever. Maybe he heard that we'd been searching the house so he came back, pretending he'd been looking for her. Maybe he hopes we won't find her and she'll be reported missing presumed dead.'

'I still think there's a strong chance that she is. Just because we didn't find a body...'

Mitch cut Nina short. 'Ok, ok. Let's stop there. As I said, we need to know where the woman is – if she's still alive. We'll put all our effort into finding her. Hazel, you said her friends were planning to rent a cottage in Wensleydale. I want you both to focus on the area round Bolton Castle. The doctor said she was near Leyburn, which fits. And check the health centre again; the woman's pregnant, there must be things she needs, aren't there, ladies?'

Hazel laughed. 'At that stage all I did was throw up.'

Nina agreed.

'Just one last thing.' Robert's tone was serious. 'I know you don't believe that the crime is terrorist related but I will be reporting back to my senior officers and we will be making our own enquiries at the garrison.' His smiled across at Nina. 'You may assure your ladies in Catterick that we will be doing our all to protect them from any further attacks.'

'Pleased to hear it, Major.' Mitch replied, grinning at Hazel as he gathered his papers and left the room.

Robert's manner had irritated Hazel: the way he addressed Mitch as "Detective Inspector" and referred to Nina as "Detective Sergeant". When he suggested they call it a day she snapped at him. 'You can if you want to, I've got to finish my report.'

'I'll go grab some groceries,' he suggested, sounding hurt.

'You've upset him,' said Nina when they were alone.

'So? We've got work to do, if Mitch wants us to cover the cottage angle. How are you fixed this weekend?'

'I can do Sunday.'

'Not tomorrow?'

'No.'

Hazel knew better than to quiz Nina on what she was doing that was so important. It was a conversation they'd had just once before. Nina had promised Nige they would have one day a week together as a family whatever happened so she might have been persuaded to work but she knew better than to push it. Hazel on the other hand was willing to spend the day with Robert in the Yorkshire Dales if Liam was happy.

'Fine. I'll tell Robert to give me a hand to look at the area and let you know if there's anything that needs urgent attention on Sunday.'

Nina had gone by the time Robert reappeared an hour later.

'What took you so long?' Hazel asked.

'I found a wonderful grocer. I have such a treat in store for supper tonight.'

'And what makes you think I'm coming to supper?' She laughed. 'You should see your face! It's a picture.'

'So you will?'

'How could I resist? I just need to make a phone call. And I'm coming on one condition.'

'What's that?'

'That you help me have a snoop round Wensleydale tomorrow.'

'With pleasure, ma'am.'

'But what about your own investigation – at the garrison?'

'I've made some calls from my cell phone while I was out. They're going to speak with some people and get back to me on Monday. If there's anything going down they'll find out.'

'Who's "they"?'

'Just the spooks that have an eye to these things.'

Chapter 18

Mills swerved, breaking hard and stalling the engine as a police car shot out of the lane down to Ivelet Bridge. She only caught a glimpse of the driver but she could have sworn it was George Herbert. She started the car, cautiously turning off the main road, over the bridge through Ivelet and up to Mossy Bank. Harry was waiting for her, his knees almost under his chin as he sat on the step by her front door.

'Was that George who nearly ran into me?'

She asked.

'Yes, he wants to get the car out of sight. He's taken it to Muker.'

'Why?' asked Mills, waiting for Harry to get up so she could let them into the cottage.

'I'm sorry about your dog,' he said, ignoring her question and following her into the sitting room, 'It must have been a horrible experience.'

'Yes.' She unloaded her bag onto the desk: files of paperwork to keep her occupied over the weekend.

'Anyway the case has moved on,' he offered.

She stopped what she was doing, giving him her full attention. 'What's happened?'

'We got a call from your young friend...'

'Fergus?'

'No, he's lying low. No-one has seen him.'

'Gareth?'

'Yep. He rang Naomi this afternoon and she called George. Apparently Fergus has asked him to bring him some clothes and food. The plan is for them to meet at the bridge down there at eight o'clock.'

Mills automatically looked across at the clock; it was only seven fifteen.

'Does Gareth know that you know about it?'

'Oh yes – he specifically asked Naomi to tell us. He wants to help catch the bastard, if you'll excuse my French.'

'Is George coming back?' Mills imagined that Fergus would put up a good fight.

'He's waiting at the Farmers Arms for my call. He'll bring the car back to collect Fergus once I've arrested him.'

'So what will happen to him?'

'We'll take him into custody at Northallerton. He could be charged under Section 4 of the Animal Welfare Act for causing unnecessary harm but the fact that he didn't survive... sorry. He could definitely be facing a jail sentence.'

'And the poison? And the red kite?'

Harry shook his head. 'Almost impossible to prove, I would say.'

Mills made him a mug of tea while Harry described how he'd decided to train as a wildlife officer. Mills was about to offer him a biscuit when he sprang up, almost spilling his drink. 'There he goes now!'

It wasn't quite twenty to eight but Gareth was walking past the cottage with a large rucksack on his back. Mills noticed that he'd reverted to his Goth clothing; his eyes were as black as ever, his face was even paler than before.

'Must go,' called Harry as he ran out. 'I'll let you know how it goes.'

For a few minutes Mills sat looking about her. The basket in the corner, the lead in the hallway, biscuit crumbs on the mat. She jumped up and made for the door. She began walking quickly but without a plan she soon slowed her pace, considering what she should do. No-one was about so she meandered down the lane as if out for an evening stroll but as soon as the bridge came into view she knew she would have to take cover. Gareth was sitting on the bench at the curve in the lane, staring at the bridge, as if expecting Fergus to appear over it. If she crossed the road to the side of the river he would see her, so she pressed herself against the dry stone wall that marked the edge of the road to consider what to do next. The wall followed the road down to where Gareth was sitting; if she climbed over and edged along inside the field, she would be hidden from view and could get quite close to the bench. The only problem was that the wall was quite low so she would have to crouch down and scuttle along if she was not going to be observed.

After several minutes of slow, careful shuffling she had travelled as far as she could. Another wall blocked her path. If she raised her head very carefully she could see across the bridge, which meant – yes – Gareth was sitting just a few metres away on the other side of the wall. She could see his back through the gaps between the stones. Very slowly she sank down with her back to the wall and listened for any sound to indicate that Fergus had arrived. It was ten to eight and another fifteen minutes had gone by when, at last, she heard a voice calling Gareth's name.

'Over here, sunshine!' The Scottish lad's accent was unmistakeable.

Mills watched through the stones as Gareth stood up and walked over to the right of the bridge, where he disappeared down onto the footpath that followed the river through the fields to Muker. At last Mills was able to stand and stretch her legs, knowing she wouldn't be spotted. She needed to move further along to see what was happening and the only way was to climb over the obstructing wall. It was a struggle to ensure that she kept out of sight as she slid over the top, grazing her hands and landing awkwardly on the muck inside an old barn that was barely more than a corrugated iron roof on stilts. To her horror she felt a hand on her arm and let out a tiny shriek as she struggled to free herself.

'Shhh! It's only me.'

She looked round to see Harry sitting alongside her in the dirt. He held a grubby finger to his lips and pointed. From where they sat she could see directly across to where Gareth was unloading packets and tins from his rucksack while Fergus hurriedly stuffed them into his own bag.

'What happens now?' whispered Mills.

Harry let go of her arm and patted her shoulder. 'Stay here,' he ordered. 'I'm going down, there's not much time.'

Mills had no chance to ask what he intended to do. Whatever his plan, it misfired badly. Both lads looked up as they caught sight of Harry piling down the hill towards them. Fergus swiftly grabbed Gareth, putting his arm round his throat and dragging him backwards. As Harry moved towards them, Fergus produced a knife, holding it to the boy's throat. He edged away from Harry, pulling Gareth with him, until he had his back against the stone of the bridge.

'Don't come any closer or he gets it!' Fergus shouted, keeping the knife against Gareth's throat.

Mills couldn't believe he would actually carry out his threat but clearly Harry wasn't going to risk it. He held up his hands in a gesture of submission and backed away.

'Ok, ok. I'm not coming any nearer.'

Gareth stood rigidly still while Harry continued to reassure his captor that he had no intention of intervening. Fergus looked anxiously around as if trying to devise a plan for his escape. Mills reckoned he'd got himself into a corner that it was going to be difficult to extract himself from.

She didn't wait to see any more. She heaved herself back up the stonework and out of the barn. This time she clambered over the wall onto the seat by the roadside and sprinted quietly up the lane until she was halfway along the bridge. From her vantage point she could see Harry and the top of Gareth's head. She edged back down until she was directly above where Fergus was standing. Harry was telling him that he should let Gareth go; that the consequences would be more serious if he didn't release him. Without any particular plan Mills picked up a large stone and rested it on the edge of the bridge. Harry, distracted by her movement, looked up and Fergus made as if to move. Without considering the consequences she pushed the stone, watching it drop directly onto his head. He fell to the ground taking Gareth with him.

Harry instantly ran forward, grabbing the knife and helping Gareth extract himself from under the motionless Fergus. Mills, horrified at what she'd done, ran down to join Harry who was leaning over the inert body.

'Is he all right?' she asked.

Harry grinned. 'No thanks to you – he's breathing; I reckon he'll be ok. Anything larger and you could've smashed his skull.'

'Don't! I don't know what I was thinking.'

'You saved my life,' said Gareth.

'That's a bit strong, but it certainly eased the situation.' Harry laughed. 'Can you get a signal here? I can't.'

Gareth handed over his mobile and Harry called George to leave the "Farmers Arms" and drive over to collect the fugitive, who was beginning to show signs of life.

'Just stay where you are, young man,' Harry instructed him. 'You're not going anywhere.' He turned to Gareth. 'Did he tell you where he'd been staying?'

'Sleeping rough, he said.'

'Well, he'll have a good night's sleep in custody tonight.'

'I want a doctor,' moaned Fergus.

'There's a very nice doctor who works for the police over in Northallerton,' said Mills. 'Gareth's aunt, Naomi. I think you've met her already. She'll make sure you're well looked after I'm certain.'

Fergus lay cursing them all in turn while Gareth and Harry restrained him. It wasn't long before they heard the police car approaching and Mills ran out to show George where they were.

'Well, well, well, who have we here?' George was clearly enjoying the situation. 'Is it the brave young man who enjoys killing defenceless animals. Feeling trapped now are we?'

Mills was relieved when Harry pulled Fergus to his feet, suggesting they take him in. The two officers escorted Fergus to their car and locked him in the back while Mills and Gareth looked on.

George came back to warn Gareth that they'd need a statement from him in due course. But then, to his obvious relief, Harry thanked him for his help and told him he was free to go. Then he came over to Mills and took her hand.

'Don't forget we're having dinner at the "Farmers Arms" tomorrow – if that's all right. I reckon I owe you for saving the day. It could have been quite a nasty outcome without your intervention. Mind you, let's hope he doesn't charge you with assault!' he added with a wink.

Mills accompanied Gareth back to the Manor. She felt it was her duty to help the boy explain the events of the evening. It was worth it to see the expression on his parents' faces when her son reached the part where Mills dropped a rock from the bridge. Penny looked horrified but Daniel was impressed and said they must take her out to dinner some time to thank her for saving their son from that nasty boy.

'I suppose we should call his parents to let them know what's happened,' suggested Daniel.

'I want nothing to do with them again,' announced Penny, shuddering in mock horror. 'I didn't really like them when I first met them,'

Daniel raised his eyebrows and shook his head.

'Well, I just wanted you to know that Gareth has been a real help. You should be proud of him,' Mills said.

'You don't have to come, you know.' Hazel wasn't sure that Robert would be a good companion on her trip to Wensleydale. So far he'd seemed only interested in the investigation if it concerned the garrison.

'I wouldn't miss it for the world, sweetie,' he called from the bathroom. The buzzing of the electric razor stopped and he appeared at the bedroom door. 'No, really, I mean it. I honestly want to help.'

Hazel had agreed the night before that they could make a leisurely start, allowing Robert to prepare pancakes for breakfast. It was a beautiful morning and she'd laid the table in the tiny overgrown garden. Already it was almost too hot to sit out in comfort.

'The maple syrup should be heated,' complained Robert.

'It's quite warm enough and you'd better take it in soon, we're attracting wasps.'

They left promptly at ten, taking the route to Castle Bolton through Masham. Hazel leaned back into the seat, enjoying the wind in her hair and the sun on the back of her neck, wishing only that she had brought sunglasses. She directed Robert to the health centre in Leyburn and then on to the chemists shop but no-one she spoke to had met Beatrice Egglington.

'We might as well start at Castle Bolton and work out,' she suggested.

The car park for Bolton Castle was busy with visitors examining the ruins and wandering along the single street of houses that made up the village of Castle Bolton. Hazel suggested she tried a few of the cottages.

'You'd better stay here,' she said as Robert locked the car.

'No way – I'm not missing out on the fun,' he said amiably.

So together they knocked on doors and talked to villagers in their gardens as they tidied their flowerbeds. No-one had seen the woman in the artist's impression.

'D'you think it looks at all like her?' Robert asked as they made their way back towards the car.

'Witnesses who saw her on the Coast to Coast path said so,' Hazel answered sharply. It was going to be a long day if Robert was going to question everything she did.

'I was just asking. Say, shall we take in the castle while we're here? It looks really old.'

'We don't have time.'

'We have time for coffee, surely?'

Hazel sighed. 'Ok, if it's quick.'

There were several free tables in the teashop and Robert ordered for them both. Hazel, reluctant to waste time, wandered over to a member of staff and showed her the picture.

'Would you or any of your colleagues have seen this woman?' she asked after showing her warrant card.

The girl took the paper, scrutinising it for a while then shook her head. 'I can show it to the girls in the kitchen,' she offered.

'If you would.'

She disappeared and Hazel returned to where Robert was waiting. Their coffee was brought in by another young woman who was carrying the picture of Beatrice Egglington.

'You asked about this woman,' she said as she transferred the cups from her tray.

'Yes, have you seen her?'

'I'm not sure. She looks a bit like her but the hair's different. She's got short hair, dyed like deep black. But her nose is similar.'

'And where have you seen her?'

'In here. She's been coming for the last week or more – several times this week. She spends ages over a pot of tea. She was here nearly all afternoon yesterday.'

'Is she always on her own?'

'Yes. Looks rather lonely.'

'Do you know where she comes from?'

The girl shrugged. 'No. I suppose she's a visitor – unless she's moved in locally. I reckon she must be quite local to walk here like she does.'

'How d'you know she walks?'

'I saw her once – when I was coming on shift. She was coming along past the cottages. She wouldn't come that way from the car park, would she?'

Hazel handed her one of her cards. 'If she comes in again today, or any time, please call me.'

The girl grinned and carried the empty tray back to the kitchen.

'So do we just wait for a call now?' Robert asked.

'No way! She might not be the Mrs Egglington anyway. As soon as you've drunk your coffee we'll move on to Redmire; it's the nearest place from here. After that it's Carperby. I'm not convinced she's got to be on foot but, assuming she's not driving, there aren't too many places within walking distance.'

They found Redmire very much bigger than Castle Bolton with far more houses. They drew a blank at the pub then spoke to some locals but it was obvious that Hazel would have to muster the troops to cover a house-to-house properly. She was becoming quite frustrated, knowing that if Nina was there they would have devised a sensible plan between them.

'What about this other place?' Robert asked. 'Carperby? Is that far?'

'No, not far. There's a pub there we could just pop in to ask.'

'Sounds like a plan. I'm getting pretty ravenous. Does your MO include eating sometime today?'

They ordered a very late lunch at "The Wheatsheaf" and discussed their total lack of progress.

'It's not surprising,' remarked Robert. 'There are so many places for people to go hereabouts. Cottages hidden round every corner. She's unlikely to visit the local hostelry if she's on her own and keeping a low profile.'

'And if she's pregnant she won't be after a drink, that's for sure.'

'There's always tomorrow.'

But Hazel had made a decision about the rest of the weekend. She had to get back for Liam later that day and Nina was free to join her the following day.

'Robert, Nina is working tomorrow. I said I'd help her. D'you mind?'

He shrugged. 'No, not if you need to help her. I can join you if you want.'

'Best not, eh?'

They enjoyed a leisurely meal before Robert drove her back to the cottage to pick up her car. As they parted, Hazel promised to get in touch before the weekend was over.

'What will *you* do tomorrow, Robert?'

'I guess I'll go deal with paperwork at Catterick later.'

'Ok. I'll call your mobile.'

'Cellphone,' he corrected her.

'We call them mobile phones over here.'

Mills had been dreading the weekend without Earl but she'd underestimated her friends. Naomi rang first thing to let her know that she'd seen Fergus in custody. She delighted in telling Mills about his sore head.

'I'm ashamed to say it was very satisfying to lob that rock onto his head but...'

'Never fear – there's no permanent damage,' Naomi reassured her. 'I just wanted to thank you for sorting poor Gareth out. He's such a nice lad but so easily led astray. By the way, I hear you're meeting Harry this evening.'

'How d'you know that?'

'He's a really nice guy, Mills. You know he was commended for saving a man from a burning car a couple of years ago?'

'No, I don't really know him at all.'

'I think he's really into the wildlife training. He's quite a sensitive bloke. Anyway, you'll no doubt find out. Have a good time and tell all about it!'

Mills had hardly had time to make toast before the phone rang again; this time it was Nina.

'Mills, I heard about Earl. You must be in pieces. Can I come over? I'll bring Rosie – we can go shopping or just hang out. It's a nice day for it.'

Mills quizzed Nina to ensure she could spare the time but she insisted she wanted a day out in the country while Nige marked some dissertations.

'All right then, Nina. Come over as soon as you like. I'll make a picnic and we'll take Rosie to the river.'

And that was how she spent the day: playing with Nina's daughter and paddling in the Swale to keep cool. Nina brought some special treats: strawberries and wine. As the afternoon wore on, Mills wondered how to tactfully tell Nina that she was going to the pub that evening. But she needn't have worried.

'I need to take Rosie back soon,' she began. 'Are you doing anything later?'

Her vague statement that she *might* be going out later resulted in loud laughter from her friend.

'When were you going to say anything, Mills?'

'What?'

'About going out with Harry?'

'How do *you* know?'

At first she pretended she wouldn't say but then she admitted that she'd asked Naomi to keep in touch about Earl and she'd let it slip.

'Everyone seems to know about it,' complained Mills, 'and it's not like it's a date, really.'

But actually, Mills admitted to herself when Nina had taken Rosie home, it was like a date. She was really nervous and spent ages getting ready, changing her clothes three times. She put on too much makeup and removed most of it again. At last she sat on the sofa waiting until it was just the right time so she wouldn't arrive too early or too late. At exactly seven twenty-five she left the cottage and drove the short distance to Muker, spending a while in the car before braving the pub.

There were several groups of walkers sitting in the sunshine outside. Harry was not among them. She went through the open door and into the bar. The tables were full with families and couples eating but there was no sign of Harry. Should she buy herself a drink and sit awkwardly at the bar or wander outside and wait, braving the groups of drinkers watching her? Preferring the former option she was waiting to be served when she felt a light touch on her shoulder.

'Hi. I'm sorry. I got stuck behind a tractor most of the way here. I realised after I should have picked you up from your house.'

'It's ok. Let me buy you a drink.'

He hesitated, as if weighing up whether it was politer to refuse the offer and insist on buying or accept. Too late, Mills asked the barman for an alcoholic ginger beer and turned to Harry.

'Old Peculier?'

'I'm driving, better make it a half of Black Sheep.'

They studied the menu and Harry ordered while they waited for a free table. He asked her about how she came to be doing forensic work when she was an archaeologist and she explained how she'd helped in some cases in the past. She sensed he was impressed. When a table became available they took their drinks and settled down comfortably while Mills asked about Harry's career in the police force.

'Nothing very interesting about that,' he replied, looking down at his beer. 'My dad was a copper and I followed in his footsteps. I didn't enjoy school very much and left as soon as I could. It seemed the best route. It's what Dad wanted, anyway.'

Mills noted he spoke of his father in the past tense.

'I bet he was proud of you.'

'Yep.' He picked up his glass and took a mouthful of beer.

He told her a little about his training days until they were interrupted by their meals arriving. Mills noticed that Harry had deftly managed to turn the conversation back to her career again and much of the evening was spent with her recounting her archaeological investigations which he appeared to find fascinating.

At ten o'clock Mills asked if they might go. She was exhausted by her busy day and the events of the previous evening. Harry understood, escorting her back to her car, waiting patiently while she searched in her bag for the keys. She was unsure what would happen next but he simply kissed her on the cheek, saying he hoped they might meet again soon? She agreed it had been a lovely evening, perhaps he would ring her? He waited beside the car until she drove off, giving a wave as she left. When she got home there was a message on her phone: it was Harry saying he hoped she'd got home safely and could he come round tomorrow afternoon?

Chapter 19

'So how was your day with Robert yesterday?' Nina asked her friend as they drove across to Wensleydale.

'I told you, it was a waste of time. That's why I want to make progress today.'

'I meant with *Robert*. You two are spending a lot of time together. Is it serious?'

'Of course not,' Hazel snapped. 'He goes away next week.'

Nina knew when to back off. 'I took Rosie to see Mills yesterday,' she began and spent the rest of the journey telling Hazel about how Mills had lost her dog. She knew her friend would be interested in how the Scottish lad had been apprehended.

'She sounds like one of the sisterhood, your friend Mills,' Hazel conceded. 'He deserved a good whack on the head!'

They spent the rest of the journey deciding on a plan of action for the day. Hazel wanted to narrow the search by questioning the staff at Bolton Castle again. It was possible that someone else had seen the mystery woman who frequented the tearoom in the village or further afield.

It was too early on a Sunday morning for visitors to be arriving, so the car park was empty except for a young couple who were putting on their walking boots before striding off in the direction of Aysgarth. Nina stretched, breathing in the fresh air, enjoying a sense of freedom from the office and, yes she admitted it, from the home.

Her friend was impatient. 'Come on Nina, we haven't got all day!'

The entrance to the tearoom was locked and, after knocking for a good minute, they were about to give up when the sound of bolts being withdrawn was followed by the creaking of the old hinges. The puzzled girl was explaining politely that they were shut when Hazel produced her warrant card and Nina followed her example.

A few minutes later they were seated with mugs of coffee while the girl continued to look for her boss. It took half an hour to establish that no-one had seen the woman in the past three days.

'So there's a good chance she might come in today?' suggested Hazel enthusiastically.

Nina was dubious. 'Are you suggesting we hang about on the off chance that she'll magically appear?'

'What's your suggestion then?' Hazel challenged her. 'D'you want to cruise around the lanes looking for her?' She could sound cruel when she was being sarcastic.

Nina always accepted her friend's suggestions, not for the reason that she was always right but because it made for a quieter life. 'All right then. Do we sit here or roam the grounds?' She giggled. 'Like spectres haunting the castle?'

'Don't be daft, Nina. We'll sit in the car park and watch for her – when we've finished the coffee. I thought I might have something to eat... it's been a long time since breakfast.'

Armed with sandwiches for later, Nina followed Hazel back to the car. She switched on the radio and they sat for several hours watching families arriving to visit the castle. Hazel wandered down to the gardens to stretch her legs, returning to take over while Nina had a stroll down the village street. She was beginning to think that Hazel's plan was a long shot when she spotted a woman who stood out like a sore thumb. She was dressed peculiarly formally in a pleated skirt and long-sleeved blouse, which made Nina think she could be a church-goer. But it was the jet-black hair against the pale complexion that made her stare. The woman kept her eyes lowered as they passed but Nina could sense a nervousness, a frailty that alerted her. She bent down, pretending to tie her shoelace so she could watch the woman's progress. As Nina expected, she walked steadily past the church, making for the door at the back of the castle that led to the tearoom.

As soon as the figure disappeared, Nina raced towards the car park. Hazel must have spotted the woman because she was coming to meet Nina.

'Is it her?' called Nina.

'If she's cut her hair short and dyed it black it could be. Shall we go in?'

'No, Hazel. Wait. She seemed, well... rather edgy. She noticed me.'

'Who wouldn't in a place like this?'

It was rare for any of her colleagues to comment on her ethnic origins and Nina had to remind herself sometimes that she did look different from the rest of the local population.

'Let's face it, girlfriend,' Hazel continued, 'anyone would notice you out here.'

'Ok, I'll stay in the car.'

'Don't worry, Nina, I'm not going to rush up to her and accuse her of being Bea Egglington, I'll just observe her. When she leaves we can follow in the car.'

Nina was happy to sit and wait quietly. It was lunch time and she envisaged Nige feeding Rosie, a spoon in one hand, TV remote in the other. There would be motor racing or some other sporting event to distract him, despite his assurances that he had "loads of marking" to finish. She watched families come and go, anticipating the day when Rosie would enjoy visiting castles, exploring the countryside, growing up into an adventurous young woman. But her daydreams were interrupted by the sight of Hazel heading full pelt towards the car. She swung open the door, flinging herself into the driver's seat.

'What's the matter?'

'She's leaving. I managed to get out while she was in the "Ladies". I tried having a friendly chat – one single woman tourist to another – but she made her excuses and left. I think I may have spooked her.'

Nina was about to reprimand her colleague when she stopped; the woman had emerged and was making her way down the stone steps and heading back up the street.

'Where's that map?' Hazel asked.

Nina pulled the ordnance survey from her bag and they examined the likely route she would take.

'I reckon she must be staying in Redmire.' Hazel sounded confident.

They waited until the diminutive figure had travelled the length of the village street and disappeared from view. Hazel drove slowly until they could see her once more then pulled up to wait again. And so they progressed to the end of the village.

'So far so good,' said Nina. 'Now she has to go as far as the road to Redmire. I'm going to sit it out for a while.'

'What if she turns off?' Nina asked.

'She won't.'

Nina found the wait unbearable, eventually insisting they continued.

'See, there she is. Now stop fussing, woman.'

Another wait, but this time when they reached a road coming in from the left. There was no sign of her.

'Damn.'

'I told...'

'Don't say it. She's not down that way – she must have gone up here.' Hazel swung the car up the road and continued a normal speed.

'There!' shouted Nina, 'I just saw her running down there.'

Hazel swung the car left onto a rough track and put her foot down as the woman disappeared into a solitary cottage at the end of the narrow lane. The noise of stones rattling under the car was deafening.

'Shall we go in after her?' asked Hazel, stretching to collect her bag from the back seat.

'Shouldn't we contact Mitch first?' Nina hated how indecisive that sounded.

To her surprise, Hazel agreed. 'You're probably right – as usual. He'll need to know what's happening. That's if she *is* Beatrice Egglington.'

Hazel tried calling on her mobile but there was no signal. Nina's was no better.

Hazel started the engine with a sigh. 'We passed a box in Redmire this morning.'

Nina climbed out and stood beside the car while Hazel made the call. The place was silent except for the birdsong. It was as if nothing could possibly be wrong on such a beautiful day... but inside that cottage was a woman who may have killed twice. Once out of extreme emotion perhaps but the second time – in cold blood.

Hazel was grinning when she reappeared. 'All systems go, kiddo. He says bring her in, whoever she is. No – only joking! If it's Mrs Egglington pick her up and bring her into Northallerton.'

They drove slowly back down the track to the cottage only to be confronted by another vehicle coming towards them.

'That's the husband,' shouted Hazel.

The car screeched to a halt and Egglington jumped out, running in the opposite direction.

'Where does that go?' shouted Nina.

'Just onto the moors. Shall I go?'

'No way, not alone. Let's just think about this for a second.' Nina sat rigid faced. 'Ok... the first thing is to make sure the other one doesn't get away.'

Hazel ran towards the cottage, Nina following. The door was open and inside on the sofa sat the woman with the black hair.

'Are you Beatrice Egglington?' demanded Hazel, trying to recover her breath.

'Yes.' The woman was ashen-faced. 'Thank goodness you've come.'

'Nina, stay here. I'm going to call Mitch again. We need back-up fast. Where's the phone?'

The woman pointed to the hallway. Nina sat beside her and did her best to calm her down. In the hall, Hazel was shouting and cursing into the phone.

'I thought he was going to kill me,' the woman sobbed.

A minute later Hazel burst back into the room, red in the face. 'I can't reach Mitch but I've called Robert. He said he'd try to get hold of him. He's ringing back in the next half hour.'

'He could be gone by then,' Nina said.

'I know but if he's hiding out, hoping we go away, it might work. I'll have a drive round to check he doesn't pop out onto the road. You stay here.'

Nina followed Hazel out onto the lane. 'I'll take a statement while you're gone,' she said.

Back inside, the woman said her name was Beatrice Avril Egglington and confirmed her address.

'In your own words,' coaxed Nina.

She began quietly. 'Larry and I met at the garrison when I visited a family from the States. They were having a barbecue and I stayed for lunch. There was wine and one thing led to another. It shouldn't have happened but it did. Except that I thought that was all it was – a foolish mistake. But he came to see me at work, brought me flowers, took me out and treated me like I was somebody. He told me he would be going away soon – it seemed like we would have just a short time together. That's when Lynn told me about Angie's cancer and said we wouldn't be doing our walking holiday. I thought it wouldn't harm to go with Larry instead. Steve wouldn't know any different.'

'So how did Steve find out?'

'He met the husband of a friend of mine in the pub when I was away and he found out about Angie undergoing treatment. He must've put two and two together because he turned up out of the blue as we were arriving at Blakey Ridge.'

She clutched the tissue in both hands.

'He came along the path towards us, smiling and waving. Larry asked who he was but by then he'd reached us. He walked right up to us and he was shaking Larry's hand but when Steve stepped back he fell to the ground and I could see the blood...'

She burst into loud, heart-wrenching sobs.

'I've been over and over it in my head, every day. I thought he was going to kill me. He made me help him drag Larry into the heather and leave him. I said

I couldn't do that but he said I must. He took me to the pub where Larry had booked a pitch for the night. He bought a bottle of whisky and he drank most of it in the hours until it got dark.'

'What happened then?'

'Steve said he wanted Larry to be found further down the path to protect me in case the police found out I was with him on the Coast to Coast walk. He said if Larry was found after the Blakey Ridge stop we could prove I wasn't with him then, that Steve and I had been together at the pub.'

She took a sip of water.

'We drove home on Monday. I didn't even get dressed the following days. I just sat in bed switching between the main channels, watching the 24 hour news. Not that there was much on the stabbing – that's what they called it. The stabbing of a young man on the North York Moors. They showed maps with arrows indicating where he'd been discovered.

Steve went off to work as if nothing had happened. He told me to behave normally, go to the gym as usual – see a friend for lunch. But it was all I could do to drag myself to the bathroom. Then he arrived home from work early with an expensive bunch of flowers: roses, lilies and spiky blue heads, saying he thought we could eat out. I couldn't do it, so he ordered a takeaway. He told me not to worry, that everything would be fine. It was as if what had happened on the Moors had been erased forever. He even used Larry's phone to send a message to his base saying he was taking extra leave to prevent them from looking for him.'

She stared out of the window across the fields, as if struggling to recall every aspect of the days following the murder.

'Finally it was there in black and white – the artist's impression. It was almost as good as a photograph. I would have been flattered in other circumstances. Steve had left the newspaper unopened at breakfast; he was in such a rush to get away that morning. He spent as much time out of the house as he could now; off to the garrison early in the morning, arriving home late, often not until closing time, leaving me to mope around the house feeling sick. He thought I was making myself ill with the worry – he still doesn't know I'm pregnant. I was sure someone would recognise my picture soon enough. I just wished I'd not mentioned that I wanted to do that damn walk. All my friends knew I wanted to, even if they didn't know I was actually doing it.'

'But you had to go back to work?'

'I knew I would have to go back sooner or later and I wondered if it would seem odd if I had my hair cut short and coloured. In the end I had it really short, even shorter than this.' She ran her fingers through the black cropped hair. 'Steve drove me in on my first day back at work. He said that they'd be so busy commenting on my new hair style, he doubted they'd be interested in what I'd been up to. As usual, he was right. Tanya was out on a visit and everyone else was so busy. I'd gone through to lunch time without anyone even commenting on my hair. Then it was only the old bat from finance when we'd passed in the corridor. Eileen, was eating her packed lunch in the office, which made my nausea worse so I went for a walk round the building to pass the time. There was a team meeting in the afternoon to discuss the new software system for purchasing. It was a bit irrelevant since I rarely ordered anything except the odd bit of stationery for the boss. But it meant I could sit without speaking; which was good because I was still shaking slightly inside.

So it wasn't until I was outside the building waiting for Steve that I finally met Tanya, arriving back from her appointment. She laughed and said "Wow, look at you. I hardly recognised you." Then she stared at me for a bit and asked why I dyed it black. Why so short and so black.'

Bea was shaking visibly now.

'She was asking lots of questions. Did I have a good time? Where did I go? What was the weather like? I was praying that Steve's car would come round the corner to save me from Tanya's incessant questions. Then she said something about looking tanned and had I been camping? She said she thought she'd seen me. I didn't wait to hear. I ran towards the entrance to the car park. She was still shouting after me when I saw Steve's car.'

She took a sip of water.

'Did you speak to her after that?'

She put the glass down and straightened her back.

'I did. She rang me that evening. I was so shocked I could hardly hold the phone. She said she'd seen me in Kirkby Stephen with Larry Wright. Before I could deny it she said I was to meet her at Black Beck ranges at nine o'clock and put the phone down. I didn't even know where Black Beck ranges was so I told Steve and he said he would go. I was to stay at home. So I did. He came back very late and wouldn't discuss what had happened.

I went in to work the next day and waited at my desk for Tanya to appear. Steve assured me there would be no trouble from her now; but he wouldn't elaborate on what had gone on between them. I knew it was foolish of me not to want to meet up with

Tanya but when Steve offered to go instead I felt such an immense sense of relief. He always knew exactly what to say. But by coffee time there was still no sign of her. Then it was lunch-time so I went down to check that Tanya wasn't due out on any visits that morning. It wasn't until Noleen came down from Finance that I heard how Tanya had been found.... I must have fainted, at least I was lying on the floor with my legs being held up on a chair by Dot. They fetched water and rang Steve.' She stopped for a minute to regain her composure, dabbing her pale face with a tissue. 'I couldn't stop crying even when he came to collect me. He just said get in the car and calm yourself down.'

'What happened then?' Hazel asked gently.

'He said we'll just pack what we need for a few days. I just lay on the bed and told him what to take from the wardrobe. If I tried to sit up I felt sick, so I lay propped up on two pillows, answering yes or no as he held up items of clothing. He said "I've found a holiday cottage that's available for at least a month. We can stay there until you feel better. When you're up to it we'll sell the house and move abroad. We could go to France, you'd like that; all that French cuisine, just up your street. I could brush up on the lingo – you'd have to speak for both of us to begin with, wouldn't you?" He actually laughed.'

She stared into the distance for a few seconds.

'Steve booked the cottage at the pub in Redmire; he paid in cash for a month in advance. I discovered later that he'd told them I'd had a nervous breakdown and the doctor said I should have rest and quiet. The owner has been very sympathetic.'

'Did you ever ask about what happened between him and Tanya?'

'No but I knew that he'd guessed that I'd drawn my own conclusions. It was a barrier between us that hadn't been there before. It wasn't that I was more frightened of him – I saw what he was capable of when he killed Larry – but I knew then that he could do it again, possibly more than twice. He was a different person then. He'd taken control of both our lives: what we ate, when we slept, when we watched TV. He didn't allow me to leave the cottage after that but went on shopping trips alone, returning with food and a fresh supply of books, magazines and DVDs to occupy our time. When it rained we sat in the cottage, if the sun shone we perched on dining chairs in the back yard, reading. What little conversation we had was polite and only when necessary. I never dared ask how long we would stay. Steve controlled my contact with the outside world and I wasn't even allowed to watch the news on TV. It was as if it had never happened and I knew that if I was his next victim, it would be the same.'

At this point she broke down and sobbed silently.

Hazel backed the car up the lane, turning uphill towards the open moorland. She couldn't second guess him and there were several routes of escape: he could have doubled back to reach the main road, perhaps hoping to get a lift from a passer-by. There was the railway line at Redmire, if he was lucky there might be a train full of visitors waiting to return to Leyburn or as far as Leeming Bar. She scanned the moors for signs of movement but soon gave up and returned to the cottage just in time to see an army wagon trundling up the road.

Hazel jumped out of the car, indicating for the lorry to stop. As it drew up in front of her, Robert jumped out and began sorting the men into groups of three or four. With Hazel's advice they were sent off in different directions to cover the main road, the station and the uplands.

'It's pretty hopeless with so few men,' Hazel commented when they had gone.

'I've asked for another twenty as soon as they can raise them,' Robert assured her. 'The instant they've confirmed the roads and station are clear they'll leave a guard and come back to join the parties out on the hills. I guess it's the place he's most likely to hunker down.'

She ran back to the cottage to tell Nina what was happening but her friend was anxious to speak to her. Drawing her into the kitchen she was looking at the woman weeping on the sofa all the time she was talking.

'It's the husband,' she said. 'He killed the boyfriend – she's given me all the details. He killed the woman because she'd seen Wright and his wife together. He sounds pretty cold-blooded.'

'Are you all right here?' Hazel asked.

'Of course. I'll stay here with her until someone brings a car. The important thing is to catch her husband.'

'I'll call in for back-up. If he's on the fells we need to find him before nightfall.'

She still couldn't get an answer from Mitch but she rang more numbers until she was promised that there would be officers with her in the next couple of hours.

'It'll be too late,' Hazel complained when she replaced the receiver. 'I'll go with Robert to organise more army lads.'

Robert introduced her to the two soldiers who were co-ordinating communications.

'They're gonna come with me so I can control the search,' he said, about to leave.

'Hey, wait for me! It is *my* investigation, remember?' she told him when she caught up.

'Don't you need to be with your friend? That woman could be responsible for Wright's death.'

'No, she's told Nina that her husband killed Wright and Stewart.'

He stopped and turned. 'In that case, honey, it's dangerous. You should stay here.'

'No way. I'm coming with you.'

They marched on in silence, Hazel silently cursing that she'd not worn walking boots. She was having difficulty keeping up with the others but was determined not to be left behind.

It was an exhausting afternoon. Robert took total control of the search, barking orders to the communications guys who transmitted them to the groups who were now all focussed on the moor. After a couple of hours the armed police arrived and took control of the roads around Redmire, ensuring that Egglington could not escape that way, unless he'd already obtained a lift out of the area. By the end of the afternoon, troops were fanned out across the fells and the whirr of a helicopter confirmed that the police were also in the skies above.

'Once night falls we'll have to go back down.' Robert was looking tired. 'The guys in the chopper will use the heat intensity camera at night so it won't help to have us all crawling about up here.'

Hazel agreed reluctantly and, after a further hour of slow progress through the heather, Robert gave careful instructions to the troops to return to Redmire forming a cordon around the village – just in case he was hiding in an outbuilding. In the distance Hazel could see men moving down the fell, a fan of inky figures in the dusk.

It was almost dark when the soldiers began congregating in the village. A handful of police officers joined them and Hazel learned that Nina was already on her way to Northallerton with Mrs Egglington in a police vehicle. Behind her, Robert was busy barking orders, commanding the troops to search the area.

'Check every barn, henhouse and sheep-pen,' he was calling.

Then he turned to join her as she leaned against the stone wall outside the cottage where Bea Egglington had been hiding.

'Your Chief Inspector is in the cottage,' he informed her. 'He's drinking tea,' he added disparagingly.

Hazel went straight in to meet him, without comment. There was nothing wrong with tea, she thought. In fact it was an excellent idea. She passed the officers gathered at the front of the house and marched in to find Mitch with two co-ordinating officers inside. He held up his hand to stop the chatter and smiled at her.

'Good job, DS Fuller. Any news from your Major?'

'No, sir. Is that tea?'

She went into the kitchen and sank down on a chair. Mitch poured her a mug of tea, adding milk and stirring it before handing it over.

'Seriously well done. Nina got me up to speed before she left. Bloody shame he shot off like that.'

'Yes, guv.'

'We've put a call out – they'll find him if he tries to leave the area.'

'The army lads have been searching the village, for what it's worth.'

'Well, he's a cool character, he might still be around. We'll maintain a presence overnight, anyway.'

'What about the army, sir?'

'Major Henderson seems to be enjoying himself, perhaps we should let him carry on playing soldiers.'

He grinned at her and she allowed herself a smile. It was true, but she rather liked the decisive, mature man she'd seen that evening.

'You'd better be getting off, Hazel. You've been on the case all day.'

'It's all right, sir. I'd like to stay and see it through.'

'In that case, take a rest. I need you to be awake if anything does kick off. There's some food in the fridge.'

She splashed her face with cold water, made herself a cheese sandwich and another mug of tea. Partially refreshed, she wandered out onto the track and down the road. Voices called from various directions and the occasional dog barked. Torches flashed then disappeared. She went back to the cottage, thinking that a quick nap would mean she'd be brighter when she was needed again.

She didn't know how long she'd dozed but woke suddenly as if disturbed by a sound. At first she couldn't work out where she was and remained prostrate on the sofa peering about her. She struggled up and lurched towards the window, thinking that Mitch might have returned. Outside, her eye was drawn to a sudden flash of light coming from

Egglington's car. She was out of the door before she remembered she'd taken off her shoes. The stones cut into her feet but she barely noticed as she ran to the car.

Egglington leapt back when he saw her and tried to climb over the wall beside him. He was caught on the barbed wire and struggled, cursing as he tried to free the sleeve of his shirt. There was a ripping sound and he fell back into the lane. Hazel was on top of him but he was a strong opponent and soon she lost her grip. He tried to scramble over the wall again, allowing her time to drag herself back to a standing position and make a lunge at him. For what seemed to be several minutes he fought to escape as she hung onto his leg. It gave her time to wrench out a wooden stake that was holding the wire in place. As soon as she'd freed it, she held it as high as she could and brought it down on his head. He slumped down to the ground and lay there looking up at her, his face contorted in the light from the cottage window.

'That was a bit silly – coming back here,' said Hazel, catching her breath. 'Did you forget something?'

He didn't answer.

'Steven Egglington, I am arresting you on suspicion of the murder of Larry Wright and Tanya Stewart. You do not have to say anything...'

'I came back for this,' he said, pointing a small pistol at her.

Chapter 20

She stood over him, weighing up the likelihood that the gun was loaded. It wasn't a risk she was willing to take – she had Liam to consider. She tried not to panic. Think what they said on the course, she thought. *Keep him talking*.

'Your wife said you killed Larry Wright. Was that because they were having an affair? I think you had a right to feel jealous. I would have done but you can't kill people for that, Steve. There wouldn't be many left would there?' She knew her laughter wasn't convincing. 'What did Bea do when it happened? Why didn't she shop you?'

'She knew I'd swear she'd done it. What do they call it – a *crime passionel*?'

'Because of the baby?'

'It was our baby. She knew it. We could have been a very happy family.'

'What about Tanya, Steve? What did *she* do to upset you?'

He shifted himself into a sitting position, still aiming the gun at her. She leaned back slowly to rest against the car; her legs were shaking so hard she feared she might fall.

'She was supposed to be a friend of Bea's but she was trying to blackmail her. She'd seen her with him and tried to get money from her to keep quiet.'

'Is that why you killed her?'

'She was threatening to ring "Crimestoppers".'

He pushed himself up the wall into a standing position and walked towards her.

'Get in the car.'

'What?'

'I said, get in the car. You're my ticket out of here.' He opened the car door with his spare hand and waved at her to get in.

Hazel's feet felt like lead as he grabbed her arm, pushing her into the car. There was an explosion behind her and for a second she thought he'd shot her. But Egglington loosened his grip and fell backwards cursing. She turned her head to see him on the ground holding his leg with one hand. She stayed motionless with her back to him as soon as she saw that the gun was still in his other hand.

'Are you ok, honey?' The accent was unmistakable. 'Take it easy, Egglington. I've got you covered.' Hazel stood transfixed as he moved slowly towards the man on the ground. There was a second shot and this time she spun round to see Egglington's body flat on his back. He'd been shot in the face.

One look at Robert showed that he was as shocked as she was. She searched his face for an explanation but there was none.

'What happened, Robert? Tell me.'

'He shot himself.' Was he telling her what had happened or what he wanted her to see had happened? 'The important thing is that you're safe.'

Soon the place was full of people and Hazel gave a brief report to Mitch before Robert insisted he drive her home.

'No, really, I'm fine. I just need to get back... for Liam,' she lied.

'Glyn! Has anyone seen Glyn?'

A technician pointed to the storeroom in the corner of the laboratory. Mills opened the door carefully, closing it behind her.

'Glyn!'

'Yes.' He didn't bother to turn round.

'I've got some good news... about the hair we thought had got mixed up.'

He put down his notebook, turned and waited with his arms folded. His face was sullen, as usual.

'The blonde hair on Larry Wright and the short black hair on Tanya Stewart *were* the same DNA.'

'How?'

'Nina, I mean Police HQ rang through to say they've found the killer.'

'So it *was* a woman?'

'No. They're his wife's hairs. She cut and dyed it to hide her identity. So it wasn't a mistake by the lab.' She smiled triumphantly, hoping for a positive response from him.

He nodded. 'Good,' he muttered.

'And I've got three bullets here, please can you confirm whether this one marked A is the same as B or C. B and C should definitely be different – they come from different guns.'

As she opened the door to leave, he said, 'Odd the hairs came from the wife when we didn't get anything from him.'

Mills pondered this as she went back to her office and when she called Nina with the results of the bullet comparison, she asked about the man's hairstyle.

'What on earth do you want to know that for?' her friend asked.

When Mills explained, Nina sounded worried. 'You think it could mean that it was the wife that killed them? It seems very unlikely since she blamed him and he admitted it.' There was a pause.

'Anyway, he had a crew cut – you know, very short, like all the army types.'

'Well that probably explains why we didn't find any loose hairs from him. I just wondered.'

'Mills, can you send me the written report on the bullets by e-mail. I know there's quite a lot riding on this.'

'Ok.'

'One last thing – it's nothing to do with work. You said your dad rented Naomi's cottage for a few days. Do you think she might let us stay in it? I've got several days leave now the case is over and I thought...'

'Of course, I'm sure she would. Give her a call.'

Hazel woke late with a bad head. Too little food and too much vodka had left her feeling sick and depressed. Liam knew she was on late shift so had left a note to say he would be at Gran's if she needed him. She looked at the ceiling, going over the events of the night before. The shot followed by the look of horror on Robert's face. If he'd meant to shoot Egglington he certainly didn't look pleased with the outcome. Perhaps he'd suddenly realised that he wasn't in the USA – that there would be consequences. She was dreading going into work later where she'd be asked to make a complete report of the shooting. This time she wouldn't get away with "there was a shot and Egglington was down," they'd want more information. She had to be fair with Robert and let him know that she would be telling it how it happened.

She showered, dressed and drank black coffee first. With a deep breath she made the call, only to find his mobile was off and the garrison telling her that he was no longer based there.

'Where is he?' she asked. She knew she sounded rude. 'I'm Detective Sergeant Fuller. I need to speak to him urgently.'

'Sorry, love. He didn't leave a number.'

She rang his mobile again. 'Robert... I... just needed to speak to you.'

If he wasn't at the garrison and his mobile wasn't functioning, he might still be at the cottage but it was already twelve-fifteen, she had to leave for work now.

'I don't know how you get yourself in these messes, Hazel,' she told herself. 'He's probably half-way to Afghanistan by now, whisked away by the secret service to avoid any "unpleasantness". Get over it.'

As soon as she entered the office, Nina was congratulating her for apprehending Steve Egglington.

'It wasn't me. I was being a whimp until Robert came to my rescue.'

'Rubbish. He tells me you were a real hero. He watched you fighting with the man for a while before he felt the need to step in.'

'You've spoken to him this morning?'

'Yes, I'm getting the statements together...'

'Is he coming in?'

'...and I had the forensics on the bullets – it was important for him to have the results.'

Hazel waited. 'And?' she asked.

Nina smiled. 'As expected, of course. Bullet in leg from Robert's gun. Bullet in head from Egglington's gun.'

'You mean it was loaded?'

'Yes. You were very lucky that Robert was there.'

Hazel sat down. 'Did you say he was coming in?'

'Yes, later this afternoon. He's got a lot of sorting out to do now.' Nina lowered her voice. 'He's flying to Libya on Thursday.'

'Libya?'

'Yes, but it's hush-hush so please keep your voice down and don't go blabbing it about. Now, I'm off for the next four days so I wanted to be certain about something.' She explained that the hairs found on Larry Wright and Tanya Stewart's clothing matched those of Bea Egglington but none were found from Steve Egglington.

'So?'

'So I'm thinking, how do we know they hadn't planned for him to take the blame so she wouldn't go to prison? There was the baby to consider.'

'He said it was his.'

'Did he? She told me he didn't know she was pregnant.'

'She's a liar. Can we force a DNA test?'

Nina gave her a quizzical look. 'We're not a police state yet, Hazel. It wouldn't prove anything.'

'So you think she might actually be the killer?'

Nina nodded. 'I've looked through all the evidence and I don't think there is anything that could be considered conclusive but I do wonder...'

'He must've helped her move Wright's body.'

'I agree.'

'He organised for her to hide. But then he reported her missing.'

'When he knew exactly where she was,' Nina added. 'She was very convincing when she gave me her statement in the cottage.'

Hazel sighed. 'Perhaps we should talk to her again. Does she know her husband shot himself?'

'Not yet. We were waiting for the results of the forensics... in case...'

'Oh don't. Honestly, Nina, I really thought that Robert...'

'Well he didn't, so cheer up and get on with your report. I want to get all the paperwork done before I'm on leave.'

'You're kidding!'

'If I don't finish it, you'll have to,' she warned.

The time dragged for Hazel, who was desperate to see Robert. There was no way she could tell him that she'd thought he'd blown a man's brains out and she couldn't reveal how she felt about him, if he was disappearing from her life so soon.

Hazel observed while he gave his account of the night to Nina.

'I think DS Fuller should be given a medal, the way she dealt with the man,' he commented as he signed the statement.

'What's this about you watching me before you stepped in,' Hazel said.

'You were managing so well,' he said. 'Doing it by the book I'd say. I only intervened when it looked as if you were being abducted.'

Nina smiled benignly. 'Well, I'm off home. I'll leave you two to carry on.'

Hazel gave her a questioning look. Nina grinned, shrugged her shoulders, picked up her bag and left.

'Are you ok, honey?' Robert looked concerned.

'I'm fine. Are you?'

'Yep.' He sighed as he came over to her and knelt beside her chair. 'I was scared last night that you'd be hurt. It surprised me how much it scared me.'

His face was so grave, his eyes so kind, she burst into tears.

'Come here, sugar.'

He dried her tears and made her laugh, so by the time they were on their way to his cottage, she felt calm again. She decided that a few last days with him was all she could expect but was happy to accept whatever the future held.

It was therefore a real surprise to her when he made her a proposal that could change her life. They were in the kitchen cooking dinner together; she was enjoying the domesticity.

'Hazel, I've been thinking,' he began. 'I know I'll be away in...'

'Libya.'

'How did you... ? Ok, so, I was thinking – when I'm back in the States – would you come and join me?'

Hazel was stunned. 'You mean for like a holiday?'

'No, not for a vacation. I mean forever.' She hadn't expected that. It caught her totally on the back foot.

'Robert, it's... it's...'

'With Liam, of course.'

There were no words to describe how she felt. She stood looking out of the window, thoughts flying round her head.

'So?' he asked, busying himself with the special pasta sauce he'd been working on.

She couldn't answer then. It was too much to take in. So she said she would give him her answer the next day and spent most of the night awake, turning over the possibilities. There was no way she could leave her job... her friends... her mother... She was a mother with responsibilities and offers like this were not for her. She'd felt so different with him, a new life with him was so tempting...'

She tried explaining how she felt the following evening and the funny thing was, he understood.

'I can't leave Mum.'

'She'll visit. She could stay as long as she wanted.'

'Liam has a girlfriend. He'd hate to leave now.'

'I won't be back for a month or too. By then he'll have had several girlfriends.'

'I'd miss my work – I'd have nothing to do.'

'Nonsense – someone of your calibre would get a job in the police force easy.'

But she didn't want to, if she was honest. The problem was that she still couldn't trust a serviceman. It could be that he never returned from Libya, at least not alive. She couldn't cope with that.

So they spent the last few evenings together, a sweet but sad time that made the moments more precious.

'Naomi!' Mills was taking Harry up to Ivy Cottage to meet Nina and Nige for the first time. She hadn't expected her friend to be there as well.

'Hello Mills. I came over to make sure Nina was settled in all right – and to see you and Harry of course.'

They were squeezed into the tiny sitting room, where Rosie was playing on the floor with Nige.

'Do you have any info on what's happened to Fergus the bogeyman?' Naomi asked when she saw Harry.

'He was given bail.'

She seemed surprised. 'Why?'

'His parents came down to collect him. They'll be keeping a close eye on him until his court appearance. I think they're pretty disgusted with him.'

Naomi laughed. 'Not as disgusted as my sister-in-law is. She refused to meet his parents when they came down; Daniel had to go alone. They were so embarrassed. They've sacked their keeper; apparently he's been using that poison in Scotland and teaching Fergus his horrible tricks.'

'So is Fergus pleading guilty?' Nina asked, picking her daughter up from the floor and putting her on her knee.

'Yes,' replied Harry. 'He even admitted to laying the poison bait out – the one that made poor Earl so ill before.'

'And what about the red kite?' Mills was suddenly reminded of the beautiful bird outstretched on the backcloth of purple heather.

'Unfortunately there's no evidence we can use against him. Even Gareth didn't know about that.'

'And how *is* Gareth?' Mills asked.

Naomi smiled. 'He's the apple of his parent's eye now, thanks to you. I'm really pleased for him. It's time he was taken seriously.'

'Is he back in full Goth again now?' Nige asked.

'Oh yes. But Penny and Daniel don't seem to mind so much now.'

When Nina disappeared into the kitchen, Mills followed.

'Let me take Rosie for you.'

'Thanks. It's only a curry. I thought we could eat it in there on our knees – there's not enough room round this table.'

'Oh, I hope you don't mind Harry coming...'

'No, it's nice to see him again – and for Nige to meet him. He's really such a nice guy.'

When they returned with the food, Nige and Harry were discussing the new football season. Naomi immediately grabbed Nina to tell her about the local places to go.

'I don't think we'll be going out much while we're here,' she said.

'Why not?' Mills asked, passing drinks round with her free hand. 'I'll be around in the evenings. I'm happy to look after Rosie. She's a poppet.'

Nige began describing the beers he particularly liked and Harry told him where to find them locally.

As they helped Nina with the washing up, Naomi asked Mills how the job at the forensic laboratory was working out.

'I've really enjoyed it, although it was my last day today.'

'That's a shame,' Nina said.

'Yes, but Brenda's back on Monday so I'll go in to hand over. She was talking about expanding the place.'

Nina nodded. 'Now the Forensic Service is winding down there'll be opportunities for labs like hers. By the way, I'm following up on those two hairs that we found on the murder victims. I think you might've had something when you said it was odd there was nothing of the husband's on the victims. But what about the archaeology, Mills? Surely you'll be carrying on working at the university now?'

'Ideally but unless they come up with an offer...'

'Have you spoken to Nige about it?' Nina was drying her hands.

'No, but...'

'Speak to him.'

When they were all gathered together again, Nige ensured everyone had a glass before preparing to make a toast.

'I have an announcement to make,' he declared. 'Nina and I have some news.'

'I knew it,' Naomi whispered to Mills, 'She's pregnant.'

'The thing is,' Nige continued, 'the thing is...'

'Come on, Nige,' Nina urged him.

'We're expecting a baby.' He looked so proud.

'Actually, that's not strictly correct, is it Nige?' Nina was laughing. 'They think it's twins.'

The women in the group spent the rest of the evening discussing the news.

'Of course it means this is probably our only holiday until they're born,' Nina said, looking over at Nige. 'Are you going away before term starts, Mills?'

'No.'

'I'm painting my flat in my break,' complained Naomi.

'Harry's doing the Coast to Coast walk,' announced Nige, enviously.

He'd known about the stabbing on the route, Harry said when the others reminded him about the lurid details of the case. For him it had simply highlighted the existence of the long distance path.

Nina admitted she had a secret desire to do the walk but somehow it was never the right time.

'Well it certainly won't be for a while,' agreed Mills.

As everyone was leaving, Nige took Mills to one side.

'I just wanted to say that there might be an opportunity for you at the university next year,' he began.

'Really?'

'Yes, you see I'm thinking about taking a sort of sabbatical when Nina has the babies. Write up some papers, look after the little ones while Nina gets back to work.'

'Right.'

'She really wants to get on in the police, you know. And I'm happy where I am. They'll need a temporary lecturer – Jake can cover the fieldwork but there will be quite a lot of other stuff that you could cover easily. We can talk about it in the autumn, there's bags of time before the babies are born.'

'What does the Dean say?'

'He was very pleased with the summer school you ran and is interested in doing more courses for the public. He's happy with the plan and wants to talk about your ideas.'

Nina carried two mugs into the interview room and closed the door. The woman seated at the table thanked her but left the tea untouched.

'I thought I was asked to come in to sign my statement,' she said.

Her tone was as lacking in personality as her grey dress and her black hair, and Nina wondered if she was in mourning for her lover or her husband. The baby didn't show yet so she reckoned they must be at similar stages of their pregnancies.

'Would you like a biscuit?' Nina asked, reaching for her bag. The morning sickness was much worse this time and she'd learned to carry biscuits to accompany the tea at all times.

'Will this take long?' the woman asked impatiently.

'Sorry, of course. Here it is.'

Nina passed the sheet of paper to her, turning it round so she could read it. There was a long pause before she reached for the pen.

'Just one thing that's been puzzling me, Bea.'

Nina hoped she sounded calm and in command; Hazel was observing her from the next room. The woman hesitated, pen poised.

'We found your hair on Mr Wright's clothing and on that of Tanya Stewart's. And yet we didn't find a single one of your husband's hairs. Wasn't that strange?'

The careful hand inscribed a signature, replaced the pen and pushed the paper back across the table in a deliberate movement.

'In fact, Bea, it worried my colleague and I so much that we started to look more carefully at your husband's movements.'

There was no reaction from the woman.

'He was a keen golfer wasn't he? Often at the club. In fact every weekend he spent more time there than at home, they say. You see, we spoke to his golfing partners and it seems he was at the club on the night Larry Wright was killed. He was there until about seven o'clock when he got a call that sent him rushing out, without even finishing his drink.'

The woman was sitting straight backed and impassive.

'We know it was a call from Blakey Ridge. We assume he drove up to help you hide the body. What did you tell him? Did you say it was self-defence? Did he even know you were having an affair?'

Nina waited for Bea to speak, to react in some way but she was looking straight ahead, as if trying not to hear.

'Ok, let's move on to the night Tanya Stewart died. She was a friend of yours, wasn't she? Steve told us she was blackmailing you. Is that why you killed her?'

'I didn't kill her. Steve went to meet her.'

'Interesting that you say that. We didn't even think to ask until we began to review the evidence. And guess what... the army have CCTV at the ranges. Not surprising really I suppose but it took a Major in the US military to point it out. So we took a look and there you are, arriving in Steve's car and leaving half an hour later.'

The grey figure seemed to slump a little as she took a sip from the mug. 'I want a solicitor.'

Hazel was jubilant when Nina joined her in the office.

'Good job, Featherstone,' she shouted across the room. 'Couldn't have done better myself.'

'We couldn't have clinched it without the CCTV.'

'I know, he's a clever guy, Robert. He'll go far. In fact he has.'

Nina knew her friend's jokes covered up a deep wound that would take a long time to mend.

'I can't help thinking about that poor baby. It'll be born in prison round about the same time that I'm...'

'She'll be fine – she'll convince them all she was wrongly convicted and they'll give her a nice place in a mother and baby unit.'

'You are so cynical.'

'She convinced her husband to cover up for her and ended up killing himself to save her – and I'm cynical?'

'I don't believe he did it for her, Hazel. I think he did it for the baby.'

'You're probably right. He seemed pretty certain the child was his.'

Brenda was sitting at her desk in a neck brace and Mills could tell by her expression that all the jokes had already been made.

'Before you ask, I missed most of the salsa classes because of this, and it rained much of the time.'

'I'm sorry to hear that.'

'I'm sure you are, Mills. I'm sure you are. Now, first I want to thank you for holding the fort. You've done a good job by all accounts.'

Mills explained progress on the work she'd finished off for Brenda and described the new jobs that had come in. She wanted to assure her boss that the apparent mix-up over the hair samples had worked out all right in the end.

'... I know Glyn e-mailed you about it.'

'The less said about that the better,' Brenda said, waving her arm awkwardly. 'It spoilt my evening, I have to say. In fact it would have been better if I *had* rushed back – it would've avoided this.' She pointed to her neck. 'Anyway I didn't want to natter on about that. I've much more important plans to make now that I've made up my mind to expand.'

'Sounds interesting.'

'It's going to be really hard work but I reckon if we get in as the first accredited forensic lab in the area we'll corner the market here.'

'Exciting.'

'Which is why I would like you to help me get started. It's going to take a year, they say.'

'What exactly is involved?'

'We'll need to decide which forensics we want to specialise in and then prove they are reliable. I'd like to keep some of our more interesting tests – like my textiles – but we need the bread and butter ones, that's certain.'

'Like DNA?'

'Exactly.' She sat smiling across the desk at Mills. 'So what do you think?'

'It sounds interesting but it would presumably be more desk work. Don't get me wrong – I've enjoyed it and I do want to stay in the science.' She was thinking about working with the sour-faced lab manager. 'I don't know if certain members of staff would...'

'You mean Glyn? Don't worry... he suggested it. He's no good with paperwork. Well, take your time. Think it over and let me know. There's no rush.' She ran her finger round underneath her brace as if to ease her neck. 'I suppose you'll be having a holiday too?'

Mills felt herself blushing. 'Actually I'm walking the Coast to Coast path next week, well next couple of weeks – with a friend.'